"You'll be all right.

Those three words we[re]... the edge. She acted on impulse. As she rose up on her tiptoes, her gaze met his, hesitantly at first, but when she saw that in that same moment he was lowering his face to hers, she closed her eyes until she felt their lips touch. That warmth that she had felt emanate from her belly now radiated all the way through her, accompanied by an even greater hunger for him. She couldn't think. She could only obey what her body and her heart were asking her to do. She pushed away thoughts of all else—Demetrios, the sanatorium, her upcoming marriage—lost in the sweetness of his taste, and touch, as she opened her mouth to take the kiss deeper.

But suddenly, she felt Erik withdraw, and his arms loosened around her. An involuntary whimper escaped her mouth.

"Thea. We shouldn't do this."

Her eyes flew open. The words were like the sting of a bee, bringing her back to the stark reality of what was her life.

Author Note

I love reading about all periods in ancient history, but Erik, the hero of this story, has been in my thoughts for some time, which is why I chose the fast-paced, action-charged period of the Vikings as the setting of my first book. However, I wanted to introduce a fresh spin on it by shifting away from the traditional locations that usually feature Vikings to much farther east, to Constantinople, the jewel of the Eastern Roman Empire.

Neighboring states constantly jockeyed for power over it given its strategic location, while internally, its courts were fraught with palace intrigue, betrayal and political scheming. But it had one unchanging feature for several centuries: the Varangian Guard. An elite group of soldiers, comprising mainly Vikings, they were unswerving in their allegiance to the emperors of Constantinople. I was captivated by what I read about the Varangians, and the idea of Erik was born.

Princess Theadora is fiery, beautiful and passionate about her work as a healer, which, coupled with her mistrust of men, does not afford much time for romance. That is, until she meets Erik... Who, she discovers, is not so different to her and whose heart is equally as closed off to love.

THE VIKING'S
ROYAL TEMPTATION

ROXY HARPER

HISTORICAL

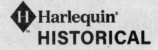

Harlequin® HISTORICAL

ISBN-13: 978-1-335-54017-1

The Viking's Royal Temptation

Copyright © 2025 by Roxy Harper

Harlequin Enterprises ULC
22 Adelaide St. West, 41st Floor
Toronto, Ontario M5H 4E3, Canada
www.Harlequin.com

Printed in U.S.A.

Roxy Harper has always been a voracious reader and from a young age especially loved the romance genre—stories that told of strong, fearless heroines and the champions who captured their hearts. She entered the world of writing with a submission to the Warriors Wanted! blitz and was thrilled when her story was selected. Spending time writing allows her to escape to the ancient worlds of her protagonists, journeying with them as they battle the external forces that strive to keep them apart, and their own personal barriers to falling in love, until they find their happy-ever-after.

Becoming a published author has been a dream come true—Roxy can't wait to write more stories for Harlequin Historical and very much hopes her readers will enjoy them!

The Viking's Royal Temptation
is Roxy Harper's debut title for Harlequin Historical.

Look out for more books from Roxy Harper,
coming soon.

First, for my mum, Lineta,
who has always been by my side, and always will be.

For my dad, Neville, who indulged my love of books.

For my husband, who told me never to give up.

For Patrick, a constant guiding hand in my writing.

For all of you who have not just played a part in
my story, but who have provided inspiration for Erik
and Thea's story—thank you, you know who you are.

Chapter One

Early summer, 979 AD, Constantinople

Thea had finished conducting her usual morning round of the ward, and was just about to begin the daily task of updating her patients' papers when the distinct clatter of armour sounded from the foyer. The wards were a place of calm and serenity, so a soldier's presence meant one of two things: someone needed urgent medical attention, or there was trouble.

She shot to her feet, instantly on the alert, and hurried in the direction of the noise, wondering what the commotion could be.

She was not unused to seeing armed men from time to time, but of late she had sensed discord in the city. She sighed. Should she be surprised? This was Constantinople, after all. Most of the aristocracy claimed a right to the crown in some way or another, and although her uncle's reign had brought some peace and stability to the kingdom, there was still the odd half-hearted skirmish and failed uprising.

Another crash brought her back to the present. She worried at her lip, quickening her steps. Putting aside the possibility of civil unrest, she knew the city also had to endure the constant threat of uninvited foreign attention. If their age-old rivals the Ottomans were not seeking to attack from the east, the Bulgarians were testing the boundaries to the west.

The thoughts sped through her mind, spurring her to move faster. It seemed as if her fears were confirmed when, on approaching the entrance hall, the sound of raised voices met her ears. She immediately recognised the shrill tones of Hilda, her head nurse. The deep timbre of the other voice she could not place, though its undertone of belligerence set her on edge. But she was not given much time to speculate, for she was soon at the doorway and able to identify its owner.

A large soldier was standing but a few feet away, his back to her. His presence seemed to fill the small atrium almost entirely, and the room immediately shrank to the size of a closet. There was his gleaming helmet, for one thing, which certainly gave him a formidable height—although Thea could tell that even without it he would be more than a foot taller than her.

Yet his height only told part of the story. As Thea appraised the length of his body she knew that the powerful build of the man who stood before her could only belong to a warrior of unparalleled strength. The expanse of his shoulders spanned the width of two ordinary men, and she could make out, even from this distance, that his thick arms were corded with enough muscle for him to wrestle a bear and win.

But of all his physical attributes it was the shoulder-length fair hair that flowed from under his helmet that stopped her in her tracks, causing terror to close like an icy fist around her belly. He was not from these parts. His complexion was lighter and his stature broader than the average

Greek soldier. She had never encountered someone of his colouring before, but knew from her studies that he must hail from the North. He could be one of the Rus—a people who came from beyond the Black Sea, who had laid siege to Constantinople on more than one occasion. The other possibility was that he was a Norseman, originating from the frozen wastelands even further beyond Kievan Rus. A race of men who were known to be enemies of Christian cities in the western part of the Roman Empire.

Neither prospect boded well, and she instinctively took a step back.

But then she registered the long, crimson-coloured cloak, trimmed with gold, that was swept over one of his shoulders, symbolising his status as a Varangian Guard, one of the elite group of warriors who had pledged allegiance to her uncle, the Emperor. He was clearly no foreign enemy of Constantinople, then. But her fear was only marginally tempered. She didn't trust men, given her past experiences—not even if those men served her uncle.

Pushing away her unease, she straightened her back and entered the foyer, side-stepping the huge double-edged battleaxe and the thick heavy blade of the sword that were scattered in disarray on the flagstones. The warrior's attention was still on Hilda, who seemed not in the slightest bit perturbed by the giant that stood before her.

'Captain or not, weapons are forbidden in the wards. You'll frighten the patients!' Hilda crossed her arms stubbornly across her chest. Hilda was a force to be reckoned with at the best of times.

'For goodness' sake, woman, we are wasting time! I'll find a bed myself if you won't help. Who is in charge here, anyway? Bring them here at once!'

It was only when the warrior turned to scan the foyer

that Thea noticed the small boy gathered in his arms. The sight of the frail child huddled against the Varangian's chest immediately caused Thea's healing instincts to take over. She squared her shoulders and stepped forward.

'You'll do no such thing.' Her voice sounded far more confident than she felt. 'And I am in charge.'

The Varangian's head turned from Hilda towards her, and his piercing blue eyes were soon sharply trained on her. She felt helpless and strangely naked under his keen appraisal, but Thea's only response to his scrutiny was to lift her chin in a gesture of defiance. She cleared her throat and tried to ignore the fact that he looked even more formidable when faced front-on.

'The boy needs to be examined for injuries first.' She locked her gaze with his, determined to demonstrate her authority. 'Besides, you're going in the wrong direction. That's the birthing ward.'

She turned on her heel and strode towards her consultation room, satisfied when, out of the corner of her eye, she saw that he was following her.

Inside her room, she indicated the pallet by her table. 'Place the boy there, please, and give us some space.'

Dutifully, the Varangian set him down and stepped aside.

'Can you sit up?' Thea enquired, tenderly cupping the boy's cheek in concern, still aware of the towering presence behind her.

He nodded shyly, before wincing in pain as he sought to adjust his position.

'There, there…you're very brave. Now, what is your name, little one?'

'Alexios,' he said weakly. His cheeks were extremely pale.

'Hello, Alexios. I can help you with the pain. Come, tell me where it hurts.'

The boy indicated his right arm. Thea looked at where he was pointing and saw the fabric of his tunic was dark with blood. She gingerly cut away the garment, and the shirt beneath, grimacing in horror at what she saw there. Large, angry welts gaped, wide and ugly, from the top of his shoulder down to his wrist. On further examination she saw that several superficial cuts and bruises also marked his body.

'Who did this to you?' Thea asked softly.

The boy looked at her, and for a moment it seemed as if he was about to speak, but then he shook his head vigorously, fear clouding his eyes.

'One of the Emperor's generals did this.' The deep voice came from behind her. 'The poor lad is afraid of him, and does not want more trouble, so will not speak about it. But I saw what happened. The general was mistreating his horse, and Alexios here simply tried to reassure the poor beast, seeing that the other horses were also becoming agitated. However, that seemed to exacerbate the general's fury, and he turned his whip on the boy instead. Fortunately, I was saddling my own horse at the time, and could intervene.'

Thea turned to face the Varangian and saw that he had removed his helmet, which he now held under one arm. She caught her breath as an exciting *frisson* tingled along her spine. Everything she had ever heard about the Varangians had made her imagine them to be battle-hardened brutes, but this one seemed to have stepped straight out of one of the Greek legends. Like Adonis himself, every line and curve of his face came together in perfect symmetry, as if sculpted out of stone, and as he stood by the window, the sun picking out the threads of gold in his shoulder-length fair hair, she could not deny that he was ruggedly handsome.

But from past experience she knew looks could be deceiving. Demetrios was handsome…just as handsome as he was cunning…

Realising she had let her thoughts run away with her and was now staring, she quickly averted her gaze from the warrior and continued her examination, thankful that his full attention was on the poor injured boy. A quick assessment revealed that the wounds were not deep, and thankfully they were clean.

'You'll make a full recovery,' she said, and smiled down reassuringly at the boy before turning to the Varangian. 'I'll administer the child a light sleeping draught, which will provide relief from the pain. But since it may be a little while until it takes effect, I will need your assistance in comforting him while I treat the wounds themselves.'

'Of course.'

Thea watched as the giant warrior set down his helmet on her work table and strode around to the other side of the pallet.

Erik helped the nurse prop Alexios against some pillows, his heart giving a small tug each time the boy winced in pain. The sight evoked the memory of another pale face that he had once looked down upon, a long time ago. Bjorn had been about the same age as Alexios when the fever had taken him. Erik would never forget how his son's body had gone limp in his arms and how the bright light in his eyes had finally dimmed…

Time had done little to diminish the memory of that fateful week, but Erik was thankful that at least he had been able to shield this boy from the grave and bring him here. He instinctively tightened his arm around Alexios and watched as the nurse began her ministrations. Her confirmation that Alexios would make a full recovery had set him at ease, so he now found more of his attention slowly drifting towards the woman herself.

He marvelled at how her slender hands moved swiftly and deftly about their task with such confidence. Something about her commanded authority, from the way she had firmly taken charge of the situation in the entrance hall, to the way she was now tending to the boy. She moved with complete assurance, he thought admiringly.

He allowed his gaze to travel upwards and saw that her hair was covered by a nurse's wimple, though he noted several tendrils had escaped to curl about the nape of her slender neck, revealing it to be a warm chestnut colour. Her lips, slightly parted in concentration, were full and bow-shaped, and the honeyed tones of her complexion were a tell-tale sign of a childhood spent further south, lending her an exotic appeal.

With a start, he realised that he had not encountered such beauty before, and for the first time in a long time the beginnings of desire flared within him. He quickly clamped down on it. He would not go down that path again.

'Would you help me turn the boy over to his side?'

She was speaking to him now. Silently reprimanding himself for letting his concentration slip, he brought himself to the present and helped the nurse shift the child's weight.

'Thank you, Captain…?'

'Captain Svenson. Varangian Guard.'

She nodded, and quickly turned her attention back to her patient, but not before Erik noticed the tiniest of shadows pass across her face. She appeared to be on edge for some reason. Was it improper for her to be in such close proximity to a man? Surely not. As a nurse, she would have found herself in such situations many a time. Perhaps she was afraid of him. After all, the foreign look of the Varangians puzzled most citizens who had not ventured outside the walls of the city. It seemed unlikely, though, since the Varangians were known to be unswerving in their loyalty to the Emperor and, by extension, to Constantinople. She must know he was not a danger to her.

He searched her face again, to see if he could ascertain the cause of her unease, but any such expression had disappeared, and she now seemed to be deep in thought as she examined the boy's wounds, her brows knitted together in concern.

Then, without warning, she met his gaze with hers, letting out an exasperated sigh.

'You say that one of the Emperor's generals did this?'

Those eyes, soft and doe-like but a moment ago, now flashed with anger.

'Yes. He—'

'Only a coward would do this to a defenceless child. Look at him! It's a mercy that the wounds are not too deep. I'll speak to my uncle about this. Whoever did this should be dismissed.'

'But what can your uncle do? Generals are practically untouchable—and this particular general reports directly to the Emperor.'

'It is fortunate, then, that my uncle is the Emperor.'

The Emperor? Her uncle?

Erik stared at the nurse, not registering her answer.

'I am Theadora. The Emperor's niece,' she added in clarification, sensing his confusion. 'Now, please pass me that vial over there.'

'But you are a princess?'

She sighed and nodded. 'Just Thea in here, though… The vial, please?' She held out her hand impatiently.

As the significance of her position dawned on him, Erik

realised he had probably broken about a dozen unwritten rules already.

He bowed as he handed her the vial. 'Apologies, Your Royal Highness, I was unaware—'

'Please, there is no need for court formalities here,' she said as she accepted the vial and applied the contents to Alexios's wounds, delicately dabbing the welts with her fine, tapered fingers.

Her lips were pursed in concentration, and she did not appear to want to offer anything further in terms of conversation. It gave Erik the opportunity to study her more closely.

Now that he came to think of it, she did bear a certain resemblance to Princess Adriana, the Emperor's daughter, though this woman's beauty was of a different sort. It was regal and classic—enduring, some might say. Whereas Princess Adriana's was softer, and of the type he considered transient. He pondered on how different the two women's characters were. Here was a woman who spent her days tending to the sick, exposing herself to life outside the palace walls, whereas Princess Adriana was like an orchid. She seemed to wilt if the world around her was not kept exactly so.

No, *this* woman was very different. Every movement demonstrated a fluid combination of poise and grace, from the way she confidently applied the salves to Alexios's wounds, to the way she skilfully cut his bandages, like a seamstress shaping material with precision. He was astonished that he had not recognised right away that this was no ordinary nurse.

'Poor boy,' she continued, sealing the vial and handing it back to Erik. 'He is exhausted. But as I said before, I expect him to recover well. He is comfortable now, in any event.'

Erik looked over at Alexios. The colour had certainly flowed back into his cheeks, and the sleeping draught the Princess had administered earlier had taken effect, for he had fallen into a peaceful slumber.

'Thank you for helping him. He has suffered a shock today,' Erik said, taking the vial from her.

Their fingers met, sending a thrill through him. She dropped her gaze to the floor, but not before he saw her colour heighten, infusing her cheeks with a rosy pink. She had felt something too. The reaction caused a faint glow of happiness to spread through him, unbidden. But what was he thinking? He was a Varangian Guard, sworn to protect the Empire, and she was a princess, born to serve it. He must remember his place.

'It is what we are here for. Alexios will need to be medicated regularly today, to manage the pain, but I expect he can be discharged tomorrow.'

The bashful young woman was suddenly gone, replaced instantly with the prim, practical nurse.

A thin veil of silence hung in the air between them. Then Erik spoke again.

'Very well. I shall take my leave now, but I'll return tomorrow to bring the boy some fresh clothes and take him back to the palace if he's well enough.'

He gave her a small nod and reached over to collect his helmet from the desk where he had set it down.

'But you're bleeding, too!'

It took a moment for Erik to realise she was addressing him, and he followed her gaze to where it had settled upon his arm. He had felt the general's whip make contact there, but he had been so focused on ensuring Alexios's safety that only now did he feel the sting of it.

''Tis nothing. Just a scratch.'

'It doesn't look like a scratch. That wound needs examining straight away!'

'I have suffered worse and lived,' Erik countered gruffly.

Again, he made for the door, but found himself held in check by the Princess, her small palm resting on his chest. The touch conferred upon him an unsettling warmth through the fabric of his tunic.

'I am sure you have, but I hold jurisdiction here, and this is not one of your battlefields.'

With a new patient to treat, it was as if she had suddenly sprung back into life.

'May I?'

Without waiting for an answer, she put her hands on him, gently examining the injury. By Thor, the woman was bossy! But something about that was strangely thrilling...

'Very well,' he conceded reluctantly. 'But perhaps one of the other nurses could do it? The situation is...improper...'

'Nonsense. As I said before, I am a nurse here—nothing more. Besides, I am the most skilled in treating wounds such as these.'

His natural stubbornness often meant he rarely gave way in an argument, whether the outcome was in his interest or not. But she was watching him with a steady gaze, one delicate eyebrow arched, and he soon realised that there was nothing for it but to comply. Those doe eyes were resolute.

Chapter Two

The Varangian took a seat by her desk, while Thea took a chair opposite. She leaned towards his forearm, which he had held out in front of him, ready for her examination, and carefully took hold of it. She saw that the wound wrapped around his arm, breaking the skin across the sinews near his elbow and continuing in a spiral to the underside of his wrist. Unlike in Alexios's case, where cloth and fabric had formed a barrier against the lashes, the whip had struck the Varangian directly on his bare skin, so his wounds were deeper and dirtier than those inflicted on the boy.

She felt a sudden pang of compassion as she imagined the pain he must be experiencing, but also admiration, knowing that he had selflessly stepped in to protect the child against his attacker.

A strange mixture of emotions started to swirl inside her. Here was a Varangian Guard, whom she knew to be no more than a fierce warrior, making her feel giddy and unnerved. But not unnerved in the way that she often felt when Demetrios looked at her, for she loathed his attention. This was different. Maybe it was the way the colour of his ice-blue eyes had taken on the warm marine hues of a mountain lake when he'd looked upon the boy in concern, or the way his presence seemed to exude strength and safety.

It was odd, because she usually wasn't easily able to feel comfortable when in a man's presence. No, her mind was surely playing tricks on her. He was a captain in the Varangian Guard, and in her experience men who held such lofty positions were not to be trusted.

She berated herself. She shouldn't let her personal reservations take hold of her. She was a healer who currently had a job to do—and a difficult one at that, since the Varangian's wounds would need some care and attention.

She gathered herself and started work, taking care not to meet his clear blue eyes. For that felt dangerous…like looking directly into the sun.

'I will need to wash this wound.'

She could feel the heat of his steady gaze on her and she hoped he couldn't hear the slight tremor in her voice.

'Of course. You're in charge.'

This time she did look up briefly, taken aback at his acquiescence. Was he being flippant? But no, he was looking at her earnestly. He was close enough for her to make out a strong, square jaw, sprinkled with the barest hint of stubble. A faint scar etched on his brow line bore evidence of his time in battle and stood in stark contrast to the beauty of his slashing cheekbones. Without his helmet, she could see that his fair hair was braided in some sections but loose and flowing in others. She noted again, with surprise, that she no longer felt as uneasy in his company as she had when she had first set eyes on him, clad in armour. On the contrary, her heart gave a flutter. It was unsettling—and puzzling.

Confused by the effect he was having on her, she looked for an excuse to break their physical contact. Gently laying his arm down on the table, she walked to the windowsill where a jug of water had been warming in the afternoon sunlight. She picked it up, then collected the pewter bowl which lay on her medicine cabinet and placed both objects side by side by his injured arm. She filled the bowl with warm water and dabbed at the surface with her fingertips to gauge its temperature. Judging it to be just right, she plucked a silver box from the pouch that was tied to her waist and sprinkled its contents into the bowl, swirling the water around in gentle, circular motions.

The mechanical, familiar movements helped settle her nerves and she soon felt less flustered. Taking her seat again, she got to work.

'Sea salt,' she explained, when she saw the warrior looking at her pouch with interest.

'You're using *salt*?' He sounded incredulous.

She tossed her head in chagrin. 'Yes, salt water prevents the wound from festering… Or would you prefer it if I covered you with honey instead?'

The words had escaped her lips without her thinking, and she wondered if her tongue had somehow become disconnected from her brain. She had simply meant the remark to show her medical knowledge, as a riposte to his incredulity, since honey had, in most parts of the Empire, been replaced with salt as a means of cleansing a wound. But instead of sounding like a sharp slap on the wrist, as she had intended, it had sounded wild and suggestive.

The image it evoked left her mortified. A warrior lathered in honey, indeed! She stared at his arm, feeling a rosy-red blush stain her cheeks. But if he sensed her embarrassment, he gave no sign of it.

'Please hold your arm over the bowl.' How she found the correct words to deliver the instruction, she did not know, but she stumbled on. 'I warn you it will sting.'

'I'm prepared.'

She took a square of white cotton from a drawer and dipped it into the water, then laid it over his wounds. The golden skin of his arm went taut over the swollen muscles as he balled his hand into one powerful fist. Instinctively her eyes followed the thin white scars that formed a patchwork from his wrist up his muscular forearm to the golden band above his large bicep.

Her pulse quickened, and she felt an unfamiliar feeling stir in her belly…a gentle heat that coiled down to her secret place below. It was warm, yet disconcerting.

Confused yet again, she reached into her medicine cabinet and fished around for a salve she didn't need, chiding herself all the while for her lack of focus. She had seen many a bare arm during her time as a healer, and this one should be no different. Except it was. It belonged to a handsome Varangian Guard who made her skin tingle at the barest of touches.

'How is the pain?' she ventured, hoping that conversation would divert her current thought process.

'It's fine. Please continue.'

Starting near his elbow, she wiped the wound in small strokes, refreshing the cloth in the salt water after each one. She followed the spiral of the wound until it curved out of sight under his arm, and then she took his tensed wrist in her free hand and turned it over. It opened like a flower, so that the palm was facing upwards, and she felt the hot beat of his pulse under her thumb.

He shifted on his stool.

'Did I hurt you?' she asked.

'No, no. Far from it.'

She continued cleaning the wound, searching for a way to break the tense silence that hung over them. Catching sight of his crimson-coloured cloak, she thought to enquire about how he had come to be a Varangian. She started with the most obvious question.

'Am I to assume that you are part of the contingent of Rus soldiers that King Vladimir sent to Constantinople last year?'

'No. I come from lands much further north. My kinsman Harald journeyed here when he was a young lad and eventually enlisted in the Guard. I followed him here a few years ago.'

Thea cast her mind back to her history lessons and to the depictions she'd seen of these Northmen. The stories differed, with historians either describing them as marauding, gold-seeking pirates, or peaceful, entrepreneurial traders. Thea knew that whatever she read in the chronicles must be taken with a pinch of salt, since most records were written with a certain agenda in mind, or to serve a political purpose for whomever was in power at the time.

Nevertheless, there was one story that held factual truth. Whether through pillaging or by peaceful assimilation, large swathes of Kievan Rus had undoubtedly come under Norse influence.

'I see. I have read about how the Northmen...*settled* in the Rus country.'

'Oh? And what have you read?' He raised his eyebrow.

Women were not taught to read, and were discouraged from being knowledgeable even if they were high born, so she was used to this reaction. But her father and mother had ensured that she was provided with the same education as any prince.

'That the Northmen came to Kiev many years ago, commingling with and marrying the local people. But now the Rus consider themselves a distinct race. Any traces of Viking descent have been assimilated into the local Slavic tribes, and the two races have become one.'

She saw that he was impressed, and a feeling of warmth washed over her.

'Yes, I suppose we do share common ancestry from trading.'

'Or from raiding…according to some sources.'

She looked up, searching his face to see whether there was any truth behind the stories she had read, which told of entire villages being plundered, and women and children taken as slaves, helpless against the sheer power and strength of the men who had kidnapped them.

He sighed. 'I agree that the line has become blurred on some occasions.'

Her heart gave a leap when she saw the remorse in his eyes.

He continued, frowning, 'I have never partaken in raids myself—though I acknowledge that there are Viking tribes that do.'

Thea appreciated his honesty about his own people, and found herself breathing a sigh of relief that he was not one of those Viking marauders who had plundered Christian cities for gold and jewels. But she found herself wondering what had led this man to enlist in the Guard. Thea knew that such men were mostly mercenaries by trade, whose previous employment had likely been less honourable than their present position as the Emperor's protectors. And yet again the familiar feeling of unease and mistrust with men took hold of her.

The Varangian Guards had styled themselves as the Emperor's personal bodyguards, and it was said that once a man became a Varangian his loyalty to the Emperor was absolute. But Thea had often wondered how absolute such loyalty would be if the Ottomans or Turks offered more gold for their services. After all, what was a Varangian if not a sell-sword?

She realised that the old demons of her past were running away with her. She must not let her scepticism regarding men get in the way of her work, and this was not the forum for such questioning. So she held herself in check and sought to make lighter conversation.

She turned to the sleeping Alexios. 'How did you become so fond of the boy?'

His expression immediately softened. 'I encountered him on our ship, coming back from Sicily. The rascal hopped on board when we had docked in Athens. He insisted on working on deck in return for his passage across the Aegean.' He chuckled as he recalled the memory. 'None of us had the heart to tell him that he wouldn't last a day working on deck if he hadn't been at sea before. But we kept him on and he proved us all wrong.'

He smiled, and she noted how his eyes crinkled at the corners. In this more relaxed state, without his helmet and weapons, the formidable warrior disappeared and was replaced by a young man at ease.

'He's certainly a tough one.'

'Yes. And he's a hard worker. When we disembarked in Constantinople I offered him a position as my squire. It didn't feel right to let him go it alone here.'

'But what of his parents?'

'Alexios is an orphan.'

'Oh…' Thea looked over at the sleeping Alexios, a shadow of pain flitting across her features.

Her heart contracted for the boy for she, of all people, knew what it was like to lose one's parents. Deep down, she still grieved for her mother and father. She was an only child, and she appreciated how lucky she was to have been taken in by her uncle and absorbed into his family. He treated her as one of his own, and she was acutely aware that not many in her position would have been as lucky. But it seemed that this boy had found such luck…

This Varangian was full of surprises. There was another layer beneath the battle-hardened warrior, it seemed…a layer that spoke of kindness and selflessness.

She reached for the purple vial that she had used when tending to Alexios and eased out the stopper. Gently, she pulled the Varangian's arm towards her so that it was closer. Steadying his forearm in one hand, she treated the raw wounds with the other, tenderly smoothing the sticky liquid in a thick layer over them.

'Is the pain manageable?'

'Yes… I—'

'Have suffered worse. I know.' She allowed herself a small smile, blushing when he let out a deep chuckle.

'I can handle a little rough treatment.'

It had clearly been said to reassure her, but his words had the opposite effect. The warm heat that had been pooling in her belly intensified, and her heart thudded furiously in her chest.

She fought for control.

'I am sure you can.' And she meant it. His body, or at least what she could see of it, was littered with scars. 'But we are almost done.'

She turned his wrist over, pressing her thumb into his open palm, her fingers cradling his knuckles. Although she channelled all her attention into applying the salve, she still could not help noting how strong his fingers felt in hers, or the pleasing roughness of his callused palms. It was a mercy that her work was nearly finished and all that remained was to wrap a bandage around his arm, for every action now seemed to require a conscious effort—as if she was doing it all for the very first time.

She had to bring matters to a conclusion before she completely lost hold of her mental faculties.

Unspooling a length of gauze from a roll, she wound it tightly around his arm in an overlapping spiral until his entire forearm was completely covered.

'There—all done.' She sat back, relieved that the task was finally complete.

'That was quick.'

Quick? To her, it had felt like an eternity.

'I hope it was not too uncomfortable.'

'Not at all. On the contrary I have never received such excellent treatment. I dare say the physicians on our battlefields could do with some of your secrets.'

He offered her a crooked smile, sending her heart soaring.

'Thank you. You've taken such good care of us.' He glanced over at Alexios. 'We are in your debt.'

His sincere gratitude caught her off guard. Her lips parted as she searched for a response, but as she looked into those brilliant blue eyes, felt the pull of his gaze drawing her to him, she felt she had no words to say. She cursed silently. All she had were her wits and her tongue, and both appeared to have abandoned her when she needed them most.

A sharp rap at the door startled her, bringing her back to herself.

'Miss Theadora, are you there? There's a new patient to see you.'

Hilda. Dear, dependable Hilda. What perfect timing!

'Be with you in a moment, Hilda. Just finishing up here.' She turned to face him, composing herself. 'Well, I've done all I need to do for now. You can return to the palace. Your arm will take care of itself.'

'Then I will be back tomorrow.'

'Tomorrow?' Unbidden, her heart leapt at the thought.

'To collect the boy.'

'Of course…' Cursing herself yet again, she hoped he hadn't caught the note of eagerness in her voice. 'We can also use the opportunity to re-dress your wound.'

'If you insist… You hold jurisdiction here.' His eyes twinkled.

'I am glad you finally realise that,' she countered primly, but a small smile tugged at her lips. 'I'll walk you out.'

She took him into the entrance hall and watched as he put on his helmet and retrieved the two heavy weapons which still lay on the floor, exactly where he had left them. Seeing him clad in steel again gave her an unexpected sensation of loss. The man she had spent the last hour with was once again a soldier, a mercenary…exactly the kind of man she did her best to avoid.

But what was it about the Varangian that had drawn her in? The man had threatened her composure, making her feel as if she was constantly testing uncharted waters. For one thing there had been that gentle pooling of heat in her belly when his eyes had met hers… It had been as if she was held captive under the intensity of his gaze. The feeling had been alien, and one which she had never before felt in a man's company.

Then there had been the way he'd shown such kindness towards the child. She'd sensed that there had been more than just concern in his gaze as he'd lain the injured Alexios down on the pallet—something much harder to read, which told of past pain. In that moment he'd seemed almost…*vulnerable*. It had surprised her, for it stood in stark contrast to all that he embodied as a mighty warrior of the Varangian Guard, to all that she knew of men.

As she watched his retreating figure disappear out of sight, her fingertips still tingling from the feel of his golden skin, she knew that there was something—*someone*—under that armour whom she wished to discover.

Erik walked up the steps to his quarters, his mind full of the Princess and the effect she had had on him. It had thrown him off guard. He prided himself on his discipline and rigour, but a short while in her company had had him tripping over himself like an inexperienced young boy. Why this woman's touch should affect him so, he had no idea.

In the years since Frida there had occasionally been women who had satisfied his physical need. But the encounters had been brief; both parties had benefited in their different ways and then parted. There had been no complexities, no entanglements—indeed nothing to deflect him from his personal oath.

But now he couldn't stop thinking about the woman he had just left behind. He recalled the feel of her fingertips on his arm, and the way her delicate eyebrows had drawn together in concern as she'd tended to his wounds. She had asked him whether he had felt any pain. He smiled ruefully. The pain had certainly been nothing compared to the jolt of desire that had shot through him every time she'd touched him. Granted, the wound was a little uncomfortable, but he had encountered a multitude of injuries more debilitating. What *had* been debilitating was the response she'd evoked in him.

The feel of those long, slender fingers on his arm had filled his imagination with the thought of them elsewhere…

He had been shocked at his thoughts, which had run wild and free in his mind despite his best efforts to tame them. Luckily, she'd seemed not to notice, mistaking his ill-restrained desire for pain, and had mercifully finished her task just when he'd thought he could take no more.

'There you are!'

A deep booming voice sounded from behind him, interrupting his thoughts. Harald, his kinsman, clapped a large hand on his shoulder, thrusting a cup of ale into Erik's hand with the other.

'What's this for?' Erik took the cup. He didn't usually drink during the day, but after the afternoon's events he could do with a distraction.

'We're celebrating!' A happy smile split Harald's face. 'You're looking at the new Commander of the Imperial Army!'

'I don't understand. That position is held by Demetrios…'

'Not any more. The Emperor is sending the scoundrel off to Macedonia. He's fed up with his mischief. He'll be serving as ambassador in Antonius's court.'

'Congratulations! That's glorious news, Harald!' Erik clasped his friend's huge forearm and wrapped his other arm around his shoulder.

'Indeed. And for a Varangian to oust a Greek… Unheard of!' Harald chuckled to himself. 'I can't tempt you to stay in the Guard? Just one more season…for old times' sake? What do you say, eh?'

Erik smiled wistfully. When he had first set foot in Constantinople he'd been just a mercenary, seeking the blind rage of battle. He had fought with enthusiasm, relishing the distraction that warfare brought. It had numbed his sorrow and provided a welcome outlet for his grief. It had been Harald who had stood by him in those dark times and supported his application for a highly coveted place in the Varangian Guard.

Over the intervening years they had risen through the ranks together, fighting side by side and back to back, becoming brothers in all but name. But recently Erik had begun to realise that fighting no longer held the appeal it once had, and the pyres of his past no longer burned as bright. His long service in the Varangian Guard had made him a wealthy man in his own right, and now, for the first time in many years, he felt free to consider what a life beyond its ranks might hold.

'I'm afraid I must turn you down this time, brother. I am set on a different path.'

'By Odin! Never has the Guard seen a warrior like you, Erik. What if I made you my second in command? You'd have free rein over the Palace Guard. Or the City Guard, if that pleases you. What about the sea? You enjoyed the Sea Guard, didn't you?' He looked at Erik eagerly.

Erik had just returned from a two-year posting in Sicily, on which most of his time had been spent on board a ship, patrolling the surrounding seas. He had enjoyed it at first, but the existence had soon become a lonely one, and he had eventually grown tired of the itinerant lifestyle.

But it wasn't just that.

He drew in a deep breath, searching for the words that would help his comrade understand.

'I've spent almost six years in the Guard, Harald. I'm tired. Tired of the bloodshed…the fighting. Of constantly moving from camp to camp or ship to ship.' He glanced at Harald's crestfallen face. 'You honour me, Harald. And I wish I could accept—'

'Then accept! What's stopping you? We could find you

an appropriate position. One that you would be happy with!'
He paused. 'What happened to us being sword brothers?'

He shot Erik an accusatory glance, causing Erik to feel
a small pang of guilt.

'I am still your brother, Harald. But my sword time is
over.' He shook his head. 'I want something other than
war now.'

'You've been a Varangian for many years, Erik. What
will you turn your hand to? Or do you mean to return to
Norway and fulfil your birthright?'

Erik paused. When the Princess had mentioned Viking
trading his thoughts had immediately gone to his father,
who had gained a significant amount of wealth as a peaceful trader in Bergen and was now the jarl. He expected
Erik to return someday and claim his birthright, since Erik
would inherit everything. But it wasn't something he liked
to make known. For one, he had always intended to make
his own way in life. More importantly, though, his birthright reminded him of loss and tragedy.

If he hadn't been the son of a jarl he wouldn't have been
contracted to marry Frida and form an alliance with her
tribe. If he had been an ordinary fisherman or farmer he
wouldn't have been obliged to marry so young, when the
fever was rampaging through the North. Frida would never
have had to travel so far from her own home. In his mind,
it was because of him that she had died, and it was a burden he would bear for the rest of his life. Maybe someday
he would return to Bergen, but now he wanted to embark
on a new chapter.

'I have no intention of returning home yet. There's much
that I can do outside of these walls and outside of being a
Varangian, Harald.' Erik gestured to the large defensive
fortifications that stood tall in the distance, encircling the

breadth of Constantinople. 'If you must know, I mean to set up a trading enterprise.'

'Trading?' Harald tapped his chin. 'That is certainly a different path! Like father like son, I suppose. It does run in the blood.' Clearly sensing that Erik's heart was set, and that there was no further room for persuasion, Harald gave up the fight. 'Very well, brother. I respect your decision.' He wagged his finger at him. 'I don't understand it, I'll confess, but I respect it. Come, join me for another drink and we can toast your new life—starting tomorrow!'

'Not so fast, brother. Our toast will need to wait one more day.'

Harald cocked an eyebrow. 'Only this morning you said you were planning to leave this very evening... Having second thoughts so soon?' He chuckled.

'No, but I had a run-in with Demetrios...' Erik recounted the incident in the stables. 'If I had not intervened, that coward would have whipped Alexios within an inch of his life. Luckily the palace wards were not far away, so I took the poor boy there. He should be well enough to travel tomorrow.'

'Despicable. You must have encountered Demetrios just after Emperor Basil had ordered him to board the next ship to Macedonia. He was in a violent mood on leaving the palace. No excuse for turning on a defenceless child, though.'

'Yes, I'm glad he's going. Anyway, I'll need to collect Alexios tomorrow, if he's well enough. And get this redressed.' Erik gestured to his wounded arm. 'So I'll stay another day, at least.'

'What happened there?' Harald glanced at Erik's bandage.

'A gift from Demetrios when I shielded the boy from his whip.'

'Hmm...' Harald looked at his friend's bandage. 'You

are going soft. You've ridden into battle with worse than that!'

'The healer insisted. She seemed to know what she was doing.'

Erik shrugged, trying to sound casual. But Harald knew him too well.

'Healer?' Harald cocked his head to the side. 'At the palace wards, you say?'

'Yes.'

Harald threw him a knowing glance.

'Well, well… Then I take it you must be talking about Princess Theadora?'

Erik schooled his features, not wanting to be drawn into conversation about the woman he had just left, and whom he couldn't stop thinking about.

'Yes. She tended to Alexios and treated my wound.'

'Aha… Well, it certainly all makes sense now. No wonder you are delaying your departure.'

'I don't know what you're talking about,' Erik retorted, a bit too quickly.

'She must have really put a spell on you if you think you need that scratch re-dressed.' Harald chuckled.

'Don't be a ridiculous, Harald. She's a skilled physician.'

Harald shot Erik a sly look.

'Only skilled? I heard she's a rare beauty…'

Erik strove for composure. If Harald only knew the effect she'd had on him… He struggled for a response, but Harald was too quick.

'What's this? Has a woman finally caught your fancy?'

Erik carefully controlled his voice, lest it betray his emotions. 'No, you know my views on that subject.'

'Oh, come on, Erik. What happened to Frida wasn't your fault. It was a terrible tragedy—'

Erik let out a dismissive grunt, and Harald knew his friend well enough to know he had touched a nerve.

'All right, all right. I'll leave off. Come, the other men are in the hall.'

'You go ahead. I'll meet you there.'

Harald disappeared into the drinking hall, leaving Erik alone with his thoughts. He pondered Harald's words. Though said in jest, he knew that there was some truth to them. He *did* want to return to the wards—and not just because he had to collect Alexios… He could not deny that the Princess had captivated him—so much so that his resolve to leave Constantinople was, for the tiniest of moments, temporarily suspended. She was magnetic. And no matter how hard he tried he just couldn't seem to get the image of those beautiful brown eyes out of his mind. Nor the feel of her small palms on his arm.

Thor's teeth! He was, or *should* be, immune to such feelings. He'd built a wall of iron around his heart since Frida died, and it was meant to be inaccessible. He'd promised himself that he would never let his love for another make him vulnerable, that he would never assume responsibility for the life of someone he loved…

He drained his cup. No, this was nothing but a passing fancy. Come morning, he'd be his old self again. The Princess *didn't* have a hold on him. He'd managed six years without feeling anything meaningful towards a woman, and he wasn't about to start now. He was just a little tired—and the day's events and what had happened to Alexios had somehow heightened his emotions.

Satisfied that he had a handle on himself, he went to join Harald and the other Varangians. He could do with another cup of ale.

Chapter Three

Dawn had cast a rosy tint across the landscape, bathing everything in a silvery cloak of pink and grey. Erik sat atop his black stallion, Mercury, and surveyed the sprawling magnificence of Constantinople from his favourite viewpoint. He lived for the mornings, when he could be alone with the sunrise and the city, away from the incessant clashing of steel that was a permanent feature of the Varangian quarters, and he'd taken to coming here whenever he needed time to think, or to order his thoughts.

He let his gaze drift to where the cluster of towers and churches formed a breathtaking silhouette against the dusky sky. In the middle of it all the Hagia Sofia assumed centre stage, dominating the skyline with the glittering peaks of its gold-plated domes. To his left, the large cupola of the Great Imperial Palace shimmered in the distance, flanked by its two crenulated turrets. It was sculpted out of rainbow sandstone, and he had always marvelled at how the hues of orange, pink and red blended perfectly to create a ripple-like effect as the sun's beams danced across the central façade.

He recalled the first time he had experienced this sunrise; it had been the day he had been accepted into the Guard. He smiled at the memory. He'd come full circle, for now it was his last day as a Varangian. Tomorrow he'd begin a new journey—one without his sword or battleaxe. The thought both excited him and filled him with a sense of nostalgia.

But there was one thing he had to do first, and his mind turned to the more pressing matter at hand. He'd spent the previous night convincing himself that the Princess was just another pretty woman with whom he had happened to cross paths…that what he had felt for her was just a momentary attraction. But the truth was she had aroused feelings in him that had been deeply buried for a long time. What was worse, she seemed completely unaware of her charm or beauty, and was therefore exactly the type of woman who needed to be kept at arm's length. Luckily, that would be easy, since he'd already purchased his fare to Cyprus and, as soon as he'd collected Alexios, would be boarding the next ship out.

Be that as it may, he could not deny that the prospect of seeing the Princess one last time filled him with a warm glow of anticipation.

He gently squeezed Mercury's flank, indicating that it was time to leave. The horse whinnied, confused by the unfamiliar path, down which Erik was now steering him.

'Easy, boy…we're just taking a short detour.'

But the stallion snorted again, tossing its black mane and stamping its hooves.

'What is it?'

Erik stroked the tensed muscle of Mercury's neck and saw that his ears were pricked forward. Mercury was an accomplished warhorse, and Erik had trained him so that he was finely attuned to his surroundings and able to sense danger over a mile away.

And then the sound of distant hoofbeats met his ears,

alerting him to the fact that they were not alone. He squinted his eyes against the low rays of the rising sun. A rider came into view, galloping at some speed towards them, and soon enough the horseman's identity was revealed. *Demetrios.* A shadow passed over Erik's features. He ought to pursue him and exact retribution for his treatment of Alexios. His hand immediately went to his sword, and he readied Mercury to charge as he drew it from its scabbard.

But the rider barely spared him a glance as he sped by in a cloud of dust, though Erik noted how his mouth was set in a grim line, and a look of hard determination was on his face. Then he saw that the cloud of dust that followed him trailed back from the direction of the wards and his heart stopped.

Alexios. Had Demetrios somehow discovered where Alexios was? Had he thought to finish off the boy while he lay on his sickbed?

Dread coursed through Erik's veins. He at once abandoned the idea to give chase, and instead hastened towards the hospital, fearing for Alexios's safety. He dug his heels deeper into Mercury's flanks, spurring on the large destrier until they were soon at their destination.

Drawing rein in front of the gates, Erik flung himself off the horse and hurried inside.

Thea tried to busy herself with anything she could. She hadn't had much sleep, and no amount of writing in her medical journals had been able to induce it. Instead, her thoughts had been filled with a certain golden-haired warrior.

When she had first set eyes on Erik she had been afraid—even when she had seen that he was in her uncle's pay. From her past experiences with Demetrios she had learnt that even if a man worked for her uncle, it did not necessarily mean he was trustworthy. Then there was the fact that he was a Varangian...

She worried at her lip. She was still wary of the mercenary-type lifestyle that led a man to enlist in the Guard, but she had to admit that at least this Varangian had a moral compass that pointed in the right direction, notwithstanding the gold and jewels he'd no doubt be collecting for his services.

The Northman had indeed been full of surprises, and had so far proved all her knowledge of men to be inaccurate and all her assumptions about Varangians to be ill-conceived. What she had seen was a brave soldier who had risked angering a general and who had put the safety of a defenceless boy before his own.

He had also exposed a sliver of vulnerability, if only for a split second, and once again she recalled the haunted look in his eyes as he'd gazed upon the injured child. For some reason, seeing that side to him had allowed her not to think of him as a man who could easily overpower her with his strength, or hold sway over her with his status, but instead as an equal, who might share the same heartaches and troubles as she.

But could it be true? After the manipulation she had suffered at the hands of Demetrios, did she dare believe this of any man?

It had all been very surprising—not least the part when she had somehow found her body responding to him in unfamiliar, not to mention wholly inappropriate ways. It hadn't just been his muscular frame which, from the parts she had seen of it, had made her feel as if a thousand butterflies were flitting around in her chest. It had been the way his blue eyes had seemed to bore right through her, rendering her speechless under the heat of his gaze…

She caught herself. This would not do! The holy sisters would be driven to an early grave if they knew what thoughts were running through her mind at this very moment.

Tossing and turning, she had eventually gave up on sleep and settled upon replenishing the mix of herbs she used for her poultices. Now she worked methodically, sorting through the different categories of plants and herbal flowers, all the while trying to make sense of her feelings. If only she could sort through them as decisively as she was sorting through these herbs! It was not like her to be so fanciful, nor to allow a man to distract her while she was at work.

Ironically, the thought caused her another lapse in concentration, and the pestle she had been using to grind the herbs accidentally slipped out of her hands. She was about to retrieve it when the subject of her thoughts came bursting in.

'Captain Svenson?'

Her startled gaze appraised his homespun garb. He was not clad in armour this time, but instead wore a plain, light tunic made from linen, cinched at the waist with a belt of woven leather, and a cloak. But he was still every inch the Varangian, since everything in his demeanour spelt danger—from the flashes of anger glinting in his steely blue eyes to the way his mouth was set in a thin line of fury.

'Alexios. Where is he?'

She got to her feet, and as she looked at him she noticed that same hint of vulnerability in his eyes she had witnessed the day before.

'Why, in the children's ward…where he's been all night.'

'Are you sure?'

'Yes—I've just been in to see him. He's had some water and is fast asleep again.'

The look of relief on his face was almost instant.

'Sorry… I did not see him in the main ward and I became concerned.'

'Whatever for? The wards are safe.'

'I know. It's just that I saw Demetrios…the general who attacked him yesterday. It seemed as if he had just left this place.'

Thea's eyes widened.

'Demetrios? *He* was the one who harmed Alexios yesterday?'

'Yes. You know him?'

She dropped her gaze to the ground.

'Yes. And if it was indeed Demetrios you saw just now, you need not worry. He was not here for the child.' She paused. 'He was here for me.'

'For *you*?'

Thea took a deep breath. She struggled to find the words to describe her connection to Demetrios. Once upon a time he had been her only companion in the city. She had come to value his friendship, for he had gone to great lengths to help her get her bearings in a city which had seemed so grand and new to her then. He'd shown her sides of it which she would otherwise never have discovered—from the secret tunnels laced with cobwebs beneath the palace's grounds, to the maze of alleyways and backstreets that criss-crossed through the heart of Constantinople. Then his behaviour towards her had slowly changed, and she'd soon sensed that it wasn't just friendship he was after.

But that wasn't a topic she wanted to address in any detail now.

'Yes. He befriended me when I came to live here. I was alone and did not know many people in the city.'

'I see. You keep some interesting company, Princess.'

His voice remained level, but there was no mistaking the accusatory tone that underscored it.

She jerked her head up sharply to meet his gaze. She could understand his anger, given Demetrios's treatment of Alexios, but he had no right passing judgement on things he knew nothing about.

Now it was her eyes that flashed with fire. 'I only meant that he showed me kindness at the time when I needed it the most. He wanted to be my...my friend. But then...' Her voice trailed off.

For a split second she considered telling Erik how she really felt about Demetrios. How she had discovered his ulterior motives for seeking out her companionship. How her rank in the line of succession had served a purpose for him. How he'd revealed a side to his character that had both frightened and repelled her. How it had changed her view of men and what to expect of them for ever.

But this was something that was personal to her, and a challenge she had to wrestle with. To explain the nature of her relationship with Demetrios to the man who stood before her now seemed futile—especially in light of how Demetrios had treated the poor boy. Erik clearly felt protective over Alexios, and revealing the extent of Demetrios's deplorable character would likely exacerbate his anger, which would not help the situation.

She looked up at him.

If he had been angry previously, it was nothing compared to the look on his face now. Those startling blue eyes had taken on a coldness she had not seen before—not even when he had arrived with the injured boy yesterday. It confirmed the need to keep the information to herself.

'Did he hurt you?'

His voice was danger...every word edged with ice. He took a step towards her, and now they were standing almost chest to chest. She could smell the faint aroma of sandalwood, and the tang of leather, and something else which she identified as unique to him. Something totally and utterly male. And, strangely, something that attracted her rather than scared her.

She wanted to answer his question. Demetrios had never harmed her—not physically, at least. But harm was not always physical... The taunting, the mental abuse, the sickly love letters, the threats... She'd suffered them all in silence. Because to respond in any way would have caused more harm than good. She didn't want to rock the political landscape. Demetrios served her uncle well, and after everything her uncle had done for her she considered Demetrios's actions insignificant in the grand scheme of things. Her uncle and his family were now *her* family, and the only people left to remind her of her mother. She couldn't risk losing them too.

No. She couldn't tell a soul.

'I—'

Before she could continue, there was a knock on the door.

'Your Highness, a letter for you.' A sentry walked in smartly. 'Demetrios sends his regards.'

He handed her an envelope and bowed out, oblivious to the building tension in the room.

Thea took the parchment and hastily set it down on her desk on top of other papers, cursing the bad timing. So *that* explained Demetrios's presence at the wards...

'Well?' Erik had not taken his eyes off her. 'Aren't you going to open your letter?'

He gestured at the spidery scrawl that she had come to know so well and to associate with Demetrios, and her gaze settled on Erik's outstretched arm, which still bore yesterday's bandage. She seized at the opportunity to change the topic of conversation.

'It is unimportant. I'll read it later. But we should re-dress that bandage.' She jerked her head at his forearm.

He did not move. Instead he continued to look at her, the expression in his eyes unreadable. But his reply left her in no doubt as to his feelings.

'If you give me the gauze I can do it myself.'

Again, she was taken aback by the iciness in his tone.

'I still need to examine it.'

'Is that necessary? You cleaned it yesterday. I am sure it is fine.'

She let out a frustrated sigh. He was nothing if not stubborn! She couldn't understand why he was behaving so. What had she done to upset him? Granted, he had not arrived in the best of moods, but she had sensed a distinct change in his attitude towards her when she had mentioned her connection to Demetrios. Perhaps he did not approve of her affiliation with him, having witnessed his treatment of Alexios.

A small wave of annoyance washed over her. He didn't know the half of it! And anyway, he had no right to concern himself with her affairs.

'It is necessary. I need to see it.' Her voice was firm.

A thick curtain of silence hung in the air between them. She felt small under the intensity of his gaze, which raked over her like a bushfire over sun-burnt grass, and she had an overwhelming desire to send the Varangian on his way and let him tend to himself.

Brushing it aside, she squared her shoulders in an attempt to stand tall—and was frustrated when the result was that she barely reached his shoulder.

After what seemed like an eternity, he spoke.

'Very well. I'll show it to you.'

'Thank you.' She ducked her head, fixing her stare on the injured arm. Holding his gaze any longer would be dangerous. 'How does it feel?' she asked.

'Better.'

'Any pain or fever?'

'None.'

'Good. Let me just—' She reached out to try and undo the bandage, but he took a step back.

'I'll do it.'

He was certainly doing his utmost to ensure she did not touch him. The realisation caused a dull ache to thud in her chest. She drew in a sharp breath, not wanting to acknowledge how it bordered strangely close to hurt.

'As you wish,' was all she could manage.

Confused by his behaviour, and her response to it, she watched as he unfastened his cloak and laid it on the back of her chair. Then he undid the knot at the top of the dressing and unwound the spiral of overlapping gauze as he held out his arm for her examination.

In spite of her feelings, she was pleased to see that the wound was indeed healing well.

'The wound looks good. But it needs some of this.'

She plucked out the healing unguent from her pouch, and before he could say a word started to apply it to the injury. She saw a muscle jump in his jaw, but he did not resist her again and allowed her to finish her task.

'I'll send you back with a supply of fresh gauze and some ointment, but otherwise...'

She searched for a way to create some lightness to the mood, since the tension between them which had been building brick by brick over the last half-hour now seemed almost as thick as the Theodosian walls which encircled the city.

'I am sure you will be happy to hear that you will not need to see me again.'

She attempted a small smile as she handed him the bundle of supplies. To no avail, for his expression was as stony as ever. She was, however, rewarded with a response, at least.

'That is helpful, since I am to leave the city tomorrow.'

'Oh...? You're being sent out on another mission?'

'No. I am leaving the Guard.'

Leaving the Guard.

She was beset by a maelstrom of emotions. So he would truly be gone from her life. She'd known him less than a day, but judging by her mind and body's reaction to the news it was as if she had known him for years. She couldn't understand it. She hoped, at least, that she was doing a competent job of masking her sadness, since it appeared that *he* was not in the slightest bit affected. In fact, quite the opposite, for it seemed as if he could not leave her company quickly enough.

'Then I wish you well.' Was all she could say.

'Thank you. I'll wake Alexios and we'll be on our way.'

'Wait.' He paused at the doorway and turned to look at her, making her heart stop. 'I—I mean, it would be wise to let him sleep. He needs the rest. You can collect him later this afternoon, when he awakes. Hilda can show you to his ward if—' She was about to say *If you do not want to see me* but stopped herself in time. 'If I am with other patients.'

'Very well. I shall return for the boy later. Here is a fresh change of clothes for him.' He handed her the bundle and reached for the door. 'Your Highness.'

He gave a small bow. His voice had taken on a cool politeness, and his use of her title, which only served to emphasise the social distance between them, bothered her.

'Thea, please.'

He inclined his head.

'Goodbye, Thea.'

Without a backward look, he left, and all that remained was the lingering scent of male musk that followed in his wake.

She had never heard him speak her name before and the sound of it uttered with that deep, velvety timbre sent a tingle down her spine, causing the sense of loss she felt as he walked out through the door to multiply tenfold. She stood motionless in her study, trying to make sense of what had just happened. Yesterday he had treated her with such warmth and respect, even praising her for her skills as a healer. But their encounter today could not have been more different. Today she had experienced the hard, cold soldier who merited his place in the Varangian Guard. Unrelenting. Unswerving. Fierce.

Yet just when she'd been about to explain Demetrios's behaviour, she hadn't been able to help but wonder whether it was concern that she saw in his eyes rather than anger. Perhaps it had been a mixture of the two. She sighed, for if it had been concern, it wasn't for her. As a Varangian, he had sworn an oath to protect the Emperor and everything that the Emperor held dear—which included her. He was just doing his duty. It had nothing to do with how he felt about her...

Felt about her? She really was in need of sleep if she was starting to think of their relationship as anything other than physician and patient! They were two strangers who had crossed paths—paths which would now diverge. His in a direction which led out of the city, and hers which pulled her within it.

Common sense prevailed. She didn't understand exactly what these feelings that this Varangian stirred in her were, but she guessed they were dangerous, and needed to be nipped in the bud immediately. Even if she *did* think this man was unlike any other, and even if he *could* be the one man who might be able to earn her trust, there was no question as to what her future held.

Her uncle had indulged her desire to be a healer and had allowed her free rein to do as she pleased. For now. Thea knew that there was a limit to the liberties he would bestow upon her.

She let out an exasperated sigh. She would be expected to do her duty, of course. Ever since she was a child she had been under no illusion as to what her role in society would entail. She was a Greek princess, a blood relative of the most powerful man in the eastern Roman empire, if not the world. Her marriage would be one that strengthened his ties with a neighbouring state, or reinforced a long-standing alliance. Marriage, for her, would not involve a man of her choosing—and certainly not a Northman who had served in the Varangian Guard.

It was unfair, and she railed against the injustice of it, but she had never questioned it because her duty to her family came first.

So whatever it was that she felt for this Varangian would

need to be extinguished as quickly as it had been ignited. She smiled wistfully. Well, that would prove easy, since he was about to walk out of her life just as quickly as he had walked out of her study.

Erik stormed out of the wards and strode to the tree where he had tethered Mercury. The horse was waiting patiently, oblivious to his master's foul mood until Erik kicked a stone away with such force that it went skittering across the courtyard, making Mercury whinny in disapproval.

Erik struggled to make sense of the scene that had just unfolded. The Princess had seemed to suggest that she and Demetrios were friends, or at least had been. Why would she involve herself with such a despicable man? And what was he to her now?

He recalled the look on her face when she'd spoken of their relationship and tried to decipher her expression. Had it been sadness? Perhaps she had learnt that Demetrios would soon be leaving the city and the news had upset her. Then there was the letter. Why was Demetrios writing her letters? Were they lovers? Was she intending to follow him to Macedonia?

A fierce wave of possessiveness surged through him, blinding him to all else. He was shocked at how visceral a response the image evoked in him, but the thought of another man touching her—especially if that man was Demetrios—set a hot rage coursing through his veins.

He knew that he had acted coldly towards her, but distancing himself from her had felt like the only way to navigate the complicated situation that he now found himself in. He was angered by her affiliation with Demetrios, but that had done nothing to temper the fierce desire that had threatened to overwhelm him. He'd let her tend his wound again—she'd given him no choice—but if he had let it go on for much longer it would have opened the floodgates to a sea of consequences…none of which he dared to contemplate. So much for his steadfast resolve.

What was he thinking?

She was a princess. He was a Varangian. Thor's blood! After today, he wouldn't even have *that* status—while Demetrios would hold a lofty post in the Macedonian court. Erik would be a common man, and a barbarian to boot. To entertain the thought of the two of them together was laughable—especially when he had the likes of a pure-blooded Greek like Demetrios to contend with. Besides, what business was it of his what the Princess did in her spare time, or who she associated herself with? Hadn't he promised himself that he would never become emotionally involved with a woman again?

He cursed silently under his breath. This morning's events were precisely the reason he had to leave Constantinople as soon as possible. He stamped down on the sharp stab of regret he felt at the thought of never seeing the Princess again, spurring Mercury faster towards his quarters. He'd pack his things, collect Alexios and board the first ship to Cyprus, where he could start his trade safely out of reach of the Princess and her beguiling charms.

Chapter Four

The sun was well past its afternoon zenith when Thea finally finished the day's tasks and returned to her consultation room. Shutting the door behind her, she leant against it and closed her eyes, letting out a slow breath. It had been a long day. Although it had been exhausting, she had welcomed the work, for it kept thoughts of Erik at bay.

But the reprieve was only temporary. Now, alone in her study, the barrage of emotions came flooding back. They'd been acquainted for less than a day, but their knowing each other for such a short space of time seemed to bear no relevance to how much he continued to invade her thoughts—nor was it proportionate to the feeling of loss she now felt. The nature of their last meeting saddened her, and the fact she would never see him again weighed heavy on her heart.

She crossed her arms loosely over her body and let out a sigh. It bothered her that he was leaving the city. It bothered her that she could have such complex feelings for someone who was practically a stranger. It bothered her that the last memory he would have of her was one which would always taint his view of her. But most of all it bothered her that he had the potential to so easily unravel the bindings around her heart which had hardened her towards trusting any man. And that in itself was unsettling—because it was something she had not thought possible.

That thought led her to ponder Demetrios's recent actions. Over the last few years she had certainly discovered the cruel and calculating streak in him. And he'd always somehow managed to find a way to make sure that she was never far from him. Sometimes, at banquets, he'd carefully engineer the seating arrangements to ensure she was by his side. She'd learned to ignore the unwanted attention, and the way his hand often grazed hers, or the way he'd place it on her thigh under the table, because she'd known he would not dare much more—not while her uncle was in close proximity. But sometimes he'd appear at the wards at an ungodly hour, feigning some injury or another, so that he could be personally examined by her, knowing that she would have assigned herself the late-night shift and would likely be one of the few nurses on duty. She had particularly loathed those scenarios, but luckily Hilda had never been far, and would often bustle in to offer assistance.

But of late he had become more daring. Demetrios was not a man who allowed himself outbursts of rage, nor outward shows of violence. Of course she'd seen him succumb to anger, but he always made sure it was disguised, however thinly, under a layer of cold manipulation. So his treatment of Alexios had shocked her. Even for Demetrios, it was out of character. She shook her head. Thankfully the boy was safe now, and likely many miles away from the city…with Erik.

Her heart gave another tug at the image of Erik departing Constantinople, but she hastily pushed it aside. It wouldn't do to dwell on the matter. Straightening her back, she dusted down her apron and turned her mind to practicalities. She ought to arrange for Alexios's bed to be changed in readiness for their next patient.

Arriving at the children's ward, she fully expected the boy's bed to be empty. But to her surprise the child was still there, playing happily with a toy she had given him that morning.

'Hello, sweetheart. I thought Erik would have collected you by now.' She scanned the ward, half expecting and— to her annoyance—half *hoping* the Viking would appear.

The boy shook his head, but did not seem unduly perturbed, so enchanted was he with his new toy. She knitted her brows together, confused. Alexios was like a son to Erik, so it was not likely he had forgotten such an important appointment. He must have been detained by a last-minute duty.

Tapping her finger on her cheek, she pondered what to do. She looked out of the window and saw the night guards taking over for their shift. It was getting late. She should take the boy to the Varangian quarters now, so the necessary arrangements could be made for his departure the following morning. It would suit her too, since the Guards' quarters were located in a building which adjoined the palace, and she could use the opportunity to call on her cousin Adriana.

'Let's go to him, shall we?'

Alexios nodded enthusiastically.

'Very well—come along.'

She gathered his belongings in a knapsack and the pair set out. As they approached the palace she looked up to where a row of copper helmets winked beneath the dying embers of the sun, accentuating the tight security under which the palace was held. Thea knew that their approach— indeed any visitor's approach—would be subject to the watchful gaze of the contingent of sentries that manned the walkways high on the roof.

She nodded a greeting to the gatekeeper as they passed through the huge bronze portcullis, and soon they were standing in front of the façade of the palace. Made of marble, its resplendent sheen glowed in the twilight hours. She smiled softly, remembering how its grandeur had overwhelmed her when she had first set foot in the palace. Her father's court in Rascia had been elegant, and pretty, but it paled in comparison to the splendour of Constantinople. Back then everything in this city had seemed to her to be made of marble—from the sculpted beasts that lined the pathway up to the grand keyhole doorway of the palace to the carved balusters that adorned the staircase at the base of the large entrance hall.

Holding Alexios by the hand, for she knew how daunting entering the palace could be, she guided him through a side wing leading to the imperial residences. Only royalty or the Emperor's closest advisors were allowed entry here, and it was one of her best-loved parts of the building. Vibrant murals lined the walls, telling tales of exotic places. Her favourite was one of a hummingbird hovering in mid-air above the shell-pink tubular flower of a honeysuckle, its metallic coloured wings beating incessantly as it claimed its nectar reward. She had never seen such a bird in real life, and it always reminded her that there was so much more to see outside of her world.

Soon they came to a courtyard, in the centre of which a tiered fountain babbled and gurgled, throwing up bubbles of spray around the fronds of forest-green plants that grew at its edges. Interspersed between them, colourful flowers nodded gently in the breeze, giving off the sweet fragrance of rose and lavender. A young woman was bent over them, pruning unwanted leaves and stems. She looked up as they approached, her eyes growing wide in recognition.

'Alexios?'

'Leonora!' The boy tugged free of Thea's hand and ran over to the woman to give her a hug.

The woman called Leonora was looking at his bandaged arm in concern, but when she registered who Alexios's companion was she at once sank into a deep curtsy.

'Your Highness.'

'Please, rise.' Thea gently placed her hand on the woman's arm. 'You are acquainted with Alexios?'

'Yes, Your Highness. My husband Harald and his guardian Erik are sword brothers and serve in the Guard together.'

Thea's heart gave an involuntary leap at the mention of Erik.

'Harald told me what happened to Alexios yesterday,' Leonora went on. 'Poor child.'

'Yes, Erik's timely intervention was fortunate. It has meant that Alexios's wounds are not grievous, and he has recovered well.' Thea paused. Saying Erik's name out loud felt strange after what had passed between them, but it didn't stop the small, familiar flutter in her belly taking hold. 'He mentioned he would collect him this afternoon, but he did not come.'

'Oh! I'm afraid Erik was summoned to see the Emperor earlier. But I can look after the boy until he returns, if you like? He can stay with my children. They know each other.'

'Of course—if it pleases Alexios?' She looked at Alexios for affirmation. The boy nodded enthusiastically.

'Very well.'

She inclined her head and handed Alexios's knapsack to Leonora, who led the boy away. Thea watched them go, her heart contracting a little at the fact that Alexios did not have any parents to go home to. But she was thankful that the boy at least had Erik, and people like Leonora, who cared about his welfare. Family was important. She was lucky that her uncle and his wife had welcomed her to the palace with open arms. She'd acquired a little sister in her cousin Adriana, too.

The thought reminded her of the purpose of her visit. She made her way to the other side of the courtyard, which opened into a large portico. Guards were dotted along the corridor, their uniforms unmistakable, marking them out as Varangians. Only they were allowed this close to the royal apartments. Thea's thoughts immediately strayed back to Erik. It was odd that he was meeting with her uncle if he was about to leave the Guard, but she supposed that was testament to her uncle's high estimation of him. He was probably being paid a substantial lump sum as a reward for serving in the Guard, she thought, as she reached the threshold of Adriana's chamber.

'Thea!' Seeing her cousin in the doorway, Adriana flung aside the piece of embroidery she had been working on and jumped up to envelop Thea in a tight embrace. 'What brings you here?'

'I had to drop off a patient in the Varangians' quarters.' Thea returned the hug and the two stepped into Adriana's chamber. 'So, I took the opportunity to visit you.'

'I am lucky, then. But you work too hard, cousin. Who's the patient, anyway?'

Thea briefly recounted the events of the previous day. She stuck to the facts, and refrained from mentioning her further encounters with Erik, for she did not want to be drawn into conversation about him. It was still too confusing, and she didn't trust her emotions. Besides, she knew that private conversations in the royal residences often made for gossip in the servants' quarters, and before dawn the maids would have spun a tale as intricate as a spider's web about their fictional love affair. Talk of her liaison with Erik would spread like wildfire through the city. Her reputation would suffer and, judging by his behaviour at their last meeting, she doubted that Erik would be best pleased about the effect it would have on his.

A fleeting expression of anger covered Adriana's usually soft, pretty features. 'Poor boy. That brute Demetrios! I am glad he is being sent away.'

Thea blinked, uncertain that she'd heard correctly.

'What do you mean?'

'Haven't you heard? Papa has asked him to fulfil the role of ambassador to King Antonius's kingdom in Macedonia. He is to leave on the first ship out, and it can't be soon enough!'

'Demetrios is leaving the city?'

'Yes, King Antonius was here last week, and Papa and he agreed that Demetrios would relocate to the Macedonian court to further strengthen our ties with Constantinople.'

Thea couldn't quite believe her luck. She would finally be free of Demetrios and his unwanted attention! She breathed a sigh of relief, though she puzzled over why her uncle would make such a decision. Moreover, for Antonius to have travelled all this way to meet with the Emperor was indeed a significant event.

'That is indeed welcome news, cousin. But why was Demetrios chosen for the role? And why was Antonius summoned?'

'Papa requested Antonius's counsel on account of Demetrios's recent behaviour, and since the matter is delicate their discussion had to be conducted in person. There are spies everywhere these days, and one cannot be sure whom to trust.' The thought prompted her to lower her voice. 'Papa thinks Demetrios is a threat. He's been wanting Papa's crown for years.'

Thea bit her lip. She knew Demetrios was ambitious, but to aim for the *crown*? The man was truly out of his mind.

Adriana continued. 'Papa says his spies have seen Demetrios stirring up trouble in the marketplaces and in the harbour. He's also becoming increasingly argumentative in Council. But Papa wants to retain Demetrios in his retinue in some capacity.'

'Why not send him into exile instead?'

'Demetrios has many supporters, and if Papa exiles him it could tip us into civil war. So Antonius suggested that Demetrios should become ambassador to his kingdom. Everyone wins. Demetrios attains a prestigious position in the mighty Macedonian court, and Papa can send him away from the city under the guise of it being a diplomatic mission, safe in the knowledge that he'll remain under Antonius's watchful gaze.'

'That sounds like a fair exchange.'

Thea supposed it could work. She tried to push aside the feelings of misgiving that surfaced momentarily. It felt too good to be true. Would she really be free of Demetrios? Perhaps that was why he had come earlier…to give her a farewell note of sorts…

'Did you hear me, cousin? He said to say hello to you.'

'Who did?' Thea brought herself to the present again.

'Antonius, silly!'

'Oh. Yes. Of course. I haven't seen him in years. How is he?'

Thea liked Antonius. He'd been sent to her father's court when he was a boy, to spend some time learning the Slavic tongue and traditions. The two were of similar age and had spent many a summer together.

Adriana sighed, a dreamy look in her eyes. 'He's so handsome and kind. *And* he's now King of one of the largest kingdoms in the East after Papa.' She shot Thea a wistful look. 'He was asking after you...'

Thea chuckled. 'Well, I should hope so—we've known each other since we were both in swaddles.'

'I suppose... I just wish he could see *me* as a grown woman. I'm no longer a little girl...and I wish Papa and everyone else would stop treating me so!'

Thea laughed, pulling Adriana into a soft embrace. 'You are the most beautiful woman at court. Everyone says so! But I didn't realise you wanted to start courting?'

'I'm bored here, Thea. Since you left, the days have become long and tedious. It's easy for you—you have your work and your patients. But I... I am alone. I am sure Papa is waiting to marry me off to some big fish, but I am tired of waiting! I want children, a home...' She let out a long, exasperated breath.

'I am sure you'll have your moment soon, my darling,' Thea said, stroking Adriana's hair.

She loved her cousin, but she couldn't fathom how different they were. Although Thea knew that the time for her to be married was drawing near, the last thing she could think of right now was an arranged marriage.

'I do hope Papa doesn't intend me to marry Cornelius, though,' Adriana continued, wrinkling her nose.

Thea giggled at her cousin's remark. Cornelius was a rather large, balding duke who had enquired after Adriana's hand a number of times. Thankfully, her uncle had kept him at bay, no doubt having set his sights on someone more influential and appropriate for his beloved Adriana.

She again thought of her own situation, and unbidden her mind presented her with the image of a tall Northman with eyes as blue as the sky and hair as light as corn… It came along with a thousand *what if?* questions. What if she hadn't been born a princess? What if she could retain her independence? What if she could choose whom she could fall in love with…?

Her thoughts were leading her down a rabbit hole, and it was of no use. She couldn't change any of it. She would do her duty to her city and to her family. Her uncle would expect her to accept whomever he chose for her and she would do it gladly, as a small repayment for all he had done for her. He and Adriana were the only family she had left, after all.

But still it didn't stop her heart breaking at the thought of losing her independence and, more importantly, her work. She'd no longer have her patients, and being a healer was the one thing that gave her life meaning. Once she became a married woman she would be expected to melt back into the mould which had been set for her since birth—that of dutiful wife.

As if reading her mind, Adriana brought the conversation around to the subject of her healing.

'I've been talking about myself too much,' Adriana chided herself. 'Will you need to tend to the boy at the Varangians' quarters tonight?'

'No, Alexios won't need further attention. Thankfully his wounds are healing well. Besides, he is due to leave the city tomorrow with the Varangian.'

She hoped Adriana had not heard the tone of sadness that underscored her voice.

'I see. Who is this Varangian? He must be even more audacious than the rest of his kind if he dared to cross swords with Demetrios.'

'I believe he goes by the name of Captain Svenson.' Thea forced her voice to remain level. 'And, yes, he's certainly brave.'

'Ah, yes, everyone knows Captain Svenson! All the ladies at court swoon over him. He has many admirers here.'

Thea ignored the involuntary dart of jealousy that pricked at her. 'I have no doubt.'

'Oh, come, cousin. Even *you* must admit that he is handsome.'

'I suppose so.'

Thea attempted a shrug. He was handsome—there was no denying that. But her reaction to him still confused her.

'You are so hard to please! One day we will find a man to impress you.' Adriana poked playfully at Thea.

Thea offered her a weak smile. She had never told Adriana about Demetrios and his behaviour towards her, but it had meant that she could never participate in the kind of harmless flirting the ladies at court often indulged in. Instead, she tried to come across as indifferent towards her suitors, and Adriana had always teased her about this.

'In any event, the Varangians are such a blessing. Papa can't speak highly enough of them. They are a true source of comfort and protection for him—and for us all.'

'Yes, they certainly are.'

Although Thea had always been dubious about the motives that a man might have for becoming a Varangian, this time she found she wasn't so sure. Because hadn't she recently come across one who had shown a depth that she'd otherwise found lacking in such soldiers?

Sensing her cousin's unease, and mistaking Thea's silence for a reluctance to talk about matters of the state, Adriana rose and skipped over to ring the servants' bell.

'Anyway, enough of this talk of Varangians. Will you stay for some supper, cousin?'

Thea nodded, thankful for the change of subject. The two women chattered for a while longer and then, after sharing a light meal with her, Thea bid her cousin a fond farewell and returned to the wards.

Spending time with Adriana had cheered her somewhat, but Thea was still drained after the day's events. She sank into her chair and felt something at the small of her back. Reaching behind her, she pulled the object round and saw that it was Erik's cloak. He'd been in such a rush to get away from her earlier that he had forgotten it!

She fingered the woollen lining, and tentatively dared to hold the fabric up to her cheek. She found herself inhaling the scent of male musk which she had in such a short time come to associate, quite unconsciously, with Erik.

With a start, she mentally berated herself.

Pull yourself together. He's leaving. You'll never see him again.

With stalwart reserve, she stood up primly and folded the cape, resolving to send it to Erik with one of the guards later on. For now, she had to finish doing her final evening round of the wards.

As she prepared to leave, she glimpsed the letter from Demetrios that still lay unopened on her desk. The sight of it made her stomach roil, and she clenched her fists until she could feel her fingernails digging into the palms of her hand. She hated receiving his letters. But at least this should be the last one.

Holding Erik's cloak in one hand, she picked up the letter with the other. Seeing the two items in her hands, side by side, created a paradoxical image. One belonged to a man whom she loathed beyond all others, and the other belonged to a man whose attention, on the contrary, she would have welcomed.

She turned her gaze to the letter. It would be easy to mistake it for a harmless missive, but... Suddenly realisation dawned on her. Erik must have thought Demetrios's note was a love letter, and had likely inferred that their relationship was something more than friendship. She didn't know the contents of the letter yet, but they certainly would not evoke in her anything close to affection, let alone love.

A hysterical hiccup of laughter escaped her mouth.

She and Demetrios.

She knew Demetrios wanted her for his wife, and the passage of time had done nothing to quell his desire or temper his determination, in spite of her attempts to repel him. If anything, they had done the opposite.

A fresh wave of anger and frustration surged through her, and it was all she could do not to march back to Erik's quarters at the palace and clear up his misunderstanding. It was madness, she knew, since they were practically strangers, but she hated the fact that their last encounter had ended so abruptly, and that he might think that she and Demetrios were lovers.

Common sense prevailed once again. If Erik's last memory of her was such, then so be it. It was probably better that way. Pursuing this further would only lead to heartache.

Wearily, she slid her finger under the seal of Demetrios's letter, breaking apart the waxy substance. She expected it to contain a cruel jibe or two—she doubted Demetrios would leave the city and her quietly—but she certainly wasn't prepared for the words that danced before her eyes as she unrolled the parchment.

This time, you won't be able to refuse me.

* * *

'What did you make of it all?' Harald asked Erik as they made their way back to the barracks.

Notwithstanding the fact that Erik would shortly be leaving the Guard, Emperor Basil had requested that he attend a secret gathering, along with Harald and some of the other Varangian commanders.

Erik hadn't expected to be called to a meeting of the Guard when the Emperor was fully aware that he was leaving. But he'd soon found out that this was no ordinary occasion. He'd arrived at Basil's private quarters to learn that the Emperor had asked the Varangians and the head officers of the national army to renew their oaths of allegiance to him, making it clear that wavering loyalties would not be tolerated and allegiance to the Emperor was to be absolute.

Erik frowned. Such a gathering only happened in two situations: when a new Emperor ascended the throne, or in times of civil upheaval. Erik knew that Constantinople's history was steeped in conflict, both as a result of internal and external foes, and the undercurrent of unrest never quite abated—it was accepted as the status quo. But if Basil was now calling for members of the national army to refresh their oaths, it meant that he was afraid of an enemy within the city. One which posed an immediate threat.

After the other commanders filed out, Harald and Erik had remained behind, and the Emperor had gone into more detail about his concerns. Although Demetrios was being sent to Macedonia—which Basil hoped would mitigate the threat of him spearheading an uprising—he was worried that Demetrios had already mustered enough support to challenge the crown, notwithstanding his physical absence from the city. So he wanted the Varangians and the army to be on alert, and to be even more prepared for a conflict than before.

Now Erik sensed the note of unease in Harald's question, and he had to admit he felt it too.

'It doesn't bode well,' Erik admitted. 'But the Guard is strong. And the army will follow its lead.'

'True. But Demetrios is sly. Who knows what he has been up to? We will need to station our spies everywhere— from the taverns down in the harbour to the market stalls in the main squares. At least until the threat of war passes.'

Erik nodded, feeling a pang of guilt that he would shortly be leaving the city and these troubles behind.

He looked skyward. The sun was setting. He needed to collect Alexios and then finish making preparation for the long journey ahead. He wondered if he would encounter the Princess again, and the thought made his heart skip a beat despite the fact that their last meeting had been charged with tension and bitterness—at least on his part.

He was still bristling at the thought of her cavorting with Demetrios, the very man whom her uncle now feared. He wondered if the Emperor knew of her liaison with him. Perhaps he ought to mention the whole affair to Basil. After all, was he not still a Varangian today? Except he wasn't exactly sure what he would be mentioning. The fact that Thea and Demetrios were friends? That they were lovers? He didn't know the specifics of Thea's relationship with Demetrios, and he certainly could not go bandying about rumours of the Princess being involved romantically or otherwise with the man who appeared to be the Emperor's opposition. Not without proof.

But it did make him wonder—had she been privy to any of Demetrios's plotting? It was possible. Inter-family feuds were not uncommon when it came to usurping the throne of Constantinople, and if Demetrios succeeded she'd be Queen. But what if she was *not* involved? That would mean he would be leaving her behind in a city that was under threat of an impending uprising...

Let sleeping dogs lie.

He tried to convince himself that after tonight the fate of Constantinople would no longer be in his hands. He would no longer be under any duty to her, as a member of the royal family. Anyway, with Harald commanding the Guard the city was in safe hands. He tried to comfort himself with the thought.

'Alexios will be waiting for me to collect him. I must take my leave, brother.' He clasped Harald's forearm. 'I'll see you later—'

But he'd hardly finished his sentence when he glimpsed Alexios in the distance, with Leonora. The boy saw Erik and hurtled up to him.

'Alexios. What are you doing here?'

'The Princess brought him,' Leonora answered, coming up behind him.

His pulse quickened at the mention of Thea. Was she still here? He scanned his surroundings. There was no sign of her.

'She left some time ago,' Leonora continued. 'She enquired after you. I think she was expecting you to collect Alexios this afternoon. I told her you were with the Emperor.'

He felt his face suddenly take on a crestfallen expression—an involuntary response, but one which Harald was quick to notice.

'I don't think I've ever seen you this bewitched by a woman, brother!' He clapped a large hand on Erik's shoulder, but quickly held up his hands when Erik threw him a deadly scowl.

'All right…all right. Come, Leonora, let's take our leave before we experience the full scale of Erik's wrath.' He chuckled and led his wife away. 'I'll see you off in the morning, Erik.'

Erik grunted, then made his way to his own quarters with Alexios. He wanted to let Harald know that it didn't matter whether or not he was 'bewitched' by this woman. He didn't belong in her world and never would.

Thea stared down at the scroll, a wave of panic rising within her. This must surely be another one of Demetrios's cruel pranks. Only a few hours ago Adriana had informed her that Demetrios was bound for Macedonia. She knitted her brows in concern. What could Demetrios mean?

This time, you won't be able to refuse me.

The familiar sense of unease gripped her belly in a tight fist. Would he defy the Emperor and refuse to locate to Macedonia? If he did that, he'd remain in the city—and that could mean only one thing… Adriana had said he had gathered meaningful support. Thea knew that that would have involved Demetrios and his followers engaging in bribery and blackmail. No stratum of society would have been left untouched—from the lowly fishmongers in the market square to the soldiers in the national army.

Come to think of it, she didn't recall seeing the usual night guards at the entrance of the wards when she had returned from seeing Adriana. Yet she could have sworn she had seen the guards change shift when she took Alexios to the palace earlier that evening…

A thin sheen of sweat formed on her forehead. She ran to the window that overlooked the palace, peering into the darkness to ascertain any sign of movement or disturbance. Nothing.

She hastened across the room to the other window, which overlooked Galata Tower, where a flame perpetually burned bright, signifying peace and security. Again, she couldn't see anything unusual.

She worried at her lip, starting to turn away, but just as she did so the flame was suddenly put out. Seconds later a horn sounded. She had never heard it before, but she knew instantly what it was.

It was the city's defence siren.

It heralded war.

Thea rushed out, her concern first and foremost for her patients. Thankfully there were only two patients tonight. Hurrying to the main ward, her heart in her mouth, she saw that Hilda was already at the helm, directing the other nurses to gather supplies and helping the patients to get dressed.

'Miss Theadora!' Hilda's eyes were wide with concern. 'You must leave this place and seek refuge in the palace. The horn has sounded. It's too dangerous for you here—'

Thea placed a firm hand on the older woman's shoulder. 'I am not leaving, Hilda. These are my people.' She gave her a reassuring nod, although reassured was far from how she felt. 'I will go once the patients and the nurses are safe.'

She ignored Hilda's disapproving look and helped her lift one of the patients out of bed. Soon, the handful of nurses and the two patients were ready.

'You know how to navigate your way through the tunnel? Here.' She thrust a pouch of gold coins into Hilda's hands. 'This should guarantee you and the others safe passage across the Marmara, plus some extra for food and amenities.'

'But my lady, what about you?'

'I will be fine. I'll go to the palace. Do not worry. Now, go!'

Thea watched as the small group clambered through the secret entrance to the tunnel that led out of the wards and burrowed deep underground beneath the city, opening out to the harbour at the Port of Marmara. After the last member of the group had disappeared from sight she carefully concealed the entrance again and made her way to her chamber.

She dared to look through the window and immediately regretted it. Smoke blotted out the sky in a thick, dark shroud suspended over the city, and even with all the entrances shut the bitter, acrid smell of burning thatch reached her nostrils.

She forced herself to peer through the thick blanket of smog and could just about make out the flickering glare of torches. She could hear the roar of the ravenous flames even above the din of weapons clashing and the clamour of shouts and screams. Her throat went dry with terror, but she strove for composure as she sought to make a mental note of the essentials she might need in the short term.

She quickly gathered some medical supplies and stuffed them in a leather bag, along with a change of clothes and two pouches of gold coins. In the hospital kitchens she located a loaf of bread, a hunk of cheese and some figs, and also a skin of water. She wrapped them up in a muslin cloth and deposited it in her satchel. Finally, she located the dagger which her father had bequeathed to her, and fastened it to her belt, grateful that he had taught her basic skills in combat.

Satisfied that she had everything she needed, she turned to leave. But just then the thud of approaching footsteps met her ears, and the large wooden door of the foyer swung back on his hinges.

'I've been looking everywhere for you.'

A terrified gasp escaped her lips as she whirled around to identify the intruder, but there was no need. She would have recognised that voice anywhere.

Chapter Five

Erik had been lying awake, staring at the timbered ceiling, unable to banish thoughts of the Princess from his mind. Never for a moment had he thought that his last night in Constantinople would feel like this, or that he might regret hanging up his Varangian's cloak. He had poured blood and sweat—quite literally—into serving in the Guard. And the success of every battle, every siege, had culminated in this very moment—the moment when not only had he earned enough coin to leave the Guard a rich man, but he had also gained the trust and admiration of the Emperor of Constantinople.

He'd fought with honour and valour, working his way to the topmost rank in the Guard. He'd even saved the Emperor's life on one occasion. As a reward for his unwavering loyalty Basil had declared him his most trusted advisor, and had even bequeathed to him with swathes of land in various parts of the Eastern Roman Empire, which would assist him in his commercial endeavours.

He wanted to make use of all the connections he had made in the region, so that he could finally set up his trading enterprise—which he hoped someday would stretch as far north as his homeland in the Northern Lands, and as far east as Persia. He should be happy. Yet there was something missing from this image of his future life. And he knew that that *something* started and ended with the Princess.

A distant knell of warning sounded at the back of his mind. Quite apart from his promise to himself that he would close his heart to love, in no reality could he hope to have even the slightest chance with her. He hailed from the North. In the eyes of the Greeks—especially those who were highborn—he was a barbarian. He'd never be seen as one of them, no matter his status back home. It was not even as if he could call upon his rank in Norway, and the fact that his father was jarl of one of the most powerful kingdoms in the Norse lands. He never would. Because, after all, it was his rank that had caused Frida's death. And how could he be responsible, yet again, for someone's life just because he was highborn himself?

Restless, he swung his legs over the side of the bed and strode over to his washstand to pour himself a cup of water.

And then he heard it.

The deep, mournful sound of a horn.

He rushed over to Alexios, who was lying on a pallet on the other side of the room, and shook the boy gently.

'Alexios, wake up!'

The boy's eyes were soft with sleep, but on seeing Erik's expression he jerked upright.

'We must go! Gather your things quickly!'

The boy dutifully did as he was told, and Erik hastily donned his armour.

'Stay close,' he said to Alexios as the two made their way through the Varangians' quarters.

They arrived at Harald's chamber, where Leonora and the children were milling about, hastily gathering clothes and food.

'Erik!' Leonora hurried over. 'Harald has just left. He has gone to the Emperor.'

'Yes, that is where I am going, too. I will need to leave Alexios in your care, if that is not too much to ask?'

'Of course not.'

'Thank you, Leonora. You and the children should stay close to the palace guard.'

'We will.' She placed a hand on his arm. 'And Erik… make sure you both come back to us safely,' she said, as once again she took Alexios into her care.

Erik nodded. 'I give you my word,' he said, and then he turned to address Alexios. He gripped his shoulder and looked down on the boy who so reminded him of Bjorn.

'I want to fight, too! I want to protect the Empire!'

'And you will—when the time comes. But for now, Leonora and her family need you to protect *them*.'

The boy nodded solemnly, pleased at this allocation of responsibility, and Erik's heart gave a tug. It was the same expression Bjorn had always worn whenever Erik had left to go trading and asked him to assume the role of head of the family to protect his mother.

'I will see you soon.'

Erik turned on his heel and sprinted to the Emperor's private quarters. Harald and a few others were already there, their expressions a mixture of surprise and joy as they recognised Erik and realised that he was going to stay and join their ranks.

'Captain Svenson.' Emperor Basil stood up. 'Thank you for staying.'

Erik nodded, and moved to sit at the table, removing his helmet and placing it in front of him.

'I was informing the others of the situation at hand,' said the Emperor. 'It is as I feared. Despite renewing their oaths of loyalty to me just this very evening, it appears that some of the captains in my army have defected. Their leader is, of course, Demetrios. He has bribed every rank. The tradesmen and many of the working class are in his pay, too. Indeed, my scouts say that the conspiracy has spread far and wide.'

'Your Majesty, give us the order and the streets will flow with the blood of Demetrios and his supporters.'

Harald's voice boomed around the chamber. It was met with cheers and the banging of fists from the other Varangians.

'Let us quash this rebellion once and for all and expose Demetrios for the rat that he is. It has been far too long since the city has witnessed a lynching.'

'I admire your enthusiasm, Harald, but the situation requires delicacy. We must avoid this escalating into a civil war. And I will not permit bloodshed, even amongst the traitors, unless absolutely necessary,' Basil decreed.

'But, Your Majesty, Demetrios cannot be allowed to run amok around the city. Who knows the extent of his treachery? He could be allying with the Bulgurs—or, worse, the Ottomans—to destroy you.'

'That is exactly why we must be careful. As you all know, the Varangian Sea Guard are in Sicily, keeping the Normans in check. As for the City Guard and the Palace Guard, strong and worthy fighters as they are, they will be outnumbered. The national army, both infantry and cavalry, cannot be counted on for support. It is unclear which legions are loyal to the crown, and which to the opposition. The same applies to the navy.'

One of the commanders stood up. 'So what are we to do if not stay and fight? Are we to flee?'

'Yes. Or at least give Demetrios that impression for now.'

Sounds of disgruntled murmuring and whispers reverberated around the chamber. It was not often that the Varangians were forbidden from doing the very thing for which they had enlisted—fighting to protect the Emperor and the Empire.

Basil held up his hand and the room fell silent at once.

'You are here because of your unswerving devotion to me. I know you yearn for the blood of traitors. But your time will come.'

The Varangians waited, their expressions expectant. Despite the situation the Emperor's voice was level, his countenance impassive. He was a seasoned warrior himself, used to a crisis. And whilst royalty were not permitted to display any form of emotion in public, his grey eyes smouldered with anger like hot flints of stone. Soon the Varangians understood why.

'The safety of my family is of paramount importance...'

He stood up and paced the room. Erik realised that this was the first major uprising since Princess Adriana's birth. The Emperor was clearly focused on protecting her.

'We go to the Macedonian stronghold in the west,' Basil continued. 'I have made a treaty with King Antonius. Macedonia and Constantinople will unite. One of the clauses in the treaty obliges him to supply us with troops and resources for just such an event as this. We will seek refuge with him, and return with reinforcements. And then you will have your fill of fighting.'

All around Varangians cheered, stamping their feet and banging their swords on their shields.

'And what has King Antonius asked of Constantinople in return?' Harald queried.

'The hand of my dear niece Princess Theadora.'

Those few words made Erik feel as if he had been

punched in the stomach a dozen times. He was grateful that everyone's attention was focused on the Emperor, for he did not trust his expression to remain impartial at this news.

So the Princess was betrothed to King Antonius. The only positive outcome of that from Erik's perspective was that it meant the prospect of the Princess continuing a relationship with Demetrios, if she'd even had one, was no longer a possibility.

'Which brings me to the next item of urgency,' Basil continued. 'Harald, Erik...your task will be to fetch my niece from the wards and bring her to the royal barge at once. The mission will require stealth, so you will go unaccompanied. Every street and pathway is likely crawling with Demetrios's men.'

'Yes, Your Majesty.'

Harald was speaking, and Erik was thankful for that, for no words seemed able to leave his mouth.

Basil went on. 'Time is of the essence. As soon as the barge is ready we will set sail. If you do not find the barge at the harbour, then you must assume we have departed. If that is the case, your orders are to travel to the Macedonian stronghold in the west with the Princess as quickly as you can. I'll send a contingent of Varangians ahead and you can meet them on the way, so you will have protection once you leave the city.'

The two men nodded in acknowledgment and got to their feet. While the thought of seeing the Princess would usually have filled Erik with excitement, now he would have given anything to be assigned any other task than this. Knowing she was betrothed, and having to rescue her and deliver her to the royal barge only for her to marry another, would leave a bitter taste in his mouth. But a Varangian's obedience to the Emperor was absolute, and he had no choice.

'Look after her, my captains. I would not entrust such a task to anyone but you. Godspeed.' Basil turned to the others. 'The rest of you will come with me and the royal household. The Queen and the Princess Adriana will need your protection, as will I. Ready the horses too—as many as the barge can carry.'

The Varangians needed no further encouragement. They leapt to their feet, rallying around the Emperor amidst shouts of encouragement and support as they prepared to escort him to the harbour.

Erik and Harald headed in the opposite direction. To the wards.

Thea felt an icy trickle of terror drip down her spine.

'Demetrios.'

'At your service, *Princess*.' He sank into a deep bow, one sardonic brow arched in irony.

'What do you want?'

'Come now…you know the answer to that.'

Thea fought the rising panic that threatened to overwhelm her. She looked at this man whom she despised beyond all others. His eyes smouldered with blood lust and physical lust in equal measure. She knew then that she was cornered. Her luck had finally run out. There really was no chance of escape, since behind him stood about half a dozen of his cronies.

She swallowed hard. 'Leave me be, Demetrios, or you will answer to my uncle.'

He laughed softly, but nothing about his expression was soft and his lips curved up in a cruel smile.

'My dear, I'm afraid your uncle has abandoned you. It's just you and me now.'

'Why are you doing this?'

Even as the words left her mouth she looked for an escape route, playing for time. She had to get out of this place. He was dangerous. Mad. Evil. But how to get past him?

A large oak cabinet stood to her right, barricading the concealed entrance through which she had sent Hilda and the patients just moments earlier, and Demetrios and his men stood in front of her. If she made any move to run, he'd be on her like a hound after a fox.

'I am doing what I should have done years ago. I'm claiming the crown. This city has fallen to pieces over the years since your uncle has held the throne. He allows foreigners from far and wide to come here and settle within our walls, stealing our trade and our women. It's despicable. No longer are our people pure-blooded Greeks.' He scowled menacingly.

She could barely find the words to speak, but she swallowed hard and summoned the only thing that Demetrios could never take from her: her dignity. She would not beg, and nor would she cower before him.

'Those *foreigners* are our strength,' she told him. 'They teach us new ways, they bring us better and innovative methods of healing. Stop this conspiracy. I am sure you and my uncle can find a compromise.'

Thea was trying to make him see sense, to put an end to this madness. But he was beyond listening to reason. He dismissed her out of hand.

'As for those filthy Varangians—they need to be banished. For too long has Constantinople emptied its coffers for the Norsemen. The Emperor's bodyguard ought to comprise only Greek soldiers. They alone have the ability to be unswervingly loyal to this city.'

'Like you?' Thea spat out. 'You've betrayed the Emperor.

Traitor! The Varangians have honour, and they have proved their worth a thousandfold.'

'So you are partial to the Varangians?' He grabbed her arm, snarling, 'I suppose you've taken one for a lover? Is that why you've spurned me all this time?'

For a fleeting moment the image of Erik presented itself to her. But the fact that he was not there only added to her misery. She was alone, but she'd fight tooth and nail until the end.

Again, she jerked out of Demetrios's grip, and suddenly she remembered the dagger that nestled against her waist. Would she dare use it?

'It's none of your business,' she said.

'Oh, it certainly is—because I expect my wife to aspire to the utmost virtue.'

'Your *wife*?' Incredulous, she let the words burst from her. 'I'd rather die than be anywhere near you. I hate you!'

'Look around, Princess. You don't have much of a choice.' He leaned towards her and thrust his face in front of hers. 'Ah, well… You might hate me now, but in time you'll see sense and you'll come to love me just as ardently as you'll warm my bed.'

He reached out in an attempt to pull at her bodice, but she slapped his hand away before his fingers made contact.

She took a step back. 'Don't touch me!'

'Oh, I will—and I'll do much more. But first you'll come with me to the chapel, so that we can make things official. Then you will take your rightful place by my side as Queen.'

The smug satisfaction on Demetrios's cruel, wolfish features made her blood curdle. Her mind recalled the last two years—the sickly love letters from him to her, his spiteful threats when those letters went unanswered, his constant loitering around the wards, the manipulation. The memories jabbed at her like tiny, painful darts, and soon a wave of emotion surged through her until it broke in a torrent of molten rage, tipping her over the edge.

'Never!'

She reached inside her cloak for the dagger and took a swipe. The knife's edge made contact with Demetrios's forearm, drawing blood. He leapt back in surprise, his features contorted with fury, turning his face a mottled red.

'You insolent witch!'

Thea's reflex was to strike out at him again, but this time he anticipated her move. Quick as a viper striking at a vole, his hand shot out and parried the blow, fastening on her wrist. The force of his grip made her gasp in pain, her eyes widening as his fingers tightened with deliberate brutality, twisting her wrist until the dagger fell with a thud to the stone floor.

Desperate, she lashed out with her free hand, her nails raking across his face. She closed her eyes and waited for his reaction—but it never came. Instead, she felt his grip loosening. Behind Demetrios a commotion was unfolding. He pushed her back roughly as he whirled around to determine the cause, and she crumpled to the floor.

Behind his men a cloud of smoke parted to reveal two Varangians, their ruby-red cloaks unmistakable even against the backdrop of the flames which were now hungrily licking at the building next door. Already two of Demetrios's men lay lifeless on the flagstones, their blood dripping off the Varangians' swords. One of them stepped forward, the glare of burning buildings glinting off his sleeveless chainmail and helmet as he stood there surveying the scene with utter composure. Broad shoulders carried the armour as if it were as light as muslin, and bare arms tanned to a golden colour bore rings just as golden, encircling his biceps.

'Beating defenceless children is not enough for you, then, Demetrios? Now you prey upon women too?'

Thea would have recognised the deep, velvety timbre of that voice anywhere.

Erik.

A tidal wave of relief washed over her. He was still several paces away, but there was no mistaking him. Thea lifted her gaze to his face. His mouth was set in a grim line, and she saw how the iciness of that cold glare bored into Demetrios. It made Thea want to cower beneath it, in spite of the fact that it appeared he was here to protect *her*. Had she not known the face that lay underneath the iron helmet she would have fled in terror, for it obscured his features, the sharp nasal strip and slanting cheek guards creating a countenance designed to terrify.

Behind him another Varangian, just as tall and almost as broad, stood at the ready.

Demetrios drew his sword and snarled.

Erik and Harald had used the secret underground tunnels from the palace to get most of the way to the wards. They'd emerged a few streets in front of it and surveyed the chaos that surrounded them. The insurgents had been busy at work, setting market stalls and taverns alight. The sound of screaming townswomen and crying babes was only rivalled by the clash of steel on steel. At any other time the pair of Varangians would have rushed to the defence of the vulnerable, but the Emperor had assigned them a specific task and they were duty-bound to complete it, so they'd moved doggedly forward.

Soon they'd arrived at their destination and seen that

the thatched roof of the building adjoining the wards was ablaze, sending plumes of smoke high into the sky. And the flames were already making their way deliberately across the first floor of the hospital.

'Blast it…' Harald had breathed. 'I hope we are not too late.'

'Wait.' Erik had held his comrade's arm in check. 'Look.'

He'd pointed at the ground floor where, through the window, he could see silhouettes of people.

Please let that be the Princess.

'We'll have to move quickly. It's only a matter of time before the building will collapse under the flames.'

Harald had unsheathed his sword as he'd followed Erik to the entrance.

Erik had seen her first. The expression of fear and anger on her face had set his teeth on edge, and his hand had instantly gone to the hilt of his sword, even as a jolt of relief and protectiveness shot through him. She was still alive. The need to protect her, to keep her safe, had almost brought him to his knees. In front of her, he'd made out the distinct form of Demetrios, who seemed to be flanked by about six men.

As if sensing the tension in his companion, Harald had stepped in front of Erik. 'Brother, I know you are fond of the woman, but she is betrothed to another. Keep your feelings buried. You cannot afford to be distracted.'

Erik had felt like a child being scolded. But he'd had to admit that Harald's words rang true. There was no room for distraction. A Varangian was trained to keep his emotions in check.

He'd schooled himself, drawing the huge iron sword he'd named Skull-Splitter.

'You are right, brother.'

The sound of their approach had been masked by the surrounding melee, and the two men at the rear of Demetrios's retinue, oblivious to their presence, were dispatched in short order. But the others, whose attention had been focused on their master's exchange with the Princess, now became aware of the Varangians and turned to face them, forming a wall in front of Demetrios.

'Beating defenceless children is not enough for you, then, Demetrios?' said Erik. 'Now you prey upon women too?'

'Hand over the Princess by order of the Emperor!' Harald bellowed.

Demetrios parted the defensive barrier that his men had formed in front of him.

'The Princess is mine, and the Emperor no longer merits that title.'

'Release her, traitor, and you will be spared. Else meet the same fate as your friends.' Harald pointed his sword to the lifeless forms.

'You are outnumbered, Varangian vermin. It is you who should beg to be spared. And as for the Princess… If you survive this night you can tell Basil that I've taken her to wife.'

Until now, Erik had kept his wrath in check. But no more. He launched himself at the man closest to him, the sheer fury of his charge driving his opponent back as the great blade of Skull-Splitter came down on him with such force that the crunch of blade on bone was heard by all.

He went down like a felled oak. Silence ensued as the rebels took a moment to register what had happened.

And then all hell broke loose.

The two Varangians braced themselves for the onslaught.

Even outmanned, they knew how to depend on each other for protection—as they had over a hundred times before.

Thea was not sure how she kept her eyes open, nor how she did not crumple under the sheer suspense of it all. Although the Varangian duo had taken down three of Demetrios's men with relative ease, the remainder were on the alert and raging with blood lust, and the air was heavy with smoke, making it difficult to see their opponents.

Thea clapped her hands over her mouth, forcing herself to watch the scene unfold—for the next opponent to face Erik was a giant.

Thea gasped. How could he defeat such a man? But gradually she saw how a Varangian's training came into its own. It was not all about brawn, but tactics. Erik used his agility as his strength, until finally the Greek giant started to show fatigue. Without hesitation, Erik drove his sword up under his guard. He staggered backwards, hitting the floor like a large sack of grain.

All around burning timber and thatch were falling from the ceiling and the roof, and the wooden beams had started to creak as if in agony. Directly above Erik, Thea saw a large, smouldering rafter that was on its last legs.

'Erik, look out!' she screamed.

He heard her, and dodged the falling debris just as it came crashing down onto the very spot upon which he had stood moments before, scattering sparks everywhere. He nodded to her in appreciation, but in a split second had refocused his efforts on the fighting.

Relieved, Thea turned her attention to where Harald was engaged in fighting two men at once and having just as much success as Erik. But suddenly his foot snagged on a piece of uneven stone, causing him to stumble backwards. With a roar of triumph his opponents rushed at him, swords outstretched, and it was all Thea could do not to join the fray.

She crawled over to where her dagger lay and wondered how to proceed. Should she intervene? Her father had taught her how to defend herself, but she would be no match for the heavily armed Greek soldiers. She'd only hinder the Varangians, she realised. So she watched, feeling helpless and frustrated.

Erik had seen the danger to his kinsman and was at Harald's side in a flash, hauling one of the attackers off so that he could draw him away and even the odds for Harald, who wasted no time. He wrestled his opponent to the ground and finally managed to overpower him, slamming his arms above his head and holding them there in a vice-like grip. Sitting astride his victim, Harald finished the task with his sword.

Thea's relief lasted only seconds.

On realising that his retinue was no more Demetrios, who had slid into the background like a lone wolf slinking away from the hunter, emerged from the shadows.

Thea saw the moment it happened. With a cruel smile, Demetrios crept up behind Harald, and at the same time a shrill shriek escaped Thea's mouth.

'*No!*'

But the warning came too late, for Demetrios had sunk his long sword into the back of the unwitting Varangian, so deep that the blade pierced him through to his chest cavity. With a sick feeling of dread, Thea saw the point emerge on the other side of his torso.

Erik was still engaged with his own quarry, but at the sound of Thea's scream he turned to see his friend and sword brother keel over. With a feral snarl, Erik kicked his opponent away with such force that the man flew into the air, hitting his head on the side of a table as he went down, unconscious.

'Demetrios!'

Thea heard Erik's voice thunder through the noise and the clamour. But she did not stop to watch, for her healer's instincts had taken over. She crawled over to Harald, trying to staunch the blood with one hand while desperately fishing around in her medicine bag for a bandage with the other.

The Varangian looked up at her, trying with his last breath to provide instruction. 'Go with Erik. Run…' he grunted.

Thea placed her hand on his lips. 'Conserve your energy, soldier.'

She worked quickly, trying to undo the heavy armour so that she could get to the source of the injury. But she knew even before she began that it was no use, for the wound was too deep and the blood loss already too great. The wound would prove fatal.

Thea held his hand in reassurance, her eyes glassing over with tears, realising that this man had risked his life to save hers. 'Thank you, Varangian.'

'Leonora… Family… Safe…' he managed with a choke.

She nodded. 'I will take care of them. I promise.'

Painfully, she watched as the light slowly dimmed from his eyes and he drew his last breath. With a sob, she gently closed his eyelids, and pulled his cloak over him in a gesture of respect.

The air was getting heavy. Thea's eyes streamed with the intensity of the heat and smoke, and trying to gulp for mouthfuls of air proved painful. Coughing and spluttering, she brought her forearm up to her nose and mouth as she scanned her surroundings. They had to leave before they were burnt alive. She looked over to where Erik was squaring up to Demetrios, but just as she saw him raise his sword another huge beam came crashing down, separating the two combatants. Demetrios was cut off from the entrance.

Thea saw him stalk back into the recesses of the wards. But not before he reached out to point his sword at her.

I will have you yet, he mouthed.

And then everything went black.

Chapter Six

Erik was torn. He desperately wanted to follow Demetrios into the flames and finish him, exacting vengeance for his cowardly attack on Harald. But duty overrode his fury. It was imperative that he delivered the Princess to safety. He looked over to where he thought he'd seen out of the corner of his eye her rushing over to Harald as he fell, and as he moved through the haze he eventually saw two seemingly lifeless bodies lying side by side.

Cursing, he hurried over, sidestepping the debris. He saw Thea first. She was on her side, and her eyes were shut, but her body evidenced signs of life as she gasped for air involuntarily, even in her unconscious state. Relieved that she was still alive, he quickly turned his attention to Harald, shaking him gently. When he remained unresponsive Erik put two fingers on the side of his neck, feeling desperately for a pulse. It only confirmed his fears. There was nothing.

He let out a gut-wrenching groan, not wanting to believe his eyes but knowing that he had to. Yet there was no time to grieve. The ceiling above was creaking menacingly, and Erik gauged that they had only minutes left until the whole building collapsed.

'See you in Valhalla, brother,' he whispered, laying Harald's sword on his chest.

Then, he gathered up the Princess in his arms, and with a final glance over his shoulder at his fallen friend stepped out into the chaos. Within seconds of their departure the building burst into flames, sending great billows of smoke skyward and spitting sparks far and wide.

Erik hurriedly stripped off his cloak and draped it over Thea, partly to protect her from the flames and partly to obscure her identity as he hastened towards the harbour.

He knew the blueprint of Constantinople and the hidden passageways and alleys that burrowed through it like the back of his hand. Avoiding the main streets which opened out into the busy thoroughfares, where the rebels would surely be out in full force, he raced onward, hoping against hope that the royal barge would still be there. He came to the small corridor that led down to the port and peered through a narrow slit between the buildings.

The royal standard on the barge rippled in the night breeze as it made its way across the Golden Horn. With a sinking feeling in the pit of his stomach Erik realised that it was at least a mile from the port. They were too late.

Erik leant against a wall and tried to order his thoughts. It would be too dangerous to try and source a boat to make the crossing now. The rebellion was in full swing, and the port would no doubt be a hub of chaos. Better to wait a few hours until the fighting had subsided and the rebels had drunk their fill before making a move.

Retracing his steps, he ducked into an alleyway and made his way to a disused wine cellar known to only a few. It was blissfully cool inside, away from the scorching flames, and he welcomed the clean air. It would prove a useful shelter for now, he thought, as he bolted the wooden door and pushed a heavy oak chair up against it.

He lay Thea down on the floor on top of his cloak and

rubbed away the dust and dirt from her mouth and cheeks. Lowering his ear so that it hovered just above her mouth, he tried to gauge the depth of her breathing. It was slow and shallow, but it was there. Good. And she would only improve now that she was out of the dense smoke.

He removed the satchel from her shoulder and sifted through it, hoping that it contained some useful supplies, and was rewarded when he located a skin of water. Grateful for Thea's foresight, he propped her head up and held the vessel to her lips. Her eyes flickered open, and so parched was she that even in her dazed state she drank deeply, coughing and spluttering, but managing to keep most of it down. Although exhaustion soon overwhelmed her, and she fell back into darkness.

Resisting the urge to curl up beside her, Erik reluctantly moved away to the other side of the small room, knowing that he needed to rest for the journey ahead. Loosening the strappings on his breast plate and cuirass, he removed the items, along with his helmet. But he kept hold of his sword and placed his shield beside him, before sinking down to the floor.

He was bone-tired, and the loss of Harald was a heavy blow. But he couldn't think of that—it would only make him more reckless. There would be a time to grieve, and it was not now. He had lost many a friend in battle, and had learned to make himself numb to such loss…for the time being at least.

So he distracted himself by mapping out their next move. He'd go to Nikos—one of his oldest friends and a man who was fiercely loyal to the Emperor. Nikos built many ships and boats, and Erik was sure he'd spare one for them…especially when he saw that his cargo was so precious. Then there was the aftermath of their crossing. The Golden Horn was an easy sail, and safe enough provided they left early, under the cloak of dawn. But when they alighted on the opposite bank they'd need horses to transport them across the countryside for the rest of the journey.

He hoped the Princess could ride...

He must have fallen asleep, for he woke up hunched on his side with a cramp in his arm. Something had roused him. Tightening his fingers around the woven leather of his sword's grip, he strained his ears for unfamiliar sounds. But Constantinople was eerily quiet. Maybe he was imagining things. But then he heard it again. A faint sound almost like a whimper. He stilled.

Thor's blood. It was the Princess, and it appeared she was crying. He immediately released his sword and pondered what to do. It had been so many years since he'd had to comfort a woman, he'd forgotten how. Damn it. This was something that her handmaidens would be much better at. Well, they weren't here, and he alone was in charge of the Emperor's niece. He'd better figure out a way to allay her fears so that she didn't scream the place down and attract attention. Not that he could blame her... She had suffered a terrible ordeal, and not many men in her place—let alone women—would have made a stand against Demetrios and his men, outnumbered as she was.

With a sigh, he stood up and strode across the room until he was standing above her. She was lying on her back, his cloak in disarray underneath her, and she seemed to be sprawled in a restless slumber punctuated every now and then by a desperate sob. She was likely deep in the throes of a bad dream. Since she wasn't awake, there was no need to comfort her. Should he let her be? He knew that sometimes it was best to let the nightmare run its course, rather than interrupt it. But there was something about her muffled gasps of terror that tugged at his heart and awakened his protective instincts.

'No, Demetrios!'

She was clawing at the air now, and at the sound of that name Erik knew he had to try and help her right away. He hunkered down by her side, and when he saw that her cheeks were moist with tears something in him twisted painfully. He immediately picked her up bodily and drew her into his arms, cradling her.

'Shh, you're safe now...' he whispered.

She was so slight, lying there in his lap, and it was easy to shift her so that her head rested against his chest, just over his heart. The very heart he had promised himself he would harden against such moments as these, but which now seemed to melt as easily as ice under the midwinter sun. He pressed his cheek into the soft brown silk of her hair, which was loose and flowing, and realised that this was the first time he had seen her hair without the nurse's wimple. He wondered how it would feel to run his fingers through it... But he resisted the urge to do so and instead brushed aside the stray tendrils that had settled on her forehead.

She let out a sigh and huddled closer into his chest, so that he could feel the warmth of her body against his pectorals. She was utterly relaxed now, and her sobs had subsided. He was glad that she was no longer in discomfort, but the cause of her nightmare set his teeth on edge. Demetrios. What had he done to her in the past? The coward had a lot to answer for... When this was all over he would hunt him down and seek vengeance for the death of Harald— and retribution for whatever he had done to make the Princess feel like this.

He looked down at the subject of his thoughts, saw her features made even more delicate under the soft light of the moon's beams that shone through the small window above them. Even in such a time of crisis the sight of her like this gave him the urge to make her his, to keep her safe.

Shaking his head, he fought for control. Her safety was the priority—not his longings.

He let out an exasperated breath. This was madness. Tomorrow he would need all his wits about him for the journey ahead. He'd need to figure out the safest way to find Nikos and obtain horses—not to mention undertake the difficult task of mapping out where they'd need to strike camp until they reached the Emperor. And yet here he was, spending a sleepless night fretting over the Princess, who no doubt was still bristling at the way he had behaved with her at their last meeting.

He felt a surge of shame. Judging by the way she had dealt with Demetrios tonight, it was clear that she held not the slightest affection for him. He had obviously misjudged their relationship, and he would need to apologise to her for that. But why had she kept that information to herself when he had confronted her about Demetrios the day before? There was definitely a history there...and one that she didn't seem willing to share. It bothered him.

He studied her features. The long eyelashes, the high cheekbones, the rosy cheeks. Even in her troubled sleep she was utterly flawless. And it felt so natural to comfort her and soothe her. It seemed to calm the incessant inner conflict that had torn at him since Frida's death. She whimpered again, and this time she nestled even closer to him. As she shifted her position one of her hands, which had previously rested limply in her lap, slid up his chest to hook around his neck. It was a completely unpremeditated move, for she was still deep in sleep, but perhaps that was precisely why it made his breath catch in his throat.

It suddenly dawned on him that he hadn't felt like this in a long, long time. More troubling was the realisation that he still yearned for this feeling. It was a tender, inexplicable sensation that he found himself admitting he'd missed. He felt himself relax, utterly content to have this warm, feminine bundle in his arms, with the scent of lavender and rose that emanated from her, and the whole world seemed to contract to just the two of them and this one, simple moment.

But nothing about this situation was simple. And the sight of his Varangian's cloak underneath a princess of the Roman Empire was a stark reminder of that. He had to release her from his hold. This was too dangerous. *She* was too dangerous for him.

He gently lay her down again, using her satchel as a pillow to replace his lap, and backed away to resume his original place. Tonight he had discovered yet more proof that he was not immune to the Princess's charms, and his personal oath would be left in tatters if he didn't get a rein on his emotions soon.

Thea sat bolt upright. Her chest was tight with fear and her mouth felt as if she had swallowed several mouthfuls of sawdust. Droplets of sweat were beading her forehead and trickling down between the valley of her breasts. Where was she? Had Demetrios captured her?

'Princess, be still.'

That voice again. The one she associated with strength and safety. Did she dare believe it? She drew her knees up to her chest and began to shake uncontrollably, not daring to turn around.

But then he was there, next to her, his arm around her shoulders.

'Shh…you are safe, Princess.'

She looked up, and her gaze locked with blue eyes.

'Erik? Is it really you?'

'Yes.'

She couldn't speak. Instead, to her horror, a loud, hacking sob of relief escaped her mouth. She couldn't believe it. One moment she was facing Demetrios, fighting for her life, and the next she was safe, with Erik. This couldn't be real. It had to be a dream. Her mind was confused, still addled with smoke, and she was weak from exhaustion.

But when she felt his arms tighten around her, and a strong hand tilt her chin upwards, she was forced to look up at him, to embrace reality.

'Princess, I swear no harm will come to you. Demetrios is gone.'

To her dismay, she felt a lone tear start to roll down her cheek. But a large thumb immediately wiped it away. It took her a moment to recollect what had happened. But then it all came flooding back. The rebellion, Demetrios, the fight… The other Varangian.

'Your friend!'

'He is in Valhalla.'

'I'm so sorry. I tried to save him, but I was too late. I—' Another sob threatened to escape her lips.

'None of what happened was your fault, Princess. And you saved my life. Had you not warned me of the falling timber I would be one of those charred items that now line the streets.' He smiled weakly. 'In any case, Demetrios was trapped inside. The building collapsed after we left.'

Thea nodded.

'You fainted when the smoke became heavy. I brought

you here. You've been in and out of consciousness and hav-ing…dreams most of the night.'

Thea dropped her gaze, embarrassed that she had been unconscious and useless all night, while he had risked his life to bring her to safety.

'Thank you, Erik. I am in your debt.'

'And I in yours.'

She dropped her gaze as a veil of silence formed be-tween them. Then she said, 'I thought you were to leave the Guard today?'

'So did I.' He smiled and shrugged his shoulders. 'But it seems like your uncle had other plans.' He stood up. 'In all seriousness, I could not abandon the city, the Emperor or the Guard at a time like this.'

He walked over to the other side of the cellar and she watched as he donned his armour.

'And Alexios?'

'He is in safe hands.'

'So what now?' she queried.

Erik looked down at the Princess, wondering how best to break the news that they had missed the royal barge, and would therefore need to journey alone, together, for a while.

'Your uncle gave Harald and me our orders. We were to meet them at the royal barge last night, once we retrieved you. But the skirmish with Demetrios delayed us and the barge was already at sea before we could reach it. We will need to join your uncle at a place which is about a week's journey from here—if we do not first find the contingent of Varangians he is sending to meet us on the way. I do not think it is possible for us to catch up with your uncle's boat now—the banks will be dense with Demetrios's men…'

He paused, remembering that he wasn't talking to one

of his soldiers, but to a princess who barely had any experience of war. He didn't want to frighten her.

He cleared his throat. 'I am sorry that we did not manage to reach the rest of your family in time, but I give you my word: I will do everything in my power to deliver you to them safely. Gather your belongings. We must leave the city at once.'

Erik was half expecting her to be dismayed at the news. But her reaction baffled him.

'Leave the city?' Her voice was incredulous.

'Yes.'

'But... I cannot!' She threw her hands up. 'There will be many who will need my help. The wards will be overflowing with the wounded.'

'Be that as it may, my orders are to take you to the Emperor.'

'I will not leave.' She folded her arms across her chest stubbornly. 'You can go. Tell my uncle that I have remained here.'

Erik stared at the Princess, who was looking at him as if *he* were the one out of his mind. He couldn't believe what he was hearing. The Emperor had ordered him to bring her to safety. He and Harald had moved mountains, parted seas, to reach her. Now Harald was dead. And here she was, defying the Emperor's orders.

He took a deep breath. 'Princess, with all due respect, your presence here right now...' he spread his hands out to signal the city '...is redundant.' He watched as her chin went up, her eyes alight with fire, like a lioness protecting its cubs from a marauding male.

'Look, I am grateful to you and your friend for saving me from Demetrios. But I cannot abandon my people or my patients. I am duty-bound to save as many lives as I can.'

'Do not speak to me of duty.' Now it was his turn to smoulder. 'I am here because of duty. Harald is dead because of duty. And you will be too, if you remain here.' He stepped forward, so that only a hair's breadth separated them. 'You will be of more use to your patients alive than dead.'

'Unlikely if I am to be taken leagues away from here!' she countered.

By Odin, she was stubborn. But so was he.

He sighed. He was not permitted to divulge the exact scope of the Emperor's orders, not even to the Princess, but perhaps by explaining some of the plan he could persuade to leave. He looked out of the small window and gauged that dawn was approximately an hour away. They didn't have much time. Their opportunity for escape was closing. It was imperative that they left now and took advantage of the darkness for their river crossing. And first they had to find Nikos, which meant venturing out onto the streets.

He took a deep breath and gently put his hands on her shoulders, as a gesture of reassurance. He locked his gaze with hers, forcing himself to soften his voice.

'Listen… Your uncle has made an alliance with Macedonia. Scouts have been sent ahead to garner support from King Antonius, who will join your uncle at an allocated stronghold. Within a sennight, the full might of Macedonia and the Varangians will descend upon Constantinople and reclaim it from the rebels.'

He saw the fire in the Princess's eyes ebb at hearing this new information.

'Antonius will help us?' she queried.

'Yes. He has given his word.'

Erik ignored the pang of jealousy he felt at what that word was associated with; from her reaction, it did not seem that she knew she was betrothed to Antonius. He felt guilty for keeping such information from her, but it was not his place to divulge it. Nor, he reminded himself, should it be any of his business.

'Now, please hurry. We must leave before dawn breaks.'

'But how can we leave unnoticed? Surely Demetrios's supporters are out in full force?'

'I have a plan. Come.' He held out his hand and watched as the Princess deliberated over what to do.

He could see an inner conflict ensue behind her big brown eyes, but what it was about he could not say. After some moments, he finally saw her hackles go down in acquiescence, but she did not take hold of his outstretched hand. Instead she bent down to retrieve his cloak from the floor in one fluid movement—but not before he noticed a shadow of doubt pass across her face at the offer of his hand.

Something was bothering her, and it wasn't just the prospect of leaving the city and abandoning her patients. He frowned.

'Very well,' she said, and placed the garment in his hand with nonchalance, as if it was obvious to anyone but him that that was what was supposed to be placed in it.

He took the cloak, puzzled at the subtle change in her attitude towards him, but reminded himself that there was no time to analyse the Princess's every movement like a callow romantic—they had to move. Though he made a mental note not to be too familiar with the Princess in the future, since it evidently made her uncomfortable.

She had wanted to take hold of Erik's hand—to surrender to the safety it offered. But her past experiences with Demetrios had made her fearful of men, and the last twelve

hours had only served to exacerbate that fear. She'd felt ut-.
terly helpless when she had been outnumbered by Demetrios and his men—they'd demonstrated, unequivocally,
that she had no control whatsoever over herself or the situation, and she'd resented that feeling of powerless. And
now—again—she had to relinquish control over her actions
to another man. And while the Varangian meant well, he
was asking her to do something against her instincts—how
could she leave the wounded behind in the city?

She knew that she was being unfair by projecting her
fear of Demetrios onto him, since all he had done from the
first moment they'd met was to look after her—and others.
Yet it felt too soon to let her guard down. The incident with
Demetrios was too fresh in her mind.

Conversely, in terms of *physical* desire, the feelings Erik
elicited in her were the complete opposite to those that
Demetrios did. Fear, resentment and repulsion were replaced with warmth, admiration and a sense of security. It
threatened her composure. *He* threatened her composure.
Apart from her uncle, who had been like a father to her
since she'd lost her parents, she had never felt beholden to
a man, or dependent on one. But she was dependent on Erik
now—and that disturbed her. More so because there was no
hope of a future with him, however much she dreamed of it.

It was all so confusing!

She quickly realised that her current train of thought
was ridiculous, given the situation they were both in. The
sooner she reached her uncle, the sooner she could return
to the city and help those in need. Instead of entertaining
subject matters of the heart, she should be directing her
mind to helping Erik.

'So, what is the plan, exactly?'

'I have a friend who is a boatwright. His place is not

far from here. We'll hire a boat from him and then row up the Golden Horn.'

'Sounds easy enough.'

She gave him a small smile, which made him chuckle.

'Do not be afraid. The city is quiet. I think the rebels have had their fill—for now at least. I warrant most are likely in a drunken stupor. But we must be quick and quiet as we leave the city. And we'll need to find horses at some point, to carry us across the countryside. Can you ride?'

She nodded, watching as he dragged the heavy oak chair away from the cellar's doorway. 'Yes. My father taught me when I was a little girl.'

'Good. Now, wait here. I will check that the street outside is clear. Watch for my signal.'

He crept out of the room, which seemed twice as big now that he had left it. She marvelled at how agile he was, given such heavy armour, and he didn't make a sound as he climbed up the narrow staircase to street level. She waited in anticipation, and soon saw him wave her up.

'Stay close behind me. If you see any movement, be as still as possible,' he whispered.

She pulled her cloak more closely around her and shivered. Dawn had not arrived, and the air was chilly and thick with the smell of burning. She did not look too closely at her surroundings, for the sight would no doubt sadden her, but she sensed that the streets were mostly deserted. She kept her eyes trained on the broad expanse of the Varangian's back. Again, that feeling of safety settled upon her, and she knew that had she been with anyone else her current situation would have been much more daunting.

Suddenly he halted in front of her, flattening his back against the wall and signalling for her to do the same. She couldn't hear anything, but he seemed to be on the alert. She strained her ears. It was hard to distinguish any sounds over the thudding of her own heart. But then she heard men's voices. They seemed to be only a street or two away. She swallowed hard as she saw Erik's hand rest on his sword's hilt. He turned round to look at her, and she could see, under his helmet, that his eyes were soft in concern. She nodded, meaning to show him that she was all right.

The voices grew nearer, and Erik tugged her further along the street, pulling her into a small alcove that was dug into a wall. It could barely fit two people, and he was holding her flush against him, so tightly that their bodies seemed as one. Her hands had nowhere to go but around his waist. Her head was resting on his chest. Her fear soon abated when she felt the steady rise and fall of it as he breathed. She closed her eyes, willing herself to match her breathing to his. The voices were now not more than a few feet away, and she felt Erik tighten his hold on her. Less than a foot…

'Surely the Hagia Sofia will still have some loot?' one of the men said. His voice was slurred. They were clearly drunk.

The two men were now standing right in front of the alcove and were in full view.

'Only one way to find out,' the other responded.

'Well, we are going the wrong way. It's that way.'

'If you say so.'

Thea breathed a sigh of a relief as the two men stumbled past them, veering off to the right. She felt Erik's grip loosen, but he didn't release her. She could have stayed like that for hours… Blast it! She had to admit that she *did* feel safe with him. And she couldn't deny that even though he was a man in a position of power, and even though the incident with Demetrios had been so recent, she didn't want to leave his company. She didn't want to join up with her uncle and Adriana. She just wanted to stay here, in this moment, in the warmth of his arms. It was the oddest feeling to allow herself to trust a man, and remain calm in his physical presence, when all her past experiences had made her feel exactly the opposite.

'I think the path is clear again. Come, Princess.'

Reluctantly, she relinquished her hold on him.

After a short while they came to a gangway, and Erik led her down some stairs to a small wooden door. Taking off his helmet, he rapped on the door, looking around furtively as he did so.

Soon she heard shuffling within, and the cover of a small spyhole was pulled back. A pair of shrewd eyes stared back at them, darting from Erik to Thea in quick succession.

'Nikos. It's Erik. Open up.'

The door immediately swung open and they were ushered inside by a small, wiry man.

'What the devil are you doing here, old friend?' He clapped Erik on the shoulder, barely reaching it. 'I thought you had left the city already.'

'I'd planned to, but—'

'Yes, that scoundrel Demetrios. Most of the buildings along this street were burnt to cinders. But I was spared. His men needed boats.'

'And that's why we are here. Nikos, this is Princess Theadora.'

At the sound of her name, Nikos's eyes widened in shock and he sank into a deep bow. 'Your Highness.'

'Greetings.' It was all Thea could manage.

'We don't have much time. Can you spare us a vessel?' Erik intervened.

'Of course. Where to?'

'I am not permitted to—'

'Yes, yes, of course... Not permitted to divulge your orders.' The small man waved his hand and scurried behind his counter. 'Let's see... Yes, I have just the one.' He pulled out a piece of yellow parchment. '*The Maiden*. She's small and discreet, but robust.'

Erik reached for his pouch.

'I wouldn't hear of it.' Nikos dismissed the gesture of payment.

'Thank you, Nikos. I am in your debt.'

'Nonsense. I've lost count of the number of times you've saved my bacon, old friend. *The Maiden* is moored at the boat yard on the south side. Take the back way, through the cellar. It will bring you up next to it, and you won't come across anybody.'

'Thank you. We'll also need horses on the other side. Any idea where we could find a pair...discreetly?'

'Hmm...' Nikos tapped his cheek. 'That will be tricky. I wager horses will be in short supply as people flee the city. But there is a place just beyond Plataea, near the Gate of Theodosia. It's a small tavern, owned by a fellow named Angelos. Tell him Nikos sent you. Godspeed.'

Erik nodded, signalling to Thea that the meeting was over, and the two of them stepped out again into the rosy grey light of dawn.

Chapter Seven

Thea sat hunched in the small boat, her legs drawn up to her chest, and gazed out towards Constantinople as it receded into the distance. Erik had made quick work of locating the vessel and unfastening its moorings, and was now quietly propelling them up the Golden Horn.

He seemed to have timed their escape perfectly.

The Golden Horn was still, and a quick scan of its banks showed no signs of movement. Erik was right. The rebels had probably sated themselves with whatever drink they'd been able to lay their hands on during the night. But it did nothing to quell the pain in her heart. How many were trapped within the city walls? How many would be in need of her help? She wondered if she had made the right decision to leave with Erik. Not that she had been given a choice, she thought, as she looked over at him.

His mouth was set in a grim line of concentration, his muscles and sinews straining as he silently rowed them onwards, each stroke accentuating the contours of his muscular arms and shoulders. Her gaze settled on his large hands, which were holding the oars in a vice-like grip... Those hands which only a short time before had been put to a different task. She recalled the pleasing roughness of his callused palms against her cheeks as he'd rubbed her tears away. She pondered that action. There was a softness in him, she decided, which every now and then he revealed—albeit inadvertently. But aside from that he remained a solid wall of hardness, as he'd demonstrated when he had refused to let her remain in Constantinople.

No, there wasn't a chance in hell of escaping him and making her way back. Besides, she begrudgingly admitted to herself, he was likely correct in his prediction that remaining there would do neither herself nor her prospective patients much good. The only way to return to her people would be to follow the plan that he had laid out for her. She'd have to wait. But it didn't stop her from feeling utterly inadequate.

With a sigh, she wrenched her gaze away from the retreating silhouette of the city. The image was too painful.

'You will return soon.'

It was as if he could read her mind. She looked up and saw that he was studying her, a frown on his face. He had stopped rowing, and she saw that the current was now carrying them along of its own accord.

'I know.' She sighed again. 'I just hope that Demetrios's supporters have the good sense to treat our citizens with dignity and respect.'

He didn't answer, but continued to survey her. His mouth twitched, as if he'd wanted to say something but had stopped himself.

'Speak freely, Varangian.'

'Very well. How did you come to be acquainted with—?'

'Someone like Demetrios?' She sighed. She had wanted to resolve the misunderstanding yesterday—to reassure Erik that she and Demetrios were neither friends nor lovers. Well, now was her chance.

'When I first came to Constantinople, after my parents

died, I didn't know anyone. The Princess Adriana was still very young then, and my uncle and his wife, although they were affectionate and welcomed me as one of their own, were often busy with affairs of state or goings-on at the palace. I didn't know anyone, and I didn't have much contact with the outside world. And I was grieving...'

She paused. She hadn't spoken to anyone about her parents' death, or how she had felt afterwards. Ordinarily, expressing herself like this would have made her feel vulnerable. Yet for some reason she couldn't quite put her finger on, she felt she could speak plainly to Erik.

'I felt completely alone,' she said. 'But one day, shortly after my arrival, I was introduced to Demetrios at court. He was very charming, and he seemed to want to be a friend to me. I'd never had an older brother, but in all honesty that's how I viewed him. He showed me the city, taught me the local dialects, and genuinely seemed to care about me. For a long time that's how it was. But...'

'But?' Erik prompted.

'His behaviour towards me slowly changed. At first it was subtle. The odd hand on my waist...orchestrated seating plans at meals. I initially brushed it off as coincidence, or gestures of affection.'

She fingered a tassel on her gown.

'But then he started making pointed remarks about our future together. He'd make excuses to come to the wards, pretending he had a wound that needed attention. Or he'd send me sickly love notes, listing all the things he would bestow upon me if I became his wife.' She shuddered. 'I never saw him that way. But I didn't want to voice my concerns. My uncle is fond of me, but accusing Demetrios would have caused an uproar in High Council. Anyway, I had never truly felt threatened physically by him. Uncomfortable, yes. Scared, sometimes… But I knew that I was out of his reach. Until recently, that is.'

She saw a muscle jump in Erik's jaw.

'I thought you said that he hadn't hurt you?'

'He hadn't. Not physically. I had not thought him capable of that. Well, not until tonight.' She drew in a deep breath. 'But over the last few weeks I had noticed that his advances were less calculated and more clumsy…more… desperate. He wanted to marry me to bolster his position at court, I imagine.'

'And when he did not succeed—?'

'Rebellion. Yes.' She wrung her hands. 'If only I had realised the extent of his aspirations I would have warned my uncle. I completely underestimated him. I never thought he was aiming for the crown.'

'Do not blame yourself. You could not have known that he would go this far.'

It was true. It had never occurred to her that Demetrios would go this far. Nevertheless, Demetrios's actions had fostered in her a deep mistrust of men and their motives. How could she be sure of someone entrusted with protecting the vulnerable if such a person then abused that position of power?

She made an effort to push these misgivings away, since they would no doubt prove unhelpful in her current situation. She had, after all, put her life in the hands of a Varangian.

'Thank you,' she managed.

'And I want to apologise for my reaction yesterday. I assumed you and Demetrios had an…arrangement. I know now that was ill-conceived, and I am sorry for assuming the worst.'

She was surprised that he'd admitted his failings. In her

experience, men often didn't like to own their mistakes. He really *was* different.

'I don't blame you for your assumption. After all, I did receive a letter from Demetrios at the most inopportune moment.' She gave a small smile, which he returned.

'But I am curious,' he said. 'Why did you tolerate him coming to the wards all these years? Why didn't you move back to the main building of the palace, where your uncle could better protect you?'

It was a good question, and one which very occasionally, when Demetrios had made her feel at her lowest, she had entertained. But it had always been a fleeting consideration.

'I couldn't leave. My patients sometimes need care through the night, and the other nurses need supervision or assistance, especially when we are understaffed. It wouldn't have been practical to live anywhere but there.' She paused, dropping her gaze. 'Besides, my work is important to me. It would have taken more than the ramblings of a man like Demetrios to send me running back to the palace with my tail between my legs.'

She sighed.

'In any case, I do not enjoy court life. Nor can I abide the hollow, artificial nature of the courtiers and ladies-in-waiting. I much prefer to be in the wards, amongst the *real* people of the city, where I am not treated as royalty but as one of them. Life there is simple. There are none of the pressures or obligations that come with being a princess—just the practical tasks of healing people and making them well again...' She shrugged. 'It's where I am happiest. And why I didn't want to leave the city, even at a time like this.'

She didn't know why she'd felt the need to tell Erik all this, but again it seemed to come naturally.

'I understand. And I'm sorry that I had to bring you with me. But—'

'You were following orders.' She gave him a small smile. 'I also understand.'

She continued to surprise him. Here was a woman who was intent on doing meaningful work, despite being high born. He was also taken aback by her dislike of court life— though it was a sentiment he empathised with. So at least they had *that* in common. He knew from experience that most ladies at court preferred to indulge in less worthwhile pursuits. In fact, he had sometimes been on the receiving end of a court intrigue or two. Bored wives and curious widows were not too shy to invite the famed Varangians, known for their unrivalled stamina, into their beds. Not that he had ever accepted.

But it was one of the reasons he'd chosen to take up posts in the Guard that did not involve living at the palace. He found the politics tedious and court dalliances certainly not worth the risk of expulsion from the Guard. Even during his short stints at court, he hadn't met a lady who was both compassionate and skilled at the same time.

The Princess certainly was a *real* person. Her general openness and honesty were endearing and refreshing. There was none of the artful flirting or doctored conversations he had experienced with other highborn women. But most of all he was drawn by her sheer determination to put other people's needs before her own—first by enduring Demetrios's endless advances so that she could reside in the wards, amongst her patients, and just now by insisting on remaining in the city, even when doing so would put her own life at risk. He couldn't help but admire her.

Another reason why he should keep his distance, he

mused. The woman had beauty, charm and intellect—a trilogy of attributes that was destined to wrongfoot him if he wasn't careful. Yet no matter how much he tried to resist feeling anything for her, he couldn't tamp down the fierce streak of protectiveness that had surged through him when she had told him of Demetrios's behaviour towards her. He hated the idea that the rogue had made her feel scared and uncomfortable. But he was grateful that he and Harald had managed to get to her on time—before Demetrios had physically harmed her.

Harald.

His heart grew heavy with sorrow once again. Harald, a mighty warrior who had faced more worthy opponents and won, had fallen at the hand of Demetrios in an act so spineless it made Erik's blood boil. Demetrios had chosen to attack him from behind, instead of to face him man to man—a cowardly act by any war code. He had probably known he would be no match for Harald in a fair fight. His friend had fought bravely, and had more than earned his place in Valhalla.

But now Erik would have the difficult task of informing Leonora of Harald's death. He sighed, dreading the moment. He'd promised Leonora—no, he'd given his word—that he and Harald would return safely. He fingered the copper pendant that Harald had worn around his neck.

His face must have reflected his feelings, for he felt the Princess tenderly place her hand on his arm.

'Did that belong to Harald?' she asked tentatively.

'Yes, it is his *mjölnir.*'

'*Myol...near?*' she repeated after him, her voice unsure.

'Almost.' He smiled and watched as she studied the piece. 'See this?' He pointed to the triangular shape. 'It is the symbol for Thor's hammer. It is worn for many reasons in our culture, but it mainly signals power and strength.'

'Thor is one of the Norse gods. I've read about him in journals,' she stated. 'And there is Odin…and Freya.'

'Yes, there are many. I know it is an alien concept when compared with the religion of Constantinople. You have one God…the Northmen have many.'

'Not so. Constantinople has been exposed to many religions in the past and, given its connection with the Greeks and Romans, we are not so unfamiliar with such concepts as polytheism as you would think. Thor is the equivalent of Zeus or Jupiter. Freya is like Aphrodite or Venus.'

'Your knowledge is impressive.'

'Thank you—but there is still much that I would like to learn about the worlds that exist beyond this one. Like yours, for instance.'

Erik usually avoided speaking of his home in Norway. In his mind, it was inextricably linked with Frida and Bjorn. And death.

'It is very different to this one,' he said carefully.

'Is that where you had intended to go when you left the Guard?'

'No. I have some other interests I would like to pursue first.'

She tilted her head, a look of puzzlement crossing her gentle features.

'Why? I would have thought that being released from the Guard would allow you to journey home unburdened? And a wealthy man to boot, I'm sure!'

The conversation was moving into dangerous territory.

He could have told her that, unlike many of the Northmen who comprised the Guard, he hadn't needed to journey thousands of miles from home all those years ago as a young man, in search of riches or status, for he had been born with all of that. And, while he had always intended to stand on his own two feet—indeed, his service in the Guard had rendered him wealthy in his own right—he didn't want to talk about his status in his homeland, or the reasons why he couldn't bring himself to go back.

He could have told her that it was exactly because of his status and wealth that he was responsible for the death of an innocent woman.

He could have told her that he'd joined the Guard to get as far as possible from the place he associated with tragedy and loss—to find a way of numbing his pain and to obtain the means to a quick but honourable death.

Now, admittedly, he was no longer driven by grief and rage. But his past life in Norway felt like a distant memory. He was set on a different path…at least for now.

But to explain all this to the Princess would elicit follow-up questions which would no doubt open up old wounds, and this was certainly not the time for him to become distracted. His senses were addled enough as it was, with how he felt about Theadora. He didn't need another reason to lose focus. He needed to direct all his attention to delivering her to safety.

He looked at her and saw her large brown eyes regarding him in enquiry. He had to admit there was something about her that made him want to tell her everything—he could see why her patients trusted her. Maybe one day he would be able to revisit his past with her, but for now it was best to let sleeping dogs lie.

'I prefer the life here in Byzantium.' He shrugged his shoulders nonchalantly. 'In any case, now that Harald has gone I will need to remain a while longer and make arrangements for his widow and family.'

She nodded. 'I am sorry that you have lost someone so dear to you.'

'Thank you. Harald died with honour, serving the Empire. I hope that will provide some comfort to his wife and children.'

They fell into an easy silence. Erik saw that they had passed the district of Plataea, so would soon be very near the Gate of Theodosia, where Nikos had said they should disembark. And, sure enough, within moments he saw the great stone arch rise in front of them.

He got as close as he could to the edge of the river and then stealthily stepped out of the boat, careful not to make any splashing sounds. He noted, with relief, that all around them there was only stillness.

The water only came midway up his leather boots, but he was sure the Princess's garments would be soaked if she stepped out of the boat, so he carefully fastened the boat to a tree trunk.

Turning to her, he held his arms out. 'I'll need to carry you over to the bank, lest you get your robes wet.'

She nodded and stood up gingerly, leaning towards him. As she hooked her arms around his neck he swept one of his arms under her legs and lifted her bodily out of the boat. In two strides he was at the bank, and set her gently down on her feet, ignoring the pang of protest he felt within as he relinquished his hold on her. Then he removed his armour and helmet and placed them in his travel bag, thinking it would be easier to travel onwards without those heavy items, as they would draw less attention. But he kept hold of his sword.

Scanning their surroundings, he looked for the signboard of the tavern, his senses acutely attuned to the sound of the Princess's footsteps behind him.

He'd asked her to pull the hood of her cloak further down her face, so that her features were obscured. The next few hours would be tricky...sourcing a horse and then travelling through the remainder of the northern part of Constantinople undiscovered. He himself had put away his Varangian cloak, knowing that there was no love lost between the Guard and Demetrios's supporters were he to be recognised. But once they were out in the open countryside and had begun their journey towards Thrace, the danger would subside. They just needed to get that far...

'Erik, look!'

The Princess was pointing to their right, where light emanated from the glow of candles burning by a window.

'Could that be the inn your friend mentioned?'

'Possibly...' Erik gauged that the building was about a furlong away—a safe enough distance for him to keep an eye on the Princess while he enquired within. 'Stay here while I investigate. I won't be long,' he said reassuringly.

She nodded, and drew her cloak more closely around her as she melted back into the shadows.

Erik strode over to the tavern's entrance. There was no need to knock, for the door was open, and an elderly man was emptying what appeared to be a kitchen slop bucket. He straightened up, wiping his brow, and a look of concern crossed his face as he caught sight of Erik.

'Can I help you?' he said, not unkindly, but Erik noted the tone of wariness that underscored the question.

'I am looking for Angelos.'

'I am he,' the man responded, as he wiped his hands on a rag that was hanging at his waist.

'Nikos sent me.' He was glad to see Angelos's expression relax at the mention of Nikos. 'He said you'd be able to provide us with horses. I need two.'

'I'm afraid they've all been purchased save for one.'

'Just one?'

'Yes, but it's a sturdy stallion. And depending on your companion, it should be able to accommodate the both of you.'

Erik considered the proposal. They didn't really have a choice. They needed a means to travel, and they needed it quickly. He supposed he could do some of the journey on foot if the horse tired.

'I'll take it.'

'Very well. Wait here.'

Presently Erik heard the sound of hooves on cobbles, and sure enough a solidly built packhorse was brought round to stand before him.

'Here you are.' Angelos led the horse by the muzzle. 'He's on the older side, but he's reliable.'

Erik studied the animal. The Princess was small, so he estimated that the horse would be able to carry them both without too much trouble for some distance at least.

'Thank you. How much?'

'One and a half *solidi*. Two if you require the saddle and mount.'

'We'll take it all.'

Erik dropped two gold coins in the man's hand and made a swift exit.

The Princess was where he'd left her.

'Can the poor beast manage us both?' She stared at him, gently rubbing the horse's muzzle.

'I think so—you are hardly a great burden. It should be able to carry us for some way before it needs a rest. And when it does, I'll go on foot.' Erik knew it wouldn't be long before the sun was full in the sky, and he didn't want to be negotiating his way through the streets in broad daylight. 'Quick, we don't have much time.'

He cupped his hands by the horse's nearside, indicating that the Princess should use it as a boost, and waited as she gripped the pommel and pushed herself up, swinging one long leg around the other side of the horse. When she was comfortable on the saddle he grabbed the cantle and easily hoisted himself up, positioning himself behind her as he reached around her to hold the reins. Gently, he squeezed the horse's sides and it responded automatically, moving forward at a surprisingly quick trot.

Neither of them spoke, and Erik could feel the tension in the Princess's body. Again, his training in the Guard came into its own, and he used his knowledge of the city to take them through several shortcuts. Although they were much further from the heart of the rebellion, the streets were becoming busier and he couldn't afford to take any risks. But in their plain clothes they blended in easily enough.

He began to relax, knowing that the hardest part of their journey was almost over. To a bystander they might have passed as a husband and wife, preparing to leave the city in turbulent times.

Husband and wife.

The thought had entered his mind so easily. Too easily. It was unsettling how natural it felt to be in her company… to consider her as his.

But she wasn't his—nor could she ever be. She was betrothed to one of the most powerful men on the continent. She couldn't be *more* out of reach.

The thought led him to wonder how she would take the news. Antonius was a good man, he begrudgingly admitted to himself, and he'd look after her well. But in the short time he had spent with the Princess he had come to understand that she was fiercely independent, and passionate about her work. Once she was married to Antonius she'd be his queen, and it would no longer be thought appropriate for her to continue life as a healer. It was not for Erik to impart the Emperor's decision to her, but that didn't stop him from feeling uncomfortable about keeping her in the dark over her upcoming marriage. She deserved to know, in order to prepare herself.

But as he thought back to the ordeal she had suffered at the hands of Demetrios, which was no doubt still fresh in her mind, he knew it was likely not the right time to inform her that she was soon to have another man foisted upon her, however respectable Antonius was. He sighed. Well, in less than a week she'd be in her uncle's care again, and hopefully better placed to accept the decision.

One week. That was all he had with her.

He recalled the softness of her body when he had held her flush up against him earlier, in the alcove, as they hid from the rebels. It had taken all his willpower not to lift her chin up and place his mouth on hers. He hadn't wanted to let her go. And now he allowed himself to wonder, just for a moment, what it would be like to hold her again. She was so easily enveloped by him, her petite body offering no hindrance to his hold on the reins. Her bare neck was only inches away, and he could see that a few tendrils of hair had come loose from her chignon and now clung to the gentle slope of her neck.

It wasn't every day that a Varangian and a princess shared a saddle, and he noticed that she kept her back rigid, in an attempt to keep some distance between them. An impossible endeavour, of course, since the saddle was not made for two. He couldn't resist breathing in her feminine scent, a mixture of juniper and jasmine, and as he felt the soft roundness of her bottom against his groin he almost groaned in frustration.

He wanted her like he had wanted nobody else. There was no use denying it.

With a silent curse, he readjusted his seat in the saddle, so that she wouldn't feel the effect she was having on him, and refocused his attention on their route. They had already skirted around the Palace of Blachernae, which was located in the suburbs of the northwest part of Constantinople. That meant they would very soon reach the open countryside, where there would be fewer people, and much less chance of encountering insurgents, so he could dismount.

Thankful for an excuse to distance himself from the proximity of the Princess's body and spare himself any further torture, he swung himself off the saddle.

Thea drew in a deep breath, trying to ignore how the warm, reassuring presence of Erik behind her had now been replaced by empty air. It felt as if every nerve in her body was screaming in protest.

She'd been enjoying the way he'd encircled her entire body with his, so that she couldn't move. All she'd been able to see were his forearms on the reins, tanned to a warm honey colour, the fine blond hairs offering a pleasing contrast to his golden skin. She marvelled at his complexion, which was so different from hers and those of her people, with their olive skin and dark hair. His build, too, was different. Greek men were lithe and nimble, but Erik was of a different ilk, with his tall stature and broad chest and back.

She had wanted to melt into his arms...to feel the warmth of that large body against hers. That gentle pooling of heat in her belly had returned—first as a gentle pulse, but then intensifying, until she'd felt her secret place below responding to the sensation and the need to have him.

Basking under the warmth of the sun, and cushioned against Erik's heated body, her mind had entered a stage between consciousness and fantasy, and she'd allowed herself to imagine what it would be like if his hands were on her waist, instead of on the reins, and how easy it would be for her to guide them downwards from there until they were in between her legs, which were conveniently parted on either side of the horse, and on that intimate area which now seemed to constantly yearn for him.

She'd been jolted out of her reverie when he'd dismounted. *What was she thinking?* Where had those wanton thoughts come from? She straightened her back and pushed away the feeling of emptiness that his absence had left, reminding herself that they were on the run. There was no time, and nor was it appropriate, to indulge in fantasies— least of all ones that had no hope of coming true.

Yet if she could so freely imagine herself being intimate with Erik, did that mean that the doubts Demetrios had instilled in her were slowly starting to melt away? It was remarkable to her that after so long being wary of men, and how they could manipulate her, here was one who had easily unravelled all that and made her feel at ease. The revelation was unsettling, and the irony wasn't lost on her since he was also unavailable to her. So she kept her eyes ahead, on the path, and they continued in silence.

After some time, she noticed that he'd slowed his pace, and that his back and shoulders had tensed.

'Captain? Is there a problem?'

She saw that they'd come to a fairly large stream, a silvery, grey ribbon which seemed to meander its way down from the mountain range ahead of them.

'There's usually a footbridge here.' He indicated in front of him. 'But it's been washed away.'

He paused as he surveyed the landscape.

'Might there be another one nearby?' she asked.

'There is one further north, but that would take us back on ourselves and add days to our journey. Also, it wouldn't be safe.'

'So what now?'

'We will have to cross. The river becomes shallower just by that ridge. Come.'

They followed the path downstream for a few furlongs and came to a part where the bank became lower and the current seemed gentler, but it still seemed quite deep. She frowned.

'The water should only be waist-deep. There is no need to worry.'

He must have sensed her unease, for he gave her a look of reassurance while he tied the horse to a tree and waited for her to dismount. She was a seasoned rider, and didn't usually need help when it came to horses, but she was accustomed to riding smaller mares. The ground seemed a fair distance away. She hesitated.

As if he sensed her uncertainty, his hands were on her waist in a flash, and he gently lifted her off and set her down as easily as if she were a sack of feathers.

'Thank you,' she managed, trying not to focus on how good it felt to have his hands on her.

'We'll need to undress. Keep just your undergarments on.'

'What?' Thea was shocked. She had only a thin silk chemise underneath her gown.

'The water will weigh you down otherwise.' He'd already started shucking off his boots and had pulled his tunic over his head, now standing before her bare-chested. 'I will avert my gaze to afford you some privacy.'

Her eyes widened in wonder and, try as she might, she couldn't help but drink in the image of him. How Demetrios could call someone like him a witless savage was beyond her, for it was as if Thor himself was standing in front of her. Her gaze raked over his broad chest, and she saw that he sported an inky black tattoo on his left pectoral muscle. The afternoon air was close with heat, and beads of sweat collected around it, almost making it come alive, and her gaze followed their movement as they rolled over his perfectly sculpted abdomen and down to…to the top of his chausses.

An involuntary sigh of disappointment escaped her lips at this abrupt end—a small Judas part of her protesting, wanting more—followed closely by an exclamatory, 'Oh!' at the belated realisation of the way she had been gawping. She felt a deep flush spread over her cheeks and wrenched her eyes away from the solid wall of hardness that stood before her.

The droplets of perspiration forming at her temples and between the valley of her breasts were not, she realised, caused by the effect of the sun, but rather by the warrior standing in front of her…by the way the wind ruffled his golden hair and how the cerulean shades of the nearby pools emphasised the blue in his eyes…by the way his muscles strained under the gold rings encircling his powerful arms…and by the way he stood before her, his long legs planted firmly on the ground, as if he were daring her to challenge his suggestion. Not that she could have even if she'd wanted to, for speech had deserted her.

Taking her silence for acquiescence, he finally turned his

attention to the packhorse, busying himself with the straps and bindings to ensure that their load was securely fastened.

Reluctantly, she began to peel off her own clothes.

Chapter Eight

'Hold on to me,' he directed, as they took their first steps into the stream and cautiously started to wade across. He held the packhorse's reins in one hand and reached out to take one of Thea's free hands with the other.

The current wasn't very strong, but one could never be certain. If he were on his own, with Mercury, he probably would have remained mounted on the horse. But he hadn't crossed here before, and he didn't know the horse well enough. And, of course, the Princess's safety was paramount.

But they reached the other bank soon enough, and without too much trouble, and finally the stream became shallow enough for him to let go of her. Thus far he had been true to his word, and made sure his gaze did not rest upon the Princess, since he knew she was scantily clad. But now, as he moved to help her up the bank, he had no choice but to turn to her.

The dampness had made her flimsy chemise cling to her like a second skin, revealing dark-tipped nipples. Part of her bodice had come undone, too, giving him a tantalising view of the gentle slopes of her small, pert breasts. He stifled a gasp, and this time he ignored the familiar knell of warning that sounded in his head at the direction of his thoughts.

She could be his. In some faraway part of him that was ruled solely by animal instinct he knew that all he had to do was take hold of her, back her up against the slab of rock that now stood behind her, and claim her. He wondered what it would feel like to put his lips on hers, to press her tenderly against the rock's slanting face, parting her legs gently with his thigh. He imagined taking hold of her small hands and bringing them up by her head, holding them there so that she couldn't escape him as he buried his face deep in her luxuriant hair. He wanted her to feel the curve of his mouth at the nape of her neck…to attend to her needs and her needs alone, to give her endless pleasure…

Of course she was totally unaware of his thoughts, and he saw her shiver. The action brought him sharply to his senses as, once again, he was reminded of his duty. He was here to protect the Princess, not indulge his desires.

'Come, Princess, there is an area over there where you can lay your clothes out to dry in the sun.' He looked skyward, gauging the time of day. 'You'll be warm again in no time.'

'Thank you, Erik. Do you think we are safe now?'

'We are safer than we were in the city. But until we reach the Varangian camp we will need to keep our wits about us.'

'How much further?'

'We should be able to reach it by dusk in another two days, if we move quickly.'

He thought he saw a shadow of disappointment cross her face. Had he imagined it? Did she feel the same way as he at the prospect of their time alone together coming to an end?

He berated himself. He couldn't let himself believe that she might consider him as anything more than her protector. It would only lead to a dead end. And yet he was sure he'd seen something akin to desire in her eyes when he'd caught her looking at him a few moments ago...

Inwardly, he decided to believe it.

Thea had chosen to journey on foot for a little while, and as they walked along in companionable silence she reflected on the last two and the paradoxical emotions that had overcome her while being in his company on this journey.

There was that feeling of calm which seemed to envelop her in a cloak of security whenever he was around... But that same cloak would unravel almost immediately at his touch, or when she saw the way he smiled at her, to be replaced by a kaleidoscope of butterflies fluttering furiously around in her chest. And she was still having trouble unpacking that strange, pleasurable sensation in her belly, which seemed to drive her to distraction at the most inappropriate times.

She looked over at him. He seemed so sure of himself. Yet she sensed that he was battling with his own demons. For one thing, his reluctance to discuss his homeland hadn't escaped her. She wanted to know more about it—more about *him*. She remembered the tattoo she'd seen on his chest when they'd forded the river. Maybe that would give her some insight into his past.

'Erik?'

'Yes, Princess?'

'Thea,' she corrected him.

'Apologies. It is a habit. Do you need something... Thea?'

'I couldn't help but notice that drawing on your...' Her mind conjured up the image of his half-naked body and the firm pectoral muscle on which the tattoo was inked. 'On your chest the other day.' She managed to finish, alarmed at how quickly her thoughts had strayed in *that* direction. She tried to recover herself. 'I do not recognise the writing. I assume it is a symbol from your homeland?'

'That is a *vegvísir*. I suppose you could call it a Viking compass. It helps with navigation.'

'How clever! I had initially thought that it might have something to do with your family. Or your name.'

He smiled. 'No, my name would be very short when written as a symbol.'

'Oh, I thought you all styled yourselves with long, fierce-sounding names…like The Fearless or The Bear-Strangler?'

He let out a booming laugh.

'No, no. It's just Erik Svenson.'

He had spoken his full name to her when they had first met, but hearing him say it like that, and knowing what she knew of him now versus then, she thought it stood in stark contrast to his mighty physique. It was simple, earthy, honest.

'And what does that mean?'

'It means Erik son of Sven… It is quite literal. Whereas your parents must have thought you extra-special to christen you with such a name.'

Thea froze at the mention of her parents. 'My parents?'

'Theadora means gift of God, doesn't it? I would have thought it a name you give a child you are deeply thankful to have received.'

'Yes, that is what it means.'

Theadora felt a lump rise in her throat. Her parents had died over five years ago, but the memory was still fresh, the grief still raw. No amount of time would diminish it. Even now, she still wondered how she had managed to get through the weeks and months after their deaths. She remembered waking up with a knot in her stomach every morning, having cried herself to sleep every night.

At first, when her father's ministers had advised that she join her uncle's court in Constantinople, she'd resisted. She didn't want to leave her home, where she would always be reminded of her parents. She had only ever met her uncle once, when she was a child, and she couldn't remember him, let alone imagine that he might replace her parents.

But then her uncle had come to visit and all her doubts had melted away at once, for he'd immediately held her in a tight embrace and told her how much she reminded him of her mother. He'd told her stories about her mother as a child, and had soon endeared himself to her. And then he'd brought his baby Adriana. As soon as Thea had laid her eyes on Adriana she'd been won over. She remembered how Adriana, only a few months old then, had looked up at her and smiled, and how she'd gently stroked her chubby cheeks and tickled her toes where they'd peeked out from under her blanket.

No one could replace her mother and father, but she had become part of a new family, and she gave thanks for it every day.

'I'm sorry, Thea, have I upset you?'

'No. No, you haven't.'

'I fear I have… Perhaps you should call me Erik The Impudent.'

Thea allowed herself a little smile, relieved at his attempt to change the tone. She gently patted the horse's muzzle.

'I'm sure we can think up a better name for you, can't we?' She pretended to address the horse. 'Erik The Impudent would be far too kind.'

'It would? Then what would you suggest?'

She tried searching for a suitable adjective to return the

joke, but when she thought of him the only words that came to mind seemed to be compliments.

Perhaps sensing her attention was elsewhere, he stepped in. 'I could suggest a few more? What about Erik The Insolent? Or Erik The Impertinent, maybe?'

She was relieved by his intervention, and she found her place in the flow of conversation again. 'All true, but they mean more or less the same… And again, all far too generous.'

'Is that so?'

'Yes. Erik the Oafish would be far more fitting.'

He let out another deep, booming chuckle that took her by surprise. 'Yes, I like that! Far more fitting!'

She studied him, yet again noting how laughter completely transformed his otherwise handsome steel-hard features.

'Then we can agree.' She, too, let out a soft laugh. 'But in answer to your question—yes, my parents gave me my name because it had taken them many years to conceive a child. They did, quite literally, see me as a gift from God. So I suppose mine is quite literal, too.'

She drew in a deep breath, wondering why she suddenly felt the urge to continue her story when she had never spoken about it to anyone before. Something about the way he looked at her in concern, and the way he cocked his head to one side, as if patiently waiting for her to go on, made her feel as if she was the only person in the world. She felt she could tell him anything.

'My parents died a few years ago in a terrible accident. I was placed in my uncle's care, and he welcomed me into the royal household in Constantinople, treating me as one of his own. Those months in the palace helped me overcome some of the grief that consumed me after my parents' death. I even gained a little sister.'

She smiled, remembering how she and Adriana had soon become inseparable.

'For a while, I was content. But as the days went by, as I think I've already mentioned, I grew tired of the hollow workings of court life, with its petty feuds and vendettas. Then one day my uncle took me into the city. I remember being just as in awe of the vastness of Constantinople as I was appalled by how many people there were in need of help. After that day I couldn't just go back to palace life, with its unnecessary opulence and luxury. I found myself searching for a purpose.'

'Is that how you came to be a healer?' he queried.

Again, it was a question to which the answer would bring her heartache, but it was also one which she felt she could speak of to him.

'Sort of...' She looked out at the rolling mountains in the distance. 'I learned the skill from my mother. When she married my father, and moved to his court in Rascia, she fell ill and was treated by one of the royal physicians who had arrived from the East. He'd journeyed along the Silk Road. My mother became intrigued at the unconventional methods he used to treat his patients, the results of which outstripped all the more traditional methods used at court, and soon her interest became a devotion.' Thea smiled with fondness at the memory. 'I often accompanied her on her visits to the sick. She encouraged me to learn the art of healing, emphasising that it was an important skill, and that everyone—especially members of royalty—should play their part in the community'.

'That is an admirable story.' He furrowed his brow. 'But...how did you manage to persuade the Emperor to allow you to conduct such a life outside of the palace? Greek princesses are precious things.' He looked at her and gave her a crooked smile that sent her heart soaring. 'From experience, I know that they rarely stray into the public eye, let alone dirty their hands healing the sick and mingling with the poor.'

'It was not easy,' she admitted. 'He refused at first, of course. But one day my uncle became sick, and none of his physicians had a clue as to the cause. I recognised his symptoms as the flux, and administered a tonic that my mother had used for such maladies. He recovered, and I took the opportunity to make my case again.' She looked up at Erik, her eyes dancing with mischief. 'I remind him of my mother, you see. She was his favourite sister. So I suppose he has a certain soft spot for me. And... I can be quite insistent.'

'I have no doubt. I've experienced it, after all.' He chuckled. 'He eventually capitulated?'

'Yes. I showed him around the wards, so that he could see for himself that it needed additional resources. There were simply not enough doctors and nurses to oversee the administrative day-to-day running of the place, let alone tend to patients. Besides, as I pointed out, the palace was only a stone's throw away... Eventually he conceded, on the condition that a small contingent of guards was always stationed in the grounds.' She paused. 'And that when I got married I would give it up.'

It was a condition that irked her, so she knew the note of bitterness that crept into her voice was only thinly disguised, and it was certainly not lost on Erik. He was frowning again.

'You think me foolish for yearning for a life outside of the palace?' she asked.

'Not at all—quite the contrary. It's just that in Norway women are treated as equal to men. They have a voice of their own, they are entitled to own land and are even taught to fight alongside men in battle. In our country you would not be expected to give up your work once you became someone's wife.'

She shrugged her shoulders. 'Be that as it may…my fate is sealed.'

Thea realised once again that she had divulged almost everything about what pained her most about her past, and even her future, but that Erik had somehow, very skilfully, deflected the subject of the conversation away from himself and his own past.

She looked at him sideways. Well, he wouldn't be able to avoid it for ever, she thought. She'd find a way to learn more about this man who seemed to have got such a hold on her in such a short space of time.

As the Princess had recounted her past Erik had thought of his own mother who, despite being the wife of a jarl, still supervised the farmlands and trained the younger women in swordplay. He hadn't appreciated how complex life could be for highborn woman in Constantinople, and he was sure that the sedentary life of a Queen would not be appropriate for someone like Thea.

Again, he felt a stab of guilt. Not just because she was destined to give up her life's work, but also because her upcoming marriage would curtail her independence much quicker than she realised…

But his thoughts were interrupted at the sight of smoke in the distance. Erik slowed down and signalled for Thea to hide herself behind a nearby tree. It was a campsite—there was no doubt about it. He could see campfires, the low lines of awnings and shelters, and signs of military emplacement. But he had to be sure that the campsite belonged to the Varangian contingent that had been instructed to wait for them halfway between the city and Antonius's stronghold.

He squinted at the ridge, and could just about make out the black raven set against a burgundy flag—the symbol of the Varangians. His knees almost buckled with relief. He had managed to get the Princess this far. The hardest part of their journey was over.

'We've arrived at the camp. Come, Princess.'

Thea marvelled at the sight before her. Varangian soldiers were everywhere. Some were practising swordplay in a makeshift arena, while others were sharpening weapons and patrolling the perimeter. Women were bent over cooking pots, or laying out clothes to dry on nearby rocks, their children running around their skirts. The camp itself was not large, given it had been made after travelling, but it was still spacious enough to hold horses and oxen and pens of pigs and goats.

As their approach was noticed a pair of mounted soldiers immediately made for them at a gallop, swords at the ready. But on recognising Erik they at once sheathed their blades and saluted him.

'Leif… Sigurd.' Erik was nodding to them in acknowledgment.

'Erik. You are safe and well!'

The one called Leif was speaking.

'We knew you'd make it!' The other Varangian, Sigurd, clapped him on the shoulder.

'This is Princess Theadora.' Erik stepped aside so that Thea could be seen.

Both men sank into deep bows. 'Your Highness.'

'Please, rise.' She inclined her head.

The two men straightened up. After a moment, the taller one looked at Erik, puzzled. 'And Harald?'

Thea saw a muscle in Erik's jaw twitch, but whatever he was feeling he kept well hidden.

'Harald is in Valhalla. He died a warrior's death.'

Leif and Sigurd looked crestfallen. 'A great loss to the Guard.'

'Where are Leonora and the children?' Erik queried.

'In their tent. It's by the campfire.' Sigurd jerked a thumb over his shoulder. 'Towards the rear.'

'Let me be the one to divulge the news to them,' Erik said softly, but with authority. 'Is Alexios with them?'

'No, he was able to board the royal barge with some of the royal household servants, so he is likely already safely at Antonius's stronghold by now.'

Thea saw Erik's features visibly relax.

'That is good news.' He nodded to each of them, and the two men strode off.

'Come, Princess. I will show you to your accommodation.'

The sun was setting, and Thea saw that the camp was beginning to settle down. The Varangians were returning to their home fires. Children were running out to meet them, their little legs pumping as they ran, and the womenfolk were laying out makeshift tables for supper, or greeting their burly fair-haired warriors with a tender kiss.

Thea felt a sense of warmth surround her, and for a split second her mind conjured up an image of *her* being the one to steal a kiss from Erik as he came home to her. She shook her head. She needed to stop letting herself get carried away with thoughts that had not the slightest hope of materialising.

Soon they came to the rear of the compound and Erik dismounted outside a fairly sturdy A-shaped tent with two apses and a hinged side wall. He hauled down the loaded saddlebags from the packhorse and handed her satchel to her, before striding off to peer inside the tent. Apparently all was as it should be, and he beckoned her inside. She saw that it was modest, but comfortable and clean. There was even basic shelving, which housed utensils and some crockery. To one side of the tent there was a pallet, and to the other a small washbasin and stand.

'It's not much, but this is the largest tent on site. The Emperor gave instructions that your comfort was of the utmost importance.'

'Nonsense, it's wonderful!' After sleeping on a stone floor and travelling on horseback for days, any bed—even one made of straw—would feel like heaven.

'Very well. I will let you settle in. Dinner will be served shortly. We usually eat together, as a community, but you will probably want some privacy. And, given your status...' He paused. 'I will send one of the girls to you with some food—'

'No, no, I would love to join you all!' she interrupted. 'I mean...that is if it's all right with everyone.'

The thought of eating out in the fresh air with these people who seemed to exude such a sense of togetherness seemed a much better option than dining on her own in the tent. It would make her feel as if she were back in the wards, among the buzz of the townsfolk.

'Very well. I will come and collect you shortly.' He turned to leave. Lifting up the flap of the tent on his way out, he paused and turned to face her, a look of seriousness on his face. 'I should mention... Please do not wander outside the camp unaccompanied under any circumstance.

These woods are home to a whole host of wild beasts and the countryside could be teeming with rebels. It's not safe.'

She nodded. 'I understand.'

He reciprocated with a slight nod, and then left her. But it seemed to her that something was weighing on him. And soon enough she saw what it was.

As she peered through the opening in the tent she saw him stop at the next tent, and shortly afterwards Leonora stepped out. Thea's heart ached, for though she could not hear the words that passed between the two, she knew that they would be difficult for Erik to utter, and even more so for Leonora to hear. She watched as he handed Leonora the amulet that had belonged to Harald and Leonora crumpled in his arms. Her sobs, as she huddled into his embrace, were intense enough to shake even his hulking frame.

After a while, Thea saw Leonora straighten up and wipe away the tears from her eyes. Erik loosened his hold on her and with a hand on her shoulder said a few final words of comfort. She would now have to break the news to Harald's children. Thea looked away. She couldn't bear to think about how they would react; she still clearly remembered the day she had been informed of her parents' deaths. She wouldn't wish that upon anyone, she thought, as she began unpacking her few belongings.

Presently, she heard footsteps outside, and the silhouette of Erik's form appeared against the tent's canvas.

'Princess, are you ready?'

'Yes, I'll be out in a moment.'

She looked at her reflection one last time in the mirror, brushed away a stray wisp of hair that had settled on her forehead, and pinched some colour into her cheeks. For some reason she was nervous. She wanted these people to like her.

She stepped out and saw that several fires were now dotted around the camp. Erik led her to one around which a few of the other Varangian soldiers were placing folding stools. Some of the older children were helping their mothers arrange the trestle tables, or carrying stacks of wooden plates, crockery and horn beakers to lay out. They looked up and smiled at her as she took her place on a stool by Erik.

'Greetings.' She nodded to the group.

'Your Highness, we are honoured,' Leif replied. 'We have heard of your tremendous work in the wards. You healed one of my sword brothers.'

'The honour is mine,' she responded. 'And I am pleased to hear it.' A warm glow of happiness filled her—especially when she saw the look of admiration on Erik's face.

Platters of bread, cheese and butter were spread out on the trestle tables, and soon Sigurd emerged with a large, steaming pot, his wife behind him, carrying some earthenware bowls and horn spoons. Erik helped distribute jugs of ale and mead, and finally one of the women ladled a spoonful of a hearty stew into Thea's bowl, accompanied by a warm bread roll. Her stomach roiled in anticipation.

The stew tasted delicious. Full-flavoured, hot and savoury, it warmed her to the core—a welcome change from the bread and cheese they had had to ration over the last two days.

She saw Erik quietly putting a few bowls of stew on a tray, with some bread and mead, and carrying them to Leonora's tent. Her heart gave a tug. He was so kind, she thought.

She spoke with a couple of the other Varangian wives.

'How long is the journey from here to the Emperor's stronghold?' she asked. Thea was eager to know when she might be able to return to her people.

'It depends on how well the camp handles the terrain—and, of course, much is dependent on the weather. But all being well, just a few days,' Sigurd responded.

'I see. And what is the plan after that?'

'I heard King Antonius has called up five hundred men to storm Constantinople and reclaim it from the rebels. They should arrive at the stronghold at around the same time as us. But we will have to wait until the wedding ceremony takes place, of course, before returning with King Antonius's forces to Constantinople. Do not worry, Princess, you will soon be home.'

'Wedding ceremony?'

Thea drew her brows together. No one had mentioned a wedding ceremony. Perhaps the Emperor had finally given Adriana's hand in marriage.

'Princess Adriana is betrothed?' she asked. She wondered why Erik hadn't said anything to her about it.

There was silence around the fire. Sigurd's face registered surprise, and Leif seemed suddenly to be deeply absorbed with something on his empty plate.

A feeling of dread crept over her.

'Whose wedding ceremony is it?' she asked, forcing herself to remain calm.

'Princess, my apologies... I—' Sigurd looked awkward. 'I thought you knew. You are to be married to King Antonius.'

Married to King Antonius.

Had she heard correctly?

'Excuse me, please.'

She dropped her spoon, stood up and ran, a wave of nausea crashing through her as she felt every mouthful of the stew she had just eaten rise up to choke her.

Chapter Nine

A thousand thoughts spun through her head as she ran. She felt as if she was suffocating. She couldn't breathe. She could only think about how her life would no longer be her own. She'd known the moment would come when she would find herself betrothed. But so soon? And to Antonius? The only feeling she had for him was the kind of affection that one would have for a good friend. There was no passion… none of the thrill she felt with…Erik.

She had always known that one day she would have to fulfil her duty by marrying for convenience, but the passage of time seemed to have had no effect on how unprepared she now felt. Of course she should have seen it coming. Hadn't Adriana told her that only recently Antonius had visited her uncle in person and asked after her? In hindsight, it seemed clear that such a meeting had not been arranged solely to discuss how to keep Demetrios at bay, but also to forge an alliance between Constantinople and Macedonia.

It made sense. Antonius would not have offered Basil a wealth of resource and aid without asking for something in return. As kind and good a man as he was, the fact of the matter was that he ruled over the second largest kingdom in the Eastern Roman Empire, so he was no doubt driven by political motives. But to ask for *her* hand in marriage was odd… Surely Adriana, as the daughter of the Emperor, would have been a far more attractive prospect?

She sighed. Whatever the reason for the decision, she had to accept that *she* was the chosen one. She railed against the injustice of it all, at being treated like a pawn, at the powerless fate to which women were assigned in this world. She had hoped her uncle would have given her some warning. She hadn't expected to be given the right to refuse, but she and her uncle were close, and she was surprised, and a little disappointed, that he hadn't at least spoken to her of his intentions.

But if it helped save Constantinople and serve her people then so be it. After all, she could not risk angering her uncle and losing the only family she had left. She had no choice. She'd have to come to terms with her marriage to Antonius and with the fact that any hope of a future with Erik, fanciful as such a hope was, would now certainly be extinguished.

Erik. He knew. He must have known. And he hadn't told her.

How could he keep something like this from her after all they had been through? She'd been a fool to trust him… to think that he was different from the others. He'd kept such a big secret from her—what else might he be hiding?

The familiar doubts took hold of her. The two most important men in her life—her uncle and Erik—had let her down. Miserable, and sick at heart, she walked on.

Suddenly her foot snagged on something, jerking her out of her misery, and she looked down to see an upturned root. Looking about her, she realised that in her distress she had inadvertently wandered into the woods that lay on the outskirts of the camp. Then she remembered Erik's words of warning.

'*Do not wander outside the camp unaccompanied.*'

She tried to suppress the wave of panic rising up within her, but the more she tried to negotiate her way through the undergrowth, seeking a way out of the forest, the deeper she seemed to bury herself in it. Her pace slowed as brambles scratched her arms and face, snagged at her hair, and she grew weary, stumbling along the uneven ground with its knotted roots.

She decided to stop; it was no use carrying on and getting lost even further. She slumped down against the trunk of a fallen tree, crestfallen. She took a deep breath and tried to gather her wits.

When she looked at the immediate landscape more closely, she noticed that the shrubs and undergrowth were more concentrated to her right, and seemed to form a dense, almost uniform line. She knew such a formation sometimes meant a water source was nearby—she'd often seen it when she'd accompanied her father on his rides into the countryside as a little girl. Mayhap a river was close.

Heartened, she scrambled towards it, and soon enough she heard what seemed to be the babble of water. Finally she saw the crest of a riverbank. She exulted silently, remembering that one of the sides of the camp's perimeter backed onto a stream. All she had to do was to follow it south, and it would hopefully lead her back to the encampment.

But just as she was celebrating her good fortune the slanting rays of the setting sun settled on a figure not far away.

She froze.

Only a few hundred feet away was a wolf.

It had not seen her yet. It was standing alert, ears pricked, its gaze seemingly intent on something in the woods. But suddenly the wind changed and it caught her scent. Horrified, she could only watch as it turned its large grey body deliberately around to face her, hackles raised. Very slowly, it began to advance towards her, emitting a low vibrating growl from deep within its chest. She prepared to flee. But where? The wolf would easily outrun her on land. She looked to the fast-flowing river, its rapids boiling and churning. She side-stepped hesitantly towards the bank, her eyes never leaving the beast. Did she dare swim across?

'Don't move.'

Erik!

There was no mistaking the tall, broad frame. It must have been Erik that the wolf had sensed just moments ago.

Thea's mouth was dry. She desperately wanted to turn and run to the safety of Erik's arms, but instinct told her that she should keep her eyes on the wolf.

'The river's current is too strong. You won't make it across.' He was addressing her now, in his deep, velvety tone, which at once made her feel safe, despite her predicament. 'And if you run the wolf will have your neck in its jaws before you took your first two steps. Do as I say and you will live.'

Thea gave the faintest of nods.

The wolf paused, unsure of the odds now. Its foreleg was bent, ready for its next cautious step, as it looked from Erik to Thea.

'Stand tall and upright. You will seem larger and more threatening to it,' Erik continued as he inched slowly towards her.

She nodded, trying her best to follow his instructions, but the urge to run was too great.

He must have sensed her fear, for his voice softened. 'You can do this, Thea. Just step backwards, very slowly, in my direction. Do not turn your back to it.'

Using every ounce of willpower, Thea obeyed, tentatively retreating, her eyes never moving from the beast. Each step felt like an eternity as she inched closer and closer towards Erik. *Almost there.* But just as she turned to Erik, to gauge the remaining distance between them, her foot snagged on an upturned root. She lost her balance and stumbled, landing on her back.

The wolf wasted no time. In a split second it sprang forward, no longer seeing the fallen woman as a threat, but as prey. Thea put her forearm across her face to shield herself. It was ludicrous, but in that moment her only thought was that if she died she would no longer be forced into a marriage she did not want. She waited for the bite.

But Erik had anticipated its move, and intercepted the wolf as it leapt into the air towards her. He blocked its bite with his shield, while at the same time drawing a dagger from his waist and slashing at the wolf's side. It immediately backed off. Erik stood tall, advancing on the wolf and brandishing his weapon and shield above his head with outstretched arms, in an attempt to make himself appear even bigger. The wolf responded with a few half-hearted howls, but soon gave up the battle, slinking away.

Erik turned to her, offering her his hand to pull her up from the ground. She took it, unable to believe that she had escaped unscathed. Once more, she was in this man's debt.

'We need to move quickly.' Erik said, as he hauled her to her feet. 'The rest of the pack will not be far away.'

He led her to Mercury, whom he'd tethered to a nearby tree, and helped her mount before hoisting himself up and making for the camp. On horseback, the journey back was short, and soon they were safe within the bounds of the encampment. Knowing that her encounter with the wolf would have been distressing, he escorted her to her accommodation, to ensure that she did not swoon from the shock of it. He helped her to her tent and stood at the entrance, observing her for any signs of weakness. It was only when he was satisfied that there were none that he allowed the maelstrom of emotions whipping up within him to take hold.

The Princess had put herself in grave danger by leaving the camp unchaperoned—especially when he'd specifically asked her not to. He had done his utmost over the last few days to ensure her safety, but it seemed as if she had little regard for it. When he'd returned from giving Leonora and the children their meal Sigurd had told him what had happened.

He was fortunate that the early-evening dew, which had already settled on the ground, had allowed him to follow her footprints and track her into the woods. If he had not found her in time the wolf would have torn her to pieces. And even if she had escaped the wolf, the forest was a well-known hideout for bandits and outlaws.

However, as much as he wanted to deny it, he knew that there was more to the intensity of his reaction than he liked to admit. The sight of Thea, her life in danger, had brought back memories that he'd kept buried for years. It had reminded him too much of the tragedy that had forced him to leave Norway. The image of Frida, lying pale and lifeless on her burial ship, before he had been tasked with setting it aflame, had danced before his eyes. Thea's close brush with death had kindled that same feeling of loss he had felt when Frida had died, and a fresh wave of frustration crashed through him now, at the thought that he might have lost her, too.

He knew he should leave, before he let his anger boil

over. He tried to stay silent, to rein in his emotions, but he couldn't help it.

'What were you thinking? Do you have any idea of the danger you put yourself in? I told you that it wasn't safe for you to leave the camp unchaperoned.'

She jerked her head up, her eyes alight with fire.

'Thank you for coming after me. I appreciate it. I truly do. I needed some space to think. After all, it's not every day you find out that you are to be married and knew nothing of it.'

She looked at him accusingly, her expression a mixture of defiance and hurt. Damn it. It made his heart flip over. Nonetheless, she had to realise that she could not behave so recklessly—not at such a precarious time, when the fate of the Empire depended on her...when *he* depended on her.

'You are a princess. You cannot go running off just because you "needed some space to think".' He spread his hands out. 'The camp is large enough—couldn't you have stayed within the perimeter?'

'I wouldn't have felt the need to "go running off" if *someone* had given me some warning about my upcoming marriage. Why didn't you tell me? I had a right to know.'

Erik bit his tongue, fighting to control his temper. On the one hand he was furious with her for putting her life in danger, but on the other hand he had some sympathy with her reaction to the news of her marriage. After all, hadn't he anticipated it? In fact, her response was a totally natural one, wasn't it? Her life was about to be upended and she had found out about it in the most flippant of ways. It wasn't how he'd wanted her to find about her betrothal— although it wasn't Sigurd's fault either, he admitted, for it must be common knowledge by now. The only reason the

Princess hadn't got wind of it yet was because she had been travelling with him for the past few days.

'You're right,' he conceded. 'I should have said something. I wanted to. Believe me, I did. But at first I felt I could not. A Varangian is not permitted to divulge information that the Emperor has given him in confidence. Sigurd should not have mentioned it—but I suppose he assumed your uncle had already told you.'

'At first…?' she prompted.

He paused. That had been his reasoning right at the beginning, when he had rescued her from Demetrios's clutches in the wards. But over the days that had followed that hadn't been the only reason why. Really, it was because he had wanted to protect her feelings.

'Later, it is true that I did not feel comfortable keeping the secret from you. But after I saw what Demetrios had done to you, and how traumatised you were, I did not have the heart to tell you. I thought that if you had a few days to recover from that ordeal, and you were amongst your friends and family, you might take the news better. Besides, Antonius is a good man…he would make you happy—'

'Do not presume to know the type of man that would make me happy.'

He held his hands up. 'All right. I'm sorry. I was only trying to protect you. I hope you can forgive me.'

'I understand. But I am a grown woman. I can handle it.'

There was a hint of reproach in her tone, but when she looked up at him again there was a warmth in her eyes that almost took his breath away. He could almost feel her resentment, which at one point had been almost palpable, melting away.

She took a step towards him, placing a palm on his chest. 'In any case, thank you for saving my life.'

He didn't know what to say in that moment. All he knew was that he was hopelessly intoxicated by her. That he never wanted her to be anywhere else but here, as she was now, by his side.

'It is my duty,' he managed, all the while resisting the temptation to pull her into his arms.

The fact that she was safe, that she had not only escaped Demetrios and made it to the encampment unscathed, but had also eluded the clutches of a wolf's jaws, was miraculous.

He tried to focus, to keep things light-hearted. 'Besides, didn't you save mine that night, when you pulled me out of the way of the burning timber?'

She laughed softly. 'I suppose we are even, then.'

And when she didn't move away, but stood still in front of him, her palm still on his chest, it felt only natural to cover it with his own. So he did.

His breath fanned her neck. A silent reminder of how close he was...of how easily his arms could offer her a place of refuge. He had protected her from Demetrios and lost his closest friend in the process. He'd brought her safely out of Constantinople, avoiding the rebels and defying all odds. And today he'd come between her and a wolf, risking his life for hers yet again.

It made her heart swell. And she believed him when he said that he had never intended to keep her betrothal to Antonius a secret. He'd done it to protect her, not to deceive her.

And now he stood before her, the warmth of his palm on hers making her want him as she had never wanted anything or anyone before. *He* was the man she wanted... she *needed*. The reluctance and the repugnance, she had felt whenever Demetrios had initiated physical intimacy with her was nowhere to be seen. With Erik, she wanted everything.

But he was a man she could never have.

It wasn't fair.

She felt her lip tremble. She willed herself to stay strong. *Don't cry.*

But it was too late.

'Thea?'

'Sorry, I… I…' she choked.

Her voice refused to work. She moved to pull away from him, but he gently exerted pressure on her palm with his, making her to stay where she was.

'Hush, Thea. You've suffered a shock… You don't always have to try to be so strong.'

His voice was so kind and his words so reassuring that she couldn't resist the temptation to seek refuge in him any longer. She buried her face in his chest, huddling deeper as she felt his arms come around her, and before she knew it deep, heaving sobs racked her body. He said nothing, but held her tighter in his vice-like grip, until eventually her weeping subsided.

'I'm sorry. This is totally inappropr—'

'Shh…' he said against her temple, and he gently pressed her head back into his shoulder and smoothed her hair with his hand.

She gave in, allowing herself to fall into the warmth and safety of his embrace. She was, quite simply, both physically and mentally exhausted. She wanted to be cradled the way he was cradling her, to be held close and told that everything was going to be all right. Even though she knew it wasn't going to be. She was bone-tired…tired of fighting against it all.

How long she stood there in his arms Thea did not know. All she knew was that the shakiness in her legs had stopped and she no longer felt the need to cry. She drew strength from the heat of his chest, from the reassuring beat of his heart and from the way he held her, so that she needed nothing else to support her. She felt both safe and yet powerless at the same time.

Then she felt him raise her chin, so she was forced to look into the depths of those deep blue eyes. She had never noticed before how they were threaded with the sweetest strands of hazel, lending his gaze a softness that she sensed was meant only for her.

'You'll be all right.'

Those words were enough to tip her over the edge.

She acted on impulse. Rising up on her tiptoes, she let her gaze meet his, hesitantly at first. But when she saw that in that same moment he was lowering his face to hers she closed her eyes, until she felt their lips touch. The warmth that she had felt emanate from her belly now radiated all the way through her, accompanied by an even greater hunger for him.

She couldn't think…she could only obey what her body and her heart were asking her to do. She pushed away thoughts of all else: Demetrios, her upcoming marriage, duty. She was lost in the sweetness of Erik's taste and touch as she opened her mouth to take the kiss deeper.

But suddenly she felt him withdraw, and his arms loosened around her. An involuntary whimper escaped her mouth.

'Thea. We shouldn't do this.'

Her eyes flew open. The words were like the sting of a bee, bringing her back to the stark reality of her life.

She took a step back. 'I'm sorry. I… I don't know what came over me.'

She felt a deep blush spread through her cheeks. What was she thinking? She'd only just found out that she was betrothed to someone, and here she was ruining the prospect of that marriage before it even had a chance.

'No, it was my fault. I'm here to protect you, not dishonour you…' He was looking at her with a pained expression. 'Thea, you have been promised to another. And while I—'

She reached out and tenderly put a finger to his lips. Whatever he was going to say, she knew it would do neither of them any good. It was no use discussing the impossible. She was the one who had overstepped the mark, and he had acted honourably by putting a stop to their intimacy before it went any further. He should not feel guilty in any way.

'You have done your duty tenfold, Erik. And I am grateful for your service. Please do not feel that you have done wrong. Your honour is intact.'

He looked as if he were going to say something but then he seemed to think better of it. In an instant she saw the shutters come down over his eyes, and that look of tenderness—the one he reserved only for her—was immediately replaced by the steel of his Varangian façade.

'I thank you, Princess. Now, I will see that someone attends to your bath. In the meantime, I would urge you to rest.'

He gave her a short bow and departed, and the sense of loss she felt at his absence almost crushed her. She put a finger to her aching lips, wanting to savour the taste of him, shocked at how much she had enjoyed being in his arms, at how desperately she had wanted that kiss to continue.

Heavens, she must be in need of some sleep, for it felt as if she was truly going mad…

* * *

Their kiss haunted him. When Thea had made her desire for him plain, reaching up to touch her lips to his, he'd felt himself harden instantly. That he had mustered the resolve to put an end to the kiss when he had beggared belief. But one brief taste of her lips was not enough. He wanted so much more. Thor's teeth! He had felt more during that tender kiss with Thea than he had with anyone for a long, long time. Because it had almost driven him to madness. And this was certainly madness. She was about to marry King Antonius. In fact, they were just days away from the Macedonian forces. And here he was, hopelessly captivated by the Princess.

'Do not presume to know the type of man that would make me happy.'

Her words haunted him. It had pained him to admit to her that Antonius was a good man. But a small part of him had leapt with joy when she had intimated that the King might not be the kind of man she desired.

What had she meant? What sort of man *would* she want?

He shook his head. Not him, that was for sure. Not a crude barbarian. And certainly not someone who lacked the pristine lineage that Antonius or even Demetrios possessed. Yes, he was the son of a jarl, and in Norway he would be respected as a leader. But that had no bearing here among the Greeks, with their rigid rules and ingrained customs. Besides, even if his status was accepted as being equal to hers, it has been the direct cause of Frida's death. It made him ashamed of his heritage, and he would never use it as a tool to lure another woman into marriage.

Yet when she had insisted on dining with him and the others, instead of choosing to keep herself separate from them, a part of him had melted. She did not seem to care about protocol and customs, nor about being in the company of common folk. In fact, she seemed to actively seek it out. Her preference to live in the wards, rather than the palace, and her dislike of court customs was proof of that.

But why had she kissed him?

It was all so confusing. And, what was worse, the more time he spent with her, the more he realised that there was a huge, gaping hole in his life.

He had to find a way to stop himself from feeling. But how?

Distracted, he blundered through the camp, almost forgetting what he had tasked himself with doing. But he soon spotted Leif's eldest daughter, which reminded him that he had promised the Princess a bath.

'Gunhild!'

The girl at once skipped over to him.

'Ask your brothers to help you take the Princess a bath.'

The little girl nodded and hurried away, happy at the important task she had been allocated, leaving Erik with the image of the Princess soaking...naked.

It set his physical desires running wild again and he kicked a stone away, annoyed at himself for acting like a green adolescent. He needed to take his mind off the Princess and the outrageous thoughts he was having about her. He'd go and see Leif and Sigurd to discuss the logistics of travelling. That should provide distraction enough.

The journey would take a few days, at least, and they'd be crossing some relatively dangerous terrain, so the sensible thing to do would be to break camp as soon as possible. From a purely selfish perspective, though, he wished he could stay here with the Princess—even if she did make him feel and act like a star-crossed lover.

He found the two Varangians patrolling the perimeter of the camp. Seeing Erik, they at once dismounted.

'Erik…sorry about what happened at supper.' Sigurd looked at his boots sheepishly. 'I thought the Princess knew about the marriage!'

'No need to be sorry, Sigurd,' Erik replied.

'Antonius is a good man—and rich to boot. She could do a lot worse,' Leif said thoughtfully.

'Indeed. And I've heard he makes the ladies swoon with his good looks, too. What more could a woman want? I know my wife would leave me in the blink of an eye to be with someone like him if the opportunity arose.' Sigurd chuckled.

The two Varangians continued to list a whole host of Antonius's positive attributes, oblivious to the effect their remarks were having on Erik. But aside from the jealousy he felt, part of him was annoyed for the Princess. Such a sophisticated woman as she should have had a choice in the matter. It bothered him. He wondered who she would have chosen if she had.

'That's all very well, but he wasn't her *choice*,' he interjected, a little too bitterly.

The two other Varangians registered surprise at his tone, but if they were curious as to the reason behind it, they gave no indication.

Thea tossed and turned all night. She'd have to come to terms with her arranged marriage. Eventually. She'd prepared herself for it, and would do anything to ensure that her family and Constantinople were safe. But now she had the more immediate problem of trying to forget the kiss she had shared with Erik, and the feel of his warm body against hers, and how he'd laid his hands gently but firmly on her waist, as if she belonged only to him.

But she belonged to another. And she'd do well to remember that.

She lay on her back, wide awake, until eventually she saw the pink-grey light of dawn filter through the tent's canvas. There was no use trying to sleep now, she decided.

Peeping through the tent's flaps, she noted that apart from the crackle of the dying embers of last night's fires, and the occasional crow of a cockerel, the camp was still.

She saw Leonora, preparing breakfast outside her tent. She wondered how she and the children were coping with the news of Harald's death. Perhaps she could offer her some words of comfort. After all, she had been the last person to speak with Harald before he died. And talking to Leonora would provide a distraction from her own troubles.

'Leonora?' She gently touched the woman on her shoulder.

She at once jumped up from her cooking pot and bowed her head.

'Princess. Apologies… You must forgive my appearance. I—' The poor woman was clearly upset, but trying to put on a brave front.

'Hush, my dear,' Thea soothed. 'I have only come to offer my condolences. Your husband was a true warrior, and he died fighting bravely.' She paused to take a steadying breath, then went on. 'Before Harald departed for Valhalla he asked that we…' Thea cleared her throat at the thought of Erik '…that Erik and I do all in our power to ensure that you and the children are looked after. And we will.'

'Thank you, Princess. That means a lot,' Leonora responded.

'Please, call me Thea,' Thea urged. 'Your husband helped

save my life, so I am in your debt. If there is anything you need, please do not hesitate to ask for it.'

Leonora nodded, wiping a tear away from her eye. Then she pointed to the cooking pot. 'Now, how about some of this porridge? The children have had their fill, and there are still a few bowlfuls left.'

Thea thought it would be nice to pass the time with this woman and learn more about her life as a Varangian's wife. Perhaps she could even learn something about Erik's past.

'I'd love some.'

The delicious smell of hot, steaming porridge wafted towards her as Leonora spooned some of the oat mix into a bowl and handed it to her.

The two women sat down to eat, and Thea listened to Leonora talk about how she'd come to meet Harald. It seemed that Thea's company was doing the other woman good, and Thea was glad to provide it. Since Harald and Erik had been sword brothers, she wondered how well Leonora knew Erik, and whether Thea would be able to glean anything about his past that would explain the curious paradox of tenderness and aloofness that seemed to colour his interactions with her.

'Erik is a good man,' she began. 'It's lovely to see how fond he is of Alexios.'

'Oh, yes. He would do anything for that boy. He reminds him of Bjorn.'

'Bjorn?' Thea queried.

'His son.'

'Oh!'

When Leonora registered the expression of surprise on Thea's face, she asked, 'Has he not told you about him and the boy's mother, Frida?'

'Not yet… That is to say, no…he hasn't mentioned them.'

'Ah, well, he keeps his troubles to himself. I am sure he will tell you when he is ready. He's a private person.'

'Yes, he is indeed...'

Thea fought to keep her voice level, her features calm, while a sick dread filled her stomach. He had a *wife*? And he'd had the audacity to let her kiss him last night. So he hadn't pulled away from her because it had been the honourable thing to do. He'd pulled away from her because of guilt! And she had been stupid enough to believe he wanted her. *Fool!*

She had to get away before her emotions overwhelmed her. She didn't want Leonora to see her crumble—it wasn't her fault that she had inadvertently divulged information that had hurt her. After all, how could Leonora have known about their kiss?

She made her excuses, said that she was feeling a bit weary, and thanked Leonora for the meal. Then she ran to her tent and threw herself on her pallet, curling her knees up to her chest and desperately trying to banish the hurt—and, worse, the mistrust. Was Leonora mistaken? Or had Erik been lying to her all this time?

Again, the old feelings of suspicion swirled within her, threatening to completely overwhelm her. Yet although she could have believed something like this of Demetrios, a small part of her protested against it being true of Erik. But Leonora's words had been clear. He had a wife and a son. And, if she thought back to their kiss, she was the one who had initiated, and he was the one who had stopped it.

She couldn't blame anyone but herself for falling so hard for a man who was now even further out of reach.

Chapter Ten

The decision had been made. They'd break camp on the morrow. In some ways, Erik was glad. Delivering the Princess to King Antonius would put an end to this hopeless situation. Which reminded him—he had better go and check on her. She'd suffered a shock, and he had to be sure that she felt well enough to travel. Despite the fact that she constantly surprised him with her determination and her will to persevere even when she had suffered great trauma, the journey was only going to get more arduous.

He tried not to think too much about the kiss they had shared. Everything about it had made his senses reel—from the sweet taste of her lips to the way her body had melted into his, as if they were made for each other. It couldn't happen again—there was no question of that—but he would hold on to the memory of it for ever. It was a bittersweet feeling.

He approached her tent. Taking a deep breath, he stood just outside the entrance. 'Thea?'

There was no answer. The memory of almost losing her last night came to the forefront of his mind and a momentary feeling of dread took over him. He shook it off. The guards were on high alert, each of them instructed to watch the tent day and night to ensure her safety.

'Thea, can I come in?'

He waited. There was still no answer, but eventually he heard movement within, and the sound of soft footsteps approaching. The inner flap was pulled aside and the Princess stood there, her expression far from welcoming.

'Yes?' She folded her arms across her chest.

Erik was surprised at the sudden change in her; just last night she had treated him with affection. Did she regret their kiss? Or was she upset with him for ending it?

'I wanted to check that you are feeling better after your ordeal, since we are going to move camp on the morrow.'

'It depends on which ordeal you are referring to.' She raised an eyebrow.

'Is something wrong?'

'You tell me. Or maybe I should ask your wife.'

'My *wife*? What are you talking about?'

Now it was his turn to bristle.

'Was it honour that made you end our kiss? Or was it because you are married?'

'Me? Married? Who told you that?'

'Aren't you?'

'Not any more.'

He saw her eyes widen...a look of shame and realisation crossing her features.

'Oh... I—' She averted her gaze. 'Leonora mentioned your wife and son and—'

'They are dead.'

'Oh, Erik, I'm so sorry! I misunderstood Leonora's words. Please, forgive me.'

She looked up at him, her big brown eyes glassy with tears. He was irritated that she had assumed he would be unfaithful—she should know him better than that by now. But he supposed it wasn't her fault if she had heard mention of Frida and Bjorn. After all, he hadn't divulged much about his past to her.

He nodded. 'It was a long time ago.'

She gently placed a hand on his arm. 'I'm sorry. It must be why you are so fond of Alexios.'

'Yes, he reminds me of Bjorn. He would have been about the same age as Alexios by now.'

'What happened to your family?'

Erik looked away, at a point beyond the Princess. He hadn't spoken about their deaths for so long. It hurt too much, and he was loath to dig up the demons of his past. But as he refocused his gaze on the Princess, and saw how genuine her concern for him was, he felt an inexplicable desire to tell her all about it. To finally relieve himself of carrying some of the burden that had been so close to his heart all these years.

She must have sensed his unease, for she held up her hands. 'You don't have to talk about it...'

'It's all right. As I said, it was a long time ago.'

He drew in a deep breath and began to tell her the story. How the fever had ravaged his home town, taking all that crossed its path, how he had been on a trade mission near the coast and had managed to avoid the worst of it. But on his return he had discovered the terrible tragedy of his wife's death. And shortly after he had held Bjorn in his arms as the life slowly left his small body, too. Not many had survived, but he remembered wishing to be among the dead, so he could join Frida and Bjorn in Valhalla.

After their funerals he'd said goodbye to his father and made for Constantinople. His only goal at the time had been to get as far away as possible from Norway, to bury his grief in the rage and bloodlust of battle. And there was no better place for that than in the Varangian Guard.

He was careful not to mention that his father was a jarl—that he had inherited that birthright and that, because of it, Frida had had to leave her home and journey across the country, live in his town, where she had met her death. He couldn't bring himself to say the words out loud...to see the reproach in the Princess's eyes once he divulged the truth.

So he finished telling his story and saw that she was regarding him with pity. But he didn't need her pity either. Since making her acquaintance he had dwelled less and less on the past, and being with her made him look to the future instead. She'd given him hope. Hope that he might meet someone, hope that his heart no longer needed to be enclosed in steel.

But it was disheartening to the point of being maddening that such a future could not be with her. He'd need to put up that steel wall around his heart once more. Just for a little while...until he handed her over to her betrothed.

'Thank you for telling me.' She was talking now. 'You have suffered greatly. I should not have made such an erroneous assumption.'

Again, she placed her hand on his arm tenderly.

'Please, do not think anything of it.'

He stepped back, ignoring the look of surprise on her face. There was something else, too. Could it be hurt? He pushed aside the twang of guilt. He needed to leave the tent before she made him do things that they both might regret.

'We'll start loading the carts at dawn tomorrow, but you don't need to be up so early. One of the girls will come and wake you with some breakfast when it's time for us to depart. Rest well today.'

He bowed, and without further ado strode out of the tent.

* * *

The waggons were finally loaded and the tents dismantled and strapped over them to shield the contents from the elements.

As she nibbled on bread and butter Thea saw Erik patrolling the lines, checking that the carts were secure and that the women and children were comfortable. At one point she saw him stop and scoop up a set of mischievous twin boys, setting them down gently in their waggon and playfully scolding them, while their parents gave him a broad smile.

Another time she saw him standing against one of the larger carts, chuckling at something Leif was saying to him. His head was thrown back in mirth and she could make out the little wrinkles around his eyes. Someone, at some point, had made him laugh enough to put them there, she mused. Frida, of course. She envied the woman who had captured his heart once, and who had been able to receive his warmth and his love.

It made her wonder how he felt about their own situation. What was she to him? She had sensed passion in their brief kiss, but could that have been because she was the first woman he had been with in a while? No, that couldn't be so. He wouldn't be short of female attention. She'd seen the sideways glances that women threw him as he walked past them, and their forlorn expressions when they were not returned.

She didn't blame them. All she had to do was cast her mind back to being in his arms, and to the feel of his lips on hers, and she felt an almost unbearable sense of loss. She felt it whenever he was not near her, or when he tried to push her away, like he had last night when she'd tried to comfort him. The sudden frostiness in his tone had been jarring. It had been as if he didn't want to let himself be drawn in by her, and it had saddened her.

'Princess? Are you ready?'

He was suddenly standing by her side. She gazed up at him.

No, I'm not ready. I'm not ready to leave you.

'Yes, I think so,' she said steadily.

'Good. The sun is climbing fast, and we need to begin our journey before the animals tire in the heat. Come.'

He led her to the front of the column, where a comfortable-looking waggon was stationed. She moved to climb up into the back, but he steered her towards the front of it.

'You'll ride with me. It's safer,' he said, by way of explanation.

She gazed up at him, looking for signs of warmth, but his usual Varangian façade was firmly in place. She sighed.

He's distancing himself from me.

'Can you manage?' he asked, as she tried to hoist herself up onto the high seat.

'I might need—'

Before she'd finished her sentence she felt a firm hand on the small of her back. She ignored the tingles that ran up and down her spine and attempted to lurch forward. But the seat was still quite a distance away, and before she knew it his hand had moved downwards to give her a boost under one buttock. She finally managed to scramble up, her cheeks a deep shade of pink. She thanked him, and took her place in the passenger seat.

'How long until our next stop?' she queried.

'It will take us the best part of the day if we move at a steady pace.'

He turned to focus on steering, indicating the conversation was over. And as if they could hear the oxen started pulling the cart and began to plod along, reacting to Erik's nudges almost immediately.

She'd never ridden on an ox-drawn waggon before, and the first few paces were uncomfortable. She made a bundle out of some blankets and stuffed it behind her back, satisfied when it offered a cushion against the hard wood of the seat. Craning her neck back, she observed the long line of carts, people and cattle, and the reality of their situation was again brought home to her.

They were on their way to Antonius's stronghold and her wedding ceremony. And the man she had such strong feelings for was sitting right next to her, pretending she didn't exist.

She shifted back and stared blankly ahead. She sighed. It was going to be a long ride.

Her proximity was intoxicating. It was getting harder and harder to ignore small details—like the way her hair was swept to one side, so that it fell over her right shoulder, or the gentle curvature of her lips when she smiled in mischief. Or the way her dark brown eyes grew soft in concern when he was in discomfort.

When he had told her about his past last night, and spoken about the deaths of Frida and Bjorn, he had felt a surge of warmth from her—as if she herself were experiencing his pain. It had made his heart contract, and yet he'd wondered if he had imagined it. But no, he had seen the same look in her eyes when he had spoken of Harald.

It was a mercy that they would soon be at the stronghold. If she was no longer in his care, or in his line of sight, it might be easier to ignore the complex feelings that he couldn't now deny, and which were getting stronger with each passing day. In any case, once he delivered her to the Emperor and Antonius there wouldn't be any reason for him to be near her. He would have fulfilled his last and final duty as a Varangian. He'd leave before the wedding ceremony took place and try to forget her.

They rode in silence, and the journey seemed to be going smoothly. Noon came and went, and they stopped briefly, to eat and give the animals a rest, before pressing on again.

Eventually Erik's thoughts turned in the direction that they usually did whenever the Princess was near. She had been quiet so far, and if he were to guess he'd think she was likely pondering her upcoming marriage. While the thought made him shrink inside, for a very different reason, he couldn't imagine how the Princess was feeling.

To have no choice in such a big life decision seemed absurd—especially in the context of the Princess's profession as a healer and the aspirations she had for the wards. She was so selfless and kind it made his heart swell. She deserved to have a choice, even if that choice did not include him. That was why he was trying his level best to remain aloof from her. Like yesterday, when she'd offered him comfort. It had pained him to spurn her, and he was well aware that he'd been abrupt...but he knew that if he had availed himself of the solace she'd been offering he wouldn't have been able to stop himself from going even further than they had before.

He was jolted out of this train of thought by the sudden gleam of light on metal among the boulders up ahead. It was subtle, but unmistakable.

Instinctively, he put out his arm to stop the line of waggons. The Varangians riding alongside the column immediately leapt forward.

'What is it?' The Princess was looking at him, her big brown eyes wide in alarm. 'Rebels?'

His eyes did not leave the cluster of rocks ahead of them.

'Unlikely. We are quite a distance from Constantinople. Probably bandits or robbers.'

He signalled to the nearby Varangians and leapt off the waggon. There was no time for armour, but he reached for his sword and shield and waited. Sure enough, armed figures burst forth from the rocks, wielding axes and swords. They wore scarves around their necks and mouths, obscuring their identity, but from the way they confidently sprang forward Erik had no doubt that they were seasoned fighters.

'Stay in the cart, Princess,' he threw over his shoulder. And without another glance he gave the sign to advance.

Having seen Erik in action before, Thea felt confident of his victory. She heard shouts and muffled grunting as the Varangians' swords found their first victims. But then the rest of the bandits, seeing the fate of their comrades, parted so that they could close in on Erik's men on both sides, forcing the group to defend themselves on multiple fronts. The Varangians on horseback were at an advantage, though. Not just from a height perspective, but also because their horses were well trained in defence.

Thea's calm turned to fear as more men emerged from their hideouts in the rocks. She cried out a warning, but there was no need. The Varangians had spotted them and were already engaging. Turning her attention to Erik, she saw that he was in his element, having felled at least two men. He was now in combat with another, and Thea watched in wonder as he parried the blows, knocking his assailant off balance, wrestling him to the floor and then rolling clear of the man's kicks in one fluid movement. A strike to the head finally laid his opponent low.

Thea glanced over at the boulders to ascertain whether any more robbers would emerge, but she saw none. Relieved, she turned her attention back to the fighting and saw that the man whom Erik had struck down had regained consciousness and was crawling to retrieve his sword, which lay a few feet in front of him. If he got to his feet he'd be able to move in on Erik's undefended back. Thea saw that all the other Varangians were fully engaged and the danger had not been spotted.

She swallowed hard, remembering her father's words during their training sessions, when he'd schooled her on tactics and swordplay.

'The element of surprise is key. Take your chance, for you may not get another one.'

She toyed with her father's scimitar, which hung on her belt.

There was no time to waste.

With stealth, she hopped off the waggon, landing on her feet with a soft thud, and immediately dropped into a crouching run towards the thug. His attention was fully trained on Erik, and just as he raised his sword to attack she struck out at him, sinking her dagger deep between his shoulder blades. His scream rent the air and he staggered back, whirling round to ascertain the identity of his unexpected assailant, his expression registering shock and rage.

When he saw that his opponent was a woman, he seemed to relax, his mouth curving into a wolfish grin. He lunged at her, his movements lithe and quick, and in a second he had snatched her to him and covered her mouth with a grimy hand, muffling her screams. She closed her eyes and waited for her punishment. It never came. Within seconds she felt herself released, and saw Erik's sword hiss through the air to make contact with her attacker, who crumpled to the ground.

It seemed he was the last of the bandits, and the surrounding area was no longer filled with the sounds of shouts and swords clashing.

'Why did you do that?' He was breathing hard. 'You could have been killed.'

His tone was harsh, but he was regarding her with that same expression that she had seen once before, when he'd saved her from the wolf. Tenderness, and something else. But, as usual, it was gone in a flash.

She paused, still in shock from her encounter with the brigand. But an image of Erik dying at his hands momentarily flashed before her eyes. She couldn't bear the thought of losing him, and for a split second she felt the same unbearable feeling of desolation that she had felt when her parents had died. But now that the danger had passed she felt silly for catastrophising the situation to such an extent.

'Instinct,' she managed to say, shrugging her shoulders. 'My father taught me some skills in combat. I had to act or he would have harmed you.'

His expression instantly softened, and he closed the distance between them in one stride. He opened his mouth to say something, but then, clearly remembering they were not alone, stopped himself.

He bowed courteously. 'Thank you, Princess. It seems I am in your debt yet again. Come.' He held out his hand and helped her back onto the waggon. 'We'll strike camp a couple of leagues from here. There's a disused settlement on a hilltop which will provide shelter and serve as a good vantage point. And then it's only two days to the stronghold.'

She tried her hardest to ignore the pang of sadness that shot through her like lightning.

Two days. That's all I have left with you.

They'd reached the small cluster of disused huts with no more trouble. Erik had shown her to a small outbuilding in the centre, which was serviceable as a chamber, if a bit musty. But after riding in a waggon all day Thea was grateful for the smallest of comforts. He'd even managed to get the fireplace to work.

But she couldn't sleep. She could only think about that moment when Erik's life had been in danger. The thought of losing Erik had been unbearable—so much so that she had risked her life for him. And yet in two days he would no longer be part of her life. In two days she would be wed to another.

She knew then that she loved this man.

The impact of that realisation hit her hard, like a perfectly crystallised shard of ice, razor-sharp and vivid and real, so that she nearly gasped out loud. Her mind careened as the truth set in, and the knowledge was swiftly followed by a bittersweet understanding that her love for him was all in vain. She could never be his, for duty bound her to someone else.

Duty! She had always done her duty—to her people, her city and her family. Would it be so wrong if she did something to please herself just once?

He had expected Thea to be asleep, but when he heard she had summoned him he entered the hut and instead saw her standing by the fireplace. The slender silhouette of her body was visible through her gown, illuminated by the gentle glare behind her. Her hands were clasped neatly in front of her, her shoulders braced, her delicate chin tilted upwards. He had come to know that whenever she took this stance she meant to appear undaunted. But her eyes belied her.

'Erik.' She nodded.

'Is anything the matter? Gunhild told me you wanted to see me.'

'I do.'

He regarded her from under hooded eyes, uncertain as to what she was doing and desperately trying to ignore how her hips swayed gently as she walked towards him until their bodies were almost touching. He noticed that she trembled slightly.

He frowned. 'Are you all right? Are you hurt? Did that robber—?'

'Hush.' She placed the palm of her hand on his chest and he saw how she drew in a deep breath, almost as if to steady herself. 'Erik, you could have been kill—' Her voice caught in her throat.

'It's all right. We got through it, and I thank you for watching my back. You'd make a fine shield maiden.' He smiled at her. 'We are safe now. We took a prisoner, and the men will interrogate him once he regains consciousness. Hopefully, it was just an opportunistic attack.'

'I know, but...'

'But what?'

She swallowed hard. 'I couldn't bear it if I lost you.'

Her words caught him off guard. But he had no time to contemplate them, for now she was gazing up at him. The hand that was on his chest moved up until it was cupping his cheek, and he felt her rise up to her tiptoes...

Thea felt light-headed at their proximity, and exhaled slowly to try and ease the nervous tension in her legs. Her voice sounded different to her own ears...more confident, despite the inner trembling that she was trying to keep at bay.

He was close now, and she felt him brush a stray hair from her forehead, his touch sending her senses spiral-ling. In the low light, the cut of his jaw was even more pronounced. Flecks of gold glanced off his hair as it glowed against the blaze of the fire. He was more handsome than ever.

'I wanted to thank you again…for everything you've done for me. For protecting me,' she whispered.

His expression was guarded, but she caught traces of fluctuating emotion. His eyes, in particular, suggested he was battling with an inner turmoil. Longing? Desire? Conflict? She wanted to ease his troubles. To let him know that this was what she wanted.

One more kiss…just one.

So she reached up and put her lips to his.

He stood stock still, but she felt him shudder. Emboldened, she nibbled at his lower lip before tentatively slipping her tongue into his mouth, not knowing where these newfound skills had come from.

He didn't respond.

This was madness! She was clearly doing it all wrong, and was incapable of seducing anyone!

But just as she was about to pull away he let out a muffled groan, and suddenly his arms were around her waist, crushing her against him, and he was taking charge of the kiss. One hand was making a journey from her neck down the side of her body, lightly grazing her breast before cupping the swell of her hip. The other hand was playing havoc with her hair, pulling and teasing it.

A tide of warmth enveloped her, making her forget everything but the feel of his hands on her skin, the feel of his lips on hers. Instinct took over, and she curled her hand around his neck, wrapping his silky hair around her fingers. His kiss went deeper, and she slowly realised that the low, mewling sounds she could hear were coming from her.

One kiss, she had promised herself. But it was not enough. She was overcome by an insatiable hunger for more.

What was she doing to him? Erik had ignored the voice of warning at the back of his mind. He knew this could only end badly. But she had kissed him and had done so willingly. He'd needed no further encouragement.

He took what she was so eagerly giving.

As his hands roamed over the contours of her slender body he realised with a start that underneath the flimsy linen she was completely naked. He could see the shapes and outlines of her intimate curves, the dark peaks of her breasts straining against the gauzy material. And now she was responding to his roaming hands by placing her own on the hard planes of his chest, unbuttoning his shirt as her palms stroked his broad shoulders, and down his muscular arms.

She wanted him. Despite their situation.

The knowledge drove him on, and now he tugged at the ribbons that were holding the front of her gown together. It fell to the floor in a scant heap and he gasped.

She was exquisite…ethereal. Like a delicate summer breeze that gently ruffled tender leaves. He gazed upon her, drinking in the sight of this woman who was like no other. Her dark glossy hair fell just low enough to cover her pert breasts, but the erect buds of her nipples peaked through the veil. Her stomach was taut, and her tiny waist only served to emphasise the fullness of her hips. He followed the contours of her long slender legs up to the apex, where they met in a dark mass of soft curls.

It seemed she had become self-conscious under his hot appraisal, because now she was covering her intimate regions with her hands.

The action brought him out of his reverie.

'You are beautiful, Thea. Don't be ashamed,' he said throatily.

Gently moving her hands away, he drew her down to the chair by the fireplace, so that she was sitting on his knee.

'Let me look at you.'

He could feel the wild fluttering of her pulse as he took her wrist.

'I will not hurt you.'

His voice was husky with need, and she sensed it even as she sat dazed, as if in a dream. She felt his thigh muscles contract beneath her bottom, noticing how her toes barely skimmed the floor. Why she chose to notice that detail in particular, when she was seated so brazenly on a Varangian's thigh, stark naked, was beyond her.

She wanted to protest. It was just meant to be one kiss!

But she had been a fool to think it would stop there. And any thoughts of resistance were swiftly stopped when his mouth came down on hers again, his palms gentling, kneading the soft mounds of her breasts, first one, then the other. If she had not been seated her knees would have buckled at the unfamiliar delight, which was amplified tenfold when his hand dropped to her thigh and he caressed the soft inner flesh of it.

He made small rotating movements, his experienced fingers knowing exactly how to arouse her. Finally, he seemed to guess that she could no longer endure the teasing, and his thumb brushed against her hooded entrance. She instinctively clamped her thighs together.

'Let me show you pleasure, Thea.'

Her senses were on fire, her mental faculties impaired, as she floundered in a sea of desire and delight.

She felt him try again with a soft touch, gently pressing at the seam of her folds with his thumb. This time she did not resist. And now it was she who was gasping. Her head fell back and she moaned, a shiver of pleasure rolling through her. He probed at her opening and she felt her dampness amplify as he stroked the little bud of her womanhood. She began to buck instinctively against his hand, digging her fingernails into his shoulder blade, and he, too, seemed to groan with need.

It was only years of discipline as a soldier that allowed him to ignore the hardness that was straining against his chausses. He must remember that she was a princess. The type of woman who had never been touched. A virgin. He knew he had no right to change that—not tonight. She was betrothed to someone else. Much as it pained him to acknowledge that, he knew it would have to be *her* decision to cut across that—a decision she would have to make with time, in the cold light of day, and certainly not after the ordeals she had suffered in this last week.

But he could at least show her how to be pleasured.

The soft moans told him that she was close, and a few more strokes had her crying out in rapture. He felt tremors roll through her slight frame, and the familiar shudders that told him she had climaxed. She was still seated on him, her head resting on his chest and her breathing harsh. She was clearly spent.

Gently, he cradled her in his arms and carried her to her makeshift bed. He smiled when she made an involuntary whimper of protest as he moved away.

'Hush, little one.'

He chuckled, striding over the fireplace to retrieve her

nightgown. He handed it to her and hunkered down to lie next to her.

'Thank you,' she said shyly, pulling the gown over her head.

He noticed that her cheeks were rosy from his pleasure-making, her eyes heavy with emotion.

'Are you all right?' he queried, hoping that she didn't regret what had just happened.

She smiled up at him as she nestled further into his chest. 'More than all right, I think…' She gave a soft laugh. 'That was…that was…incredible.'

'Good. Now sleep, Princess. We have a long day tomorrow.' He covered her with a fur throw.

'Do we have to leave?' she murmured, snuggling against the luxury.

'I'm afraid so.'

He looked down on the Princess. Her lips bore a faint smile of contentment, and his heart contracted at how beautiful she looked as she slept, how peaceful she seemed. It stood in stark contrast to earlier in the day. An image of her in the clutches of the robber came to his mind. The fact that she had wanted to protect him and risk her life in doing so almost brought him to his knees.

His heart swelled with love. Yes, love. He could no longer deny it. He was in love with her—deeply and absolutely. But he didn't deserve her. And he couldn't have her.

A deep tide of sadness overwhelmed him at the certain knowledge that she would never be his. So he dropped a gentle kiss on her forehead and, with a final glance back at her, made his way out into the darkness.

Chapter Eleven

Stray shafts of sunlight pierced through the gaps between the curtains, bathing the chamber in a tangle of dappled gold. Thea awoke slowly, rubbing the sleep from her eyes and stretching lazily under the covers of her makeshift bed. But as consciousness returned, and she observed the empty expanse stretching out beside her, she propped herself onto her elbow with a start.

It had not been a dream.

A hot flame of shame mingled with desire crept up her body as she recalled images from last night... He had stroked and touched every inch of her, and had allowed her to reach heights of pleasure she had never thought possible, taking none for himself.

The realisation suddenly made her question why. Did he not think her attractive? Did his heart still belong to Frida?

Tiny darts of doubt began to prick at her, and she felt her throat constrict... Was this what being in love was meant to feel like?

Extracting herself from the tangle of sheets, she got dressed and walked over to the basin to splash her face with water, studying herself in the looking glass. Her eyes were large and bright, and her cheeks flushed with a rosy tint. She felt different.

'Princess? Can I come in?'

An urgent rap on the door jerked her out of her musings. It was Erik's voice.

She quickly smoothed down her gown before hurrying over to open the door. He was dressed in a kaftan, which was loosely buttoned and exposed some of his chest, and baggy trousers fell to his booted feet. It was the traditional casual dress worn by men in the region, as it kept them cool in the hot, sticky climate. The attire suited him and he looked as handsome as ever.

Her heart gave an involuntary lurch.

'Good morning,' she said uncertainly, unsure how to interact with him after their encounter last night.

But if he shared her unease, he gave no sign of it. Instead, there was something in his expression which told her something was not right.

'Is anything the matter?'

'It's Leif. He suffered an injury yesterday, during the skirmish, and he seems to have developed a fever from the wound. We need your expertise.'

'Of course. I'll come right away.'

She grabbed her medicine bag and followed him to the hut next door. Leif was lying on a pallet, his forehead drenched in sweat. One leg was propped up, and Thea immediately saw the gash that snaked down his flesh. She examined it, and was relieved to see that although it was indeed festering, the wound was superficial. She was confident she'd be able to get the infection under control quite quickly with a mix of camomile and flax seeds.

She searched through her bag and found the tincture, but with a sigh of dismay realised that it was almost empty. Quickly, she applied what was left in the vial to the wound and then turned to Erik.

'This should start to ease the infection. It will be enough for today. But I'm afraid we will need more if we are to contain the spread until we reach…' Her words trailed off.

Until we reach Antonius. And my wedding ceremony.

Leif let out a groan and she pulled herself together, chiding herself for not putting her patient before herself.

'Is there a meadow or pastureland nearby? Camomile is common, so I am sure we'll be able to find some.'

'Yes, there's an area about three leagues from here. If we leave now we should be back before noon. We can take horses.'

'Very well.'

The camp was fairly quiet, with only the Varangians who had kept watch during the night awake. She followed Erik as he wound his way through the pens and coops until they arrived at the makeshift stables.

'Come, let me show you your mount.'

He led her to one of the stalls and Thea gasped in delight, for in front of her stood the most beautiful white horse she had ever seen.

'An Arabian!'

'Yes, an elegant breed. She was a gift from the Emperor. Her name is Belle.'

Erik rubbed the mare's forehead and it whickered softly, clearly a little disgruntled at the early-morning start. He held out a carrot and the horse eagerly crunched away, placated. Erik signalled for Thea to approach. She gently stroked the mare's nose, letting out a little laugh as it whinnied, butting her head against Thea's hand in search of more treats.

'She likes you,' Erik observed. 'She is biddable, and not as spirited as others of her kind, but she has pace.' He held Belle's reins and signalled to a small stool by her side. 'Here, let me help you mount her.'

He held out his hands, but Thea instinctively retreated. She couldn't help but be reminded of their encounter last night. She furrowed her brow, uncertain about how to broach the subject and ask whether she had displeased him. It was silly, but she felt she needed some sort of reassurance as to why he had not pleasured himself.

She tentatively looked up at him, but was surprised to see that his eyes seemed to betray uncertainty.

A thin veil of silence hung between them until finally, he spoke.

'Thea? What's wrong?'

'Nothing. That is to say… Well, last night…'

'Did I upset you?'

'Upset me? No, of course not. It's just that I… I…' She swallowed. 'I wondered why you did not take your share of pleasure, as I've been led to believe all men do in such situations. Do I not please you?'

He was at her side in a second, and he let out a hearty laugh.

'On the contrary—you please me very much.'

Her brown eyes were dull with confusion. 'So why did you not avail yourself?'

'Princess, you are the most beautiful woman I have ever seen…' He paused, and her heart gave a flutter. 'But I cannot dishonour you while you are betrothed to another. You are not mine to take.'

A tide of relief washed over her. So it wasn't because she was inept at the art of love! It was because he was abiding by duty and honour. She admired him for that, of course. But the decision was hers, and she knew what she wanted. Nevertheless, he'd made his thoughts on the subject clear.

She was aware that as a Varangian he lived by a certain moral code, and that was something it would be difficult for him to break.

She locked her gaze with his. 'I understand,' she said carefully.

Although she didn't understand how he could have been so intimate with her last night, so tender and affectionate, while today he seemed able to completely detach himself from the situation. She was sure she had felt something in his touch last night…something that went beyond affection. But she knew that if she asked him—if she interrogated him about how he really felt about her—he would close up almost immediately.

Changing the subject, she turned to Belle, who was waiting patiently for her to mount.

'I think I can manage Belle on my own,' she said, as she stepped onto the block and swung herself up.

Belle snorted, eager to be let loose at a gallop.

'Whoa. Easy, girl. Easy.'

Erik gently patted the mare's neck, concerned that Thea might be frightened, but she seemed perfectly at home in the saddle.

'Why don't you take her for a few turns around the paddock while I saddle Mercury? You should get to know each other, since we'll be doing a fair amount of riding today.'

Thea nodded and with a click of her tongue gently squeezed Belle's sides and trotted off in a circle around the enclosure.

True to her word, she was an accomplished rider, and Erik watched as horse and woman moved as one. They would have no trouble covering ground today, he thought, as he walked to the back of the stables where Mercury was tethered. The more pressing issue was how he would get through the day without being distracted. Sleep had proved elusive, and when it had come his dreams had been full of her and memories of the way her body had responded to his touch...

He gave himself a mental shake. He could not allow his thoughts to move in that direction.

'Come, Princess.'

He led them away from the camp, following a path across the fields towards an area of countryside about three leagues distant.

He gave Mercury his head and the stallion leapt forward in response. Erik looked over to the woman riding alongside him. The ride seemed to exhilarate her, and she gave Belle a little more rein. The mare burst forward, her speed causing the wind to whip Thea's hair across her face, and she laughed with joy. He'd never see her like this...so carefree. She looked magnificent.

'Here we are,' Erik said finally. 'This expanse of meadowland is known for its range of herbal plants.'

He led them to a nearby tree, where he tethered Mercury, and held Belle's reins while Thea dismounted.

'Yes, I can see that it will yield results,' she said happily, surveying the land.

Erik passed her a sack and took one himself, and she instructed him on the appearance of the herbs she was looking for.

'We will need large quantities of everything, because the mixture will have to be boiled and herbs shrink,' she explained.

He tried not to think about the closeness of her body as she chopped and cut at the grass nearby, selecting the most mature herbs. The faint scent of lavender—a scent he now associated with her alone—wafted over to him, bringing back memories of the night before. But again he stopped the direction of his thoughts. To revel in them would only lead to more complexity.

After an hour of foraging, she seemed satisfied.

'I think we have everything needed for the mixture. It should be enough to cure Leif and see him through the remainder of the journey,' she said confidently, dusting the soil and grime off her robe.

But something had made him pause. There was a certain stillness in the air... He put his hand to his forehead, squinting into the horizon. If his instincts were right, they were going to need to move quickly. He strode over to a cluster of creosote bushes nearby and sniffed their leaves, knowing that they usually gave off a distinctive smell if rain was coming along with a thunderstorm. He wrinkled his nose as the familiar smell reached his nostrils and his fears were confirmed. In the distance, bright flashes of lightning already lit up the sky, and he saw that a thick curtain of rain was fast approaching.

'What is it?' Thea frowned, and looked in the direction of Erik's gaze.

'Thunderstorm,' he muttered. 'Quick, get Belle ready.'

Erik helped Thea onto the mare, and then secured the sacks of herbs on Mercury's back. He hastily untethered the great stallion, and in one bound was sitting astride him.

'Follow me! And don't look back!' he shouted as he squeezed Mercury's side, sending the horse leaping forward.

He glanced over his shoulder, to ascertain how close the storm was, and saw that relentless sheets of rain were hurtling across the valley floor, besieging everything in their path.

'Faster!' he commanded.

He knew there was a disused woodcutter's hut next to some ancient ruins, not far from the mouth of the valley. If they could make it there, they would be sheltered.

They pushed on doggedly and Thea looked over at Erik. Despite the storm approaching from behind, she saw the grim determination in his eyes and it told her that he would deliver them to shelter.

'Come on, Belle,' she whispered into the mare's ears. 'Just a little further.'

The sun was now well and truly blotted out, and everything in her path began to fade from view. It seemed as if the whole surface of the ground was rising in response to some upward force beneath. Belle neighed in discomfort as a spray of rain and grit lashed at her. The wind had now become a deadly opponent, and all around Thea could see that it was only a matter of time before debris would become dislodged.

Soon a small cottage with a sagging thatched roof came into view and they drew rein. Thea felt Erik's arms around her waist as he lifted her down from Belle and led her inside.

'I have to shelter Mercury and Belle, but I won't be long. There is a wall of ruins just yonder—they can be tethered behind it while we wait for the storm to die down.'

Thea nodded and hurried inside. The door slammed shut behind her. It was a tiny one-room hut, overrun with cobwebs, and the wooden floor was strewn with bits of straw and other detritus. It was, however, a welcome haven from the thunderstorm outside.

Mentally exhausted from the nerve-racking ride, she wanted only to sink down to the floor in a heap. But she guessed that they would have to shelter here for a while. She spied a broom by the fireplace and set about sweeping the floor in an attempt to make it clean, if only for a short period of time.

Mere minutes passed while she waited for Erik, but it felt like an eternity. Soon, though, she heard a loud rapping on the door, and she practically leapt towards it to wrench it open.

'Oh, Erik!' She hugged him tightly, tears of relief pricking her eyes.

'Can a man breathe?'

He smiled down at her as he handed her his satchel. Thea peered inside and saw a water skin and a small bundle which, upon unwrapping it, she discovered contained some cheese and bread.

'This should be enough food and water for the afternoon.'

Thea nodded. She wasn't hungry yet, but it was likely going to be some time before it was safe to resume their journey, so she was grateful for Erik's forward thinking.

She looked up to see him standing by the window, a frown on his face.

'What is it?' she queried, coming to stand beside him.

She followed his gaze. In the distance, a thin veil of fog wrapped around the mountain range, but Thea could make out the large sloping sides and steep ridges of the hills.

'Antonius's forces lie just beyond those mountains. We should arrive in a day.'

Neither of them spoke.

So close. So soon.

The knowledge hit her hard. In just one day she would be tied to another man, while the man she really wanted stood beside her, less than a foot away.

It was too much to bear. The previous night had not been enough. She wanted more. More of him. More of *them*. She needed one last memory to get her through the years ahead.

He made her feel safe. She'd never been able to feel so free and at ease in a man's company before—certainly not physically. Indeed, it felt as if all the demons of her past had completely melted away. Erik had given her that. And now she wanted to give herself to him—wholly and completely. Yes, she would marry Antonius. Duty commanded it. But today she would push duty to the back of her mind. Today was hers—free of duty, free of responsibility.

Tentatively, she took his hand and led him away from the window so that they were standing in the centre of the room.

'Thank you for keeping me safe.'

'As long as you are under my protection you will always be safe.'

She gazed up at him and saw that he meant it. Suddenly, all the emotion, anxiety and tension of the past week came together and culminated in a mountain of feeling, and she let herself surrender to the waves of love and sadness that crashed into her, with deep, wrenching sobs that shook her slender frame to its core. For she knew that their romance could never last.

And now it was he who was tending to her. He drew her to him and stroked her hair, soothing her as he spoke soft, comforting words in her ear, and she let herself get lost in his deep velvety voice.

Instinctively, she reached up and tipped her face to one side, so that his mouth was on her lips. It felt only natural to have his arms around her, to have his kisses on her eyes, her nose, her lips. It felt right to answer his kisses with passion, to awaken the desire that had built up since he had touched her the night before.

She did not wait for him to lead this time. Driven ever further by her own need, she felt her body react on instinct, and with an urgency she had not known she possessed. Her surroundings dissolved into a blur as her hands went to his kaftan and she tugged it upwards. She saw his eyes widen in surprise at her seemingly bold gesture, but it was apparent he needed no second bidding. He raised his arms and let her lift it over his head, revealing the expanse of his perfectly sculpted chest. She felt his hands, in turn, go to the fastenings of her gown and he disrobed her, baring her body to him as he planted hot kisses all over her.

She shuddered in anticipation of what was to come, recalling the pleasure he had provided last night with his touch, and all the while knowing that today she wanted more.

He was fluid in his motions as he gathered her to him, lifting her into his arms with one hand while with the other he spread her discarded garments over the floor. Then he carefully laid her down atop the soft makeshift cushion. Her hands roved voraciously over the hard planes of his chest, tangling in his hair, and snaking around his torso to grab at his shoulder blades. She felt his muscles, hard as flint, moving and shifting under her palms, and when she looked into his eyes and saw the longing there, she slowly slid her hands down to the shape that was straining against his trousers.

'It is unfair that you are still clothed,' she said half playfully, half huskily, pulling at the obstructive garment.

She heard him chuckle as he shucked off his boots and trousers, finally displaying his arousal. Her eyes widened in surprise, but she felt him come to lie beside her and caress her tenderly, almost in reassurance, as he trailed hot kisses down the slope of her neck. She felt his callused palm reach up to cup her breast, gently kneading it, and when she answered by gasping aloud she felt his lips move down to where his hand was, capturing the taut, dark-peaked nipple in his mouth.

She convulsed as a bolt of delight shot through her. But there was more. He sucked and nipped gently at the erect bud, seemingly encouraged by the half-cry, half-moan that escaped her, and then she felt his weight move downwards, so that he was kissing her belly, her hips, and the sensitive skin of her upper thigh. He continued his tender ministrations, this time flicking his tongue over the nub of her womanhood, which she could tell was now swollen with arousal.

Shocked at this new, intimate act, she propped herself up on her elbow to peer at him, clamping her legs together in shyness, not believing that this was something a man should do to a woman.

'Relax, Thea. Let me taste you.'

'Taste—?'

Any questions she had were swiftly silenced as he opened her legs and licked at her mound in slow, deliberate movements, like a cat lapping leisurely at its milk bowl. It sent her to even newer heights of bliss, and she urgently fisted her hands in his hair, not wanting him to stop. She felt as if she was about to explode as she writhed wantonly on the floor, her back arched in pleasure.

Just as she thought she could take no more, he pulled away, shifting his position. Mistaking this for the end, she heard herself let out a little whimper of frustration.

Erik felt every muscle in his body stretched taut and tense. He had been with women before, but since Frida none that he had truly loved. But here was a woman who had finally, after all these years, captured his heart, and he wanted to show her pleasure so that she would never forget him.

He gazed up at her, checking to see whether she was still enjoying herself. His senses were on the alert, watching for even the slightest bit of discomfort or, worse, reluctance. But there was none. Her head was thrown back, her eyes closed. Her rosy lips were gently parted and emitting soft, mewling sounds. Delighted by the pleasure he was giving her, he carried on.

'Don't stop! Erik... I... I need you. I want you. Please...'

There they were. The words he'd needed to hear—which were also the words he'd hoped she'd never say, for now he would not be able to deny her.

She pulled him towards her until he was lying on top of her, his arms either side of her, supporting his weight, and then she hooked her legs around his waist in affirmation, urging him closer.

'Thea... Are you sure you want this? If I continue, I will not be able to stop. Even I have my limits...'

'I am sure. I have never been more certain of anything, Erik.'

If she had not voiced those words, the expression in her eyes would have told him. He felt her pull his face down to hers and kiss him. And in that kiss he felt that she meant what she said. So his mouth answered her kisses, deeply and passionately, while his hand freely roamed over her soft curves, caressing the underside of her breasts and squeezing the sweet swell of her hip.

'There may be some pain to begin with, *ástin mín*,' he said softly.

'I am ready,' she said again, in reassurance.

With a soft groan he nudged at her entrance, gently prob-
ing. The expression on his face was that of a man fighting to maintain control. He could feel her wetness, and it
confirmed that she was ready for him. He kissed her tenderly, pausing to allow her to get used to the feel of the full
length of him, and then he gently pushed himself into her.

Ástin mín.

Thea's eyes flew open—not because she was afraid of
the pain, for she'd expected that, but because he had whispered an endearment, though she knew not what it meant.
What she did know was that it was a big step for him, a
man who up until now had seemed to suppress any display of emotion. It reinforced her love for him, and as she
felt the largeness of his manhood pressing against her she
welcomed him eagerly inside her, wincing only a little at
the sting of his entry.

The discomfort was fleeting, and soon obliterated by the
waves of sensation that crashed into her with each stroke
as he began his rhythm. The pain did not return, but rather
subsided as need overcame her, and she felt herself stretch
to accommodate him, revelling in the sensation of being
utterly filled and possessed by this man.

Soon, instinct took over and she was answering his
rhythmic thrusts with tilting movements of her own hips,
welcoming him into the tight heat of her body. Sweet, honeyed yielding invaded every fibre of her being, softening
muscles that had tensed even as he pushed deeper, until
he was inside her to the hilt. Finally, brought to the very
edge of ecstasy, and thinking she could no longer bear it,
she felt her inner flesh clench around him while she rode
the crest of a pleasure wave so tall that she cried out. It
seemed that her body shattered into a million tiny pieces.

And a heartbeat later she felt him let go of his restraint, withdrawing from her before giving in to his own climax with a cry of savage joy.

Dazed, Erik collapsed onto his forearms, his breathing ragged, every part of him utterly and wholly satisfied. But he realised that he could not afford the luxury of relaxing. It was her first time, and he needed to ensure she was comfortable.

He rolled from her, bringing her with him so that they were lying side by side. She clung to him and he gazed on her, searching her face for signs of worry or regret.

'Are you all right?' he asked tentatively.

She nodded.

'Did I hurt you?' He brushed a stray hair away from her eyes.

'No, you did not, Erik.'

She looked up at him, her eyes full of emotion. His heart gave a lurch. Was it regret?

He forced himself to question her. Whatever the answer was, he had to know. 'Do you have any misgivings?'

She lifted a hand to his cheek, cupping it. 'Nay, I do not, Erik. That was…wonderful.'

And the smile she gave him almost took his breath away. Relief, happiness, joy—all coursed through him.

He gathered her to him, dropping tender kisses on her temple. He didn't think he could be happier. The physical intimacy had, of course, been incredible. But he knew in his heart of hearts that what had made it extra-special for him was the fact that he was in love with her.

She'd done what no other woman had managed to do since Frida; she'd allowed him to feel love again.

But he could never have her.

The irony was not lost on him.

His heart gave a lurch, but he tried to push the thought to the back of his mind, so that they could enjoy each other's company even if only for this afternoon. Because if that was all they had he wanted to make sure they built memories they could both cherish for ever.

'You've made me so happy.' He stroked her cheek. 'Now, come, let's eat. It will be a while yet before the storm subsides, and you must be hungry.'

He brought the bread and cheese from his satchel, broke each item in two, and handed Thea her share. He watched her eat heartily, her energy no doubt spent by their lovemaking. When she was finished, she stretched out lazily on the makeshift bed of discarded garments.

'Tired?' he asked.

'No. Just…happy.' She smiled softly at him. 'And you?'

'The same.'

He came to lie beside her so that they were facing each other, and his hands rubbed small circles on her back. She instantly sidled nearer to him—a gesture of her desire. He certainly wanted her again, but for a moment or two he let himself drink in the beauty of the body beneath him. The small, pert breasts, the lean, firm stomach and the long, tanned legs…the pleasing way her dark skin contrasted with his fairness.

He took his time, stroking and caressing her body with his hands, slowly fanning the fire of their mutual desire. He caught the unmistakable look of want in her brown eyes as she felt his arousal nudge against her, and she moaned softly when his hands found the secret place between her thighs.

He knew she might be sore, untried as she was, so he made sure his touch was delicate. But then he felt her heat, and the slickness inviting him in, assuring him that she was ready for him again. The scent of her—a mixture of honey and something unique only to her—made him heady with desire, but he resisted the temptation to pursue his own craving for a few moments while he stroked her sex, eliciting from her one lusty moan after another. She wrapped her arms tightly around his neck and he heard her speak his name, pleading for more.

He smiled. 'Shh…you'll get what you want, sweet one,' he whispered, gathering her to him.

He turned her around so that her back was against his stomach. Then he continued to touch her, squeezing her bottom, palming her breasts and teasing her nipples to attention, all the while trailing hot kisses down her neck. She was writhing against him now, begging him to take her. In response, he gently lifted her top leg, so she could open herself to him. He was barely holding on to his control now, and the softness of her buttocks rubbing against his manhood was driving him crazy.

When she arched her back in carnal invitation he could wait no longer, and he entered her gently, while still rubbing the little nub of her womanhood with his fingers. She gave out a throaty cry, and soon she was whimpering as he slid in and out of her. He let the rhythm build gradually, each stroke becoming stronger and deeper, all the while willing himself to remember that she was small and tight, unused to the wilder acts of passion.

One day, in the unlikely event that they ever had another chance, he would show her the boundaries of lovemaking, he thought. But today he would be orthodox. So he held back, putting her pleasure before his, and he was soon put out of his misery when he heard her let out a cry of sheer delight. He felt her flesh clench around him again as she achieved her climax. And then he let go of his own restraint and surrendered to the pleasure, withdrawing from her just as he peaked in a gush of molten fire.

Thea lay beside him, feeling the pounding of his heart against her back. Her body was still resonating with the little bursts of pleasure that formed the aftershocks of her climax. The women in the palace had often spoken about the act of lovemaking as if it were purely one-way—a base act that often left the woman in discomfort. Pleasure was out of the question. But apart from the dull ache between her thighs Thea felt perfectly fine. Never in a thousand years would she have guessed the heights of pleasure and joy a man and a woman's joining could attain. Was this how lovemaking would be always? Or was she only so blissfully happy because she loved him? Because he'd allowed her to free herself of her mistrust of men?

He shifted behind her and she felt him gently turn her so that she was facing him. He kissed her tenderly on the mouth. It seemed that neither of them needed any words. So she lay her head on his chest and snuggled closer into his warmth, feeling his strength surround her, not wanting this dreamlike afternoon ever to end as she listened to his heart beating strongly…a steady, comforting sound.

Outside, the leaves still rustled, and the gentle tapping of branches against the window produced a soporific effect. As he stroked her hair, his tender caresses and the warmth of his body allowed her to drift off into a comfortable sleep…

Chapter Twelve

She was uncertain what had woken her at first…until she felt the light stubble of a man's chin on her shoulder, followed by a soft kiss. She smiled, remembering what had passed between them this afternoon.

'We must get ready to leave, little one,' he whispered.

'Must we leave now?' she mumbled sleepily, snuggling deeper into his warm embrace.

He chuckled. 'Not immediately, but soon. First I need to see to the horses.'

'Oh, yes. I do hope they are all right!'

Thea suddenly felt a little guilty that she had managed to spend such a pleasurable afternoon in the hut when poor Belle and Mercury had had to weather the storm outside.

'I am sure they are. Horses are resilient.' He smiled at her as he dropped another kiss on her forehead. 'I'll be back shortly.'

He pulled his shirt and chausses on, gave her a tender smile, and closed the door behind him. She squeezed her eyes shut and brought her hand to her lips. They were still swollen with his kisses. She wanted to savour the memory of their time together. Not for a moment did she regret what had happened. It had felt totally and utterly right. But that was where it would have to end, she told herself. This afternoon had been a fairy tale, and she could not hope for it to be anything more—not while Constantinople still needed saving.

Her heart broke at the thought of honouring a treaty with a man she knew she would never love. Because a little voice inside her told her for certain that she would never love another like this.

She sighed. At least some part of Erik would always be with her—although of course there would be no child from their union. She knew enough about the act of a man and woman joining to understand that Erik had been careful not to spill his seed inside her. Even so, they had shared something which was beyond special, and which she knew she would cherish for the rest of her days. It was bittersweet. But it would have to get her through the years ahead.

How was it possible for a person to make another person so happy and so heartbroken at the same time? she thought miserably, as she gathered her discarded clothes from the floor and got dressed.

She wondered whether she was the only one to feel these tumultuous emotions, or whether Erik did too.

Ástin mín. He'd whispered that softly in her ear while they'd made love. It was obviously in the Norse language, but what did it mean?

She made a mental note to ask Leonora later. It was an endearment, to be sure. And his actions towards her were affectionate and tender. But he never seemed to speak about how he felt or what he was thinking. Those two words were all she had.

She sensed that he was still holding something back from her—some part of him. And she knew that it had everything to do with what had happened to him in Norway, with Frida and Bjorn. She wished she could ask him about his true feelings for her, so that she would have even more to remember their time together by, but that was something he would need to tell her freely. It was certainly not something she was minded to coax out of him—what would be the point?

She turned as the door opened and Erik entered.

'The horses are fine and saddled.'

'That's good. The rain seems to have stopped, too.'

She wanted to say so many things to him, but instead here she was, talking about the weather. She wrung her hands, not knowing what to say or do.

'Yes…' He seemed to sense her anxiety, and he was by her side in one stride. Gently, he tipped her chin up so that she was looking at him. 'Princess? Are you all right?'

He was looking at her with such concern and warmth it took her breath away.

'Yes. It's just that…' She struggled to find the words to express how she felt.

'What is it? You can tell me,' he urged her, gently.

'I… I wish things could be different.'

It was all she could manage. What else could she say? That she loved him? That she couldn't imagine life without him? That she was going to have to go ahead with a marriage of convenience because she couldn't let down her family, nor her people?

But she reminded herself that she was talking to a Varangian. If anyone could understand her obligation of duty, it was him.

'So do I, little one.'

She felt a lump rise in her throat as a single hot tear rolled down her cheek. He instantly thumbed it away and drew her to him.

'Don't cry,' he was saying as she felt him tighten his embrace. 'You'll be all right.'

She drew her head back and gazed up at him.

'Will I?'

'Yes. Antonius is a good man. He will look after you.'

'Please...stop! I can't bear to hear it.'

She knew that what he was saying was sensible, but hearing him not only voice it, but also accept it almost unequivocally, made everything seem more final. It was absurd, but it hurt her. How could he be so emotionally disconnected it from it all? So stoic, when she was crumbling inside? Indeed, it felt as if her whole world was collapsing. Evidently, he didn't share her feelings at all.

'Thea... The Norns wish it this way.'

'So this is our fate?'

'It seems so.'

'I'll never forget you,' she mumbled. 'And what we shared today.'

She looked up at him and saw something flicker in his eyes.

'Nor will I, Princess.' He stroked her hair tenderly. 'You are the most wonderful, beautiful and kind woman I have ever known.'

He led her outside and she gave the hut one last, nostalgic look before closing the door on her fairy tale.

The Princess had made him feel the joy of love again—that indescribable feeling of belonging to another, of wanting to do anything for that person. Yes, anything. He would risk his life for her if he had to, and it would be well worth it.

But that same love also brought heartache, for with it came the bitter, certain knowledge that he was, in fact, about to lose her. Not in the same way he had lost Frida, of course, but arguably in a way that was much worse. Unlike after Frida, who had passed on to the next world, this time he'd have to live his days knowing that Thea was alive and well but out of his reach, joined to another man. It would be another man who would wed her and love her and warm her bed every night.

The realisation crashed into him like a sledgehammer driving through stone.

And yet, she had helped him to remember something of the love that he had shared with Frida, something of the happy times he had spent with her and Bjorn, together as a family. He had vowed that he would never seek that arrangement again…that he would never put himself in a position where he could lose those he loved and cherished. But he had done precisely that. And, what was worse, he couldn't even enjoy it—because she was going to be taken away from him.

Would he ever be able to find it with someone else? He doubted it.

'Captain?'

He turned to see Sigurd riding by his side.

'Yes?'

'The prisoner has not regained consciousness, but he seems to be in good health otherwise.'

'You dealt him quite a blow to the head. Those sorts of wounds take time to heal. Inform me at once if he awakens. I want to ensure it was an opportunistic attack by bandits, rather than a more meditated one by a splinter group of rebels.'

'Of course, Captain.' Sigurd paused and looked to the horizon. 'It appears we are not far from the stronghold. Likely just two leagues away. Look.'

Erik followed Sigurd's gaze.

Sure enough, the outline of battlements and parapets could be seen directly ahead of them, along with the profile of a large fort.

'Send riders ahead to inform the Emperor and King Antonius of our arrival.'

'Right away.'

Sigurd turned his horse around and rode back to carry out the task, leaving Erik alone with his thoughts again.

His stomach knotted at the sight of the fortress in front of him. It signalled the end of his journey with Thea. For once they arrived at the stronghold it would be deemed inappropriate for them to be in each other's company. He would have fulfilled his duty, and there would be no reason for him to be by her side again. No doubt the Emperor and King Antonius would arrange for the wedding ceremony to take place as soon as was reasonably practicable.

'I'll never forget you.'

He recalled the words she had whispered to him yesterday, as they'd left the woodcutter's hut, and they made his heart swell with joy so that it almost burst. He knew that she'd meant what she said, and it had taken him every ounce of his willpower to resist the urge to proclaim his feelings for her—to ask her to choose him, to admit how much he loved her and ached for her.

But what was the use? He couldn't be selfish. Constantinople needed her, and she was betrothed to King Antonius. And *he* was just a Varangian, sworn to do the Emperor's bidding. The fact that he had shared her bed was dangerous enough as it was. Dangerous—and stupid. But, oh, so blissful! He couldn't believe she had given him the opportunity to be the first to make love to her. It still seemed like a dream...

He had fallen, and fallen hard, in spite of his promise to himself. The one woman who was out of his reach was the one to capture his heart. The woman he must shortly hand over to another man. The woman whom he knew was perfect for him.

So this morning, when they had set out on the final day of their journey to Antonius's stronghold, he had decided that it would be an easier parting if he kept his distance from her. He had delegated the driving of the Princess's ox cart to Leif, whose wound was healing nicely but who still needed rest, while he took Mercury and rode out ahead of the camp.

And now they were at the great gatehouse, and the portcullis was heaved upwards immediately as news of their arrival became known.

Instantly Erik was approached by an official-looking steward.

'Captain Svenson?'

'I am he.'

'And Princess Theadora?'

'In the cart at the front of the line.'

The attendant nodded. 'The Emperor summons you and the Princess to his chambers. The King is also present. Follow me.'

Erik's heart sank. This was the one situation he had wanted to avoid above all others. Being in the same room as the Princess, his beloved, and her betrothed. But luckily his Varangian training would come in useful. He could slip on a mask when needed and make his features unreadable.

He nodded. 'As the Emperor commands.'

It had been the longest morning of her life. Erik had not spoken a word to her after they had returned to the camp yesterday. Instead, he'd taken himself away to his own tent, and apart from a curt nod in greeting, when she'd risen to break her fast today, he hadn't acknowledged her presence. Leif had taken Erik's place on the ox cart, and Thea had seen, with a sinking feeling, that Erik had chosen to ride at the front of the column on horseback.

It was obvious what he was doing, of course. And she didn't blame him. They had to distance themselves from each other, for to do anything else would be risky. Today they would arrive at Antonius's stronghold, and she needed to mentally prepare herself for what was to come. And so did he.

She sighed, slumping back in her seat and drawing her veil over her face. She should at least try to get some rest; she hadn't slept a wink during the night. She had lain awake for hours, reliving her time with Erik in the woodcutter's hut. She wanted every moment to be permanently imprinted on her brain...every kiss, every touch. She wanted to remember every tiny detail about him—from the little crinkles around his eyes to the stubble around his chin, the calluses on his palms. Those palms which had cupped and kneaded her breasts so tenderly, and whose touch had been made even more sensual by their pleasing roughness.

A faint smile touched her lips as her mind brought forth memories of their blissful afternoon. Yes, those memories might just be enough to get her through the coming days.

She fell into a restless sleep, but was jerked awake as the oxen came to a halt. Her eyes flickered open and she hoped she was still dreaming. But she wasn't. In front of her was a tall, imposing fort, and the flags of Macedonia and Constantinople rippled on their poles on the balustrades.

They'd arrived at Antonius's stronghold.

Out of the corner of her eye, she saw Erik approach.

'Princess, you are summoned.'

He held out his hand to help her down and she took it, forcing herself to forget where else that hand had been, and how his touch had sent shocks all over her body the day before.

She stepped down from the cart and followed him to where one of her uncle's advisors stood waiting.

'Your Highness.' He gave a deep bow. 'I hope you have had a pleasant journey. Your chamber is ready, but first the Emperor and the King wish to see you.'

All she could do was nod and smile politely, all the while aware of Erik's presence behind her. Her pulse quickened as the steward led them through a long stone-flagged corridor until they finally came to a large wooden door. He knocked, and she recognised her uncle's voice bidding them enter.

The room was lavishly decorated, for a military fort, displaying the wealth and might of Macedonia. She saw her uncle first, who was sitting on a grand wooden chair in the centre of the room. Beside him was Antonius. Both men stood up at once and her uncle hurried forward, to gather her up into an embrace.

'My little Thea! Thank goodness you're safe!'

'Thank you, Uncle. Yes, thanks to Er—' She righted herself. 'Thanks to Captain Svenson.'

She turned to him and gave him a smile, but it was difficult to make out his expression behind the nose guard of his helmet.

'Of course. I had no doubt you would be safe with Captain Svenson.' He turned to Erik. 'My eternal gratitude, Captain. And I am sorry about Harald. I heard the news. He was a great fighter. He will be missed.'

'Your Majesty, thank you—and it was a privilege.'

Thea noticed Erik glanced at her briefly.

'And the journey was uneventful?' her uncle asked.

'Fairly. We encountered some trouble two days ago, but we overcame it without any issue or casualties. We took a prisoner. We are still waiting for him to recover from his head injury. It was likely that they were outlaws, trying their luck, rather than rebels, but I'd like to rule that out.'

'And that is why I trust you with my life,' the Emperor declared.

Erik inclined his head. 'If there is nothing else, Your Majesty, I will take my leave.'

'Not so fast!' Her uncle chuckled. 'At ease! And take that helmet off.'

Thea watched as Erik did as he was told.

Her uncle continued. 'You are amongst friends. And I believe one little friend in particular has missed both you and Princess Theadora.'

Thea watched as Alexios came running in, taking both her and Erik by the hand and gazing up at them.

'Erik! Princess!' the little boy squealed with delight.

Thea saw the warmth in Erik's expression as he ruffled the boy's hair, but otherwise the impassive mask stayed firmly in place.

'Hello, Alexios.' Thea knelt down and cupped his cheek in her hand. 'I see your wounds have healed nicely.'

The little boy nodded happily.

Her uncle turned to Erik. 'Now, I want you to meet King Antonius. You and he will be joining forces, and I want you to work together to train the new recruits. With the Varangians leading the cavalry and the Macedonians the infantry, Demetrios's rebels will have no chance!' He clapped Erik on the shoulder. 'What say you?'

Thea bowed her head. This was a disaster! Erik and Antonius were to work together! Fate was indeed cruel.

'Your Majesty, now that I've fulfilled my final task of delivering the Princess to safety I was hoping to be released from the Guard...'

Erik's voice was even, she noticed, but she sensed an undertone of brittleness in his voice.

'Leave the Guard? Now?' her uncle queried, raising an eyebrow. 'Well, if that is what you wish... But I was hoping that you'd join us in one last battle...'

It was, of course, a command. One didn't refuse the Emperor.

'Yes, of course, Your Majesty.' Erik stepped forward. Then he turned to Antonius and bowed. 'King Antonius, it is an honour.'

Antonius nodded. 'I look forward to our working together, Captain. I have heard much about your skill with the sword.'

'Wonderful! Wonderful!'

Her uncle clapped his hands and turned to Antonius, and Thea saw him wink and gesture at him. She sighed. He'd never been good at hiding anything. And now her heart thumped as Antonius took his cue and slowly walked over to her, a smile on his gentle, handsome features. If she had never come across Erik—if she hadn't been so besotted with him—she was sure the prospect of marriage to Antonius would have filled her with contentment, at the very least. For he was a good man, and he would treat her well.

Please don't ask me to marry you here, now, in front of Erik.

'My dear Theodora.' He took her hand in his and kissed her on both cheeks in the customary greeting. 'I am so happy to see you safe and well.' The concern in his green eyes was evident. 'It has been a while... I don't think I've seen you since we played *tabula* in Adrianopolis!'

'King Antonius.' She bobbed a curtsy. 'Indeed—and you played well.'

She could not bring herself to meet his gaze, and she saw a small frown form on his brow. He knew her well, as they had practically grown up together. No doubt he could sense that something was amiss.

But if he did, he didn't press her. 'You must be weary from your journey, Princess. Please, take your rest. The maids will have some refreshments ready in your chamber.'

'Thank you…you are most kind.' A wave of relief crashed through her. It seemed he was going to wait to talk to her about their betrothal.

'Of course. Perhaps you would like to have dinner with me this evening?'

She glanced at Erik and saw his back stiffen. Her own stomach clenched, for she knew what their dinnertime conversation was going to entail.

'Of course, Your Majesty.'

'Anton,' he corrected. 'Since when have you ever addressed me by my title?' He smiled at her.

All she could do was nod and paint a smile on her own face, before she was shown out by one of the female attendants. She tried to catch Erik's eye, but he was staring straight ahead. They might have been strangers for all that passed between them. Her heart gave a tug as she left the room.

'Now, Antonius, Erik…let's discuss strategy…'

She heard her uncle's voice trail off.

Erik wasn't sure how he had managed to get through the past few hours. First having to watch the exchange between Thea and Antonius, which had been painful and difficult in itself, without the added complication of knowing that this evening they would have a very intimate dinner, and next having to spend hours with Antonius, meticulously planning the week's training schedule for the young soldiers.

The memory of Alexios standing between him and Thea earlier, holding their hands, almost brought him to his knees. It was so easy to think of them as a family...to think of her as his wife.

It was as if he were in a dream—one which with each passing minute was becoming harder and harder to endure. It would have been much easier to despise Antonius if he had been pompous and rotund, or air-headed and foolish. But the man was handsome and pleasant—and, judging by the splendour of the Macedonian court, a successful diplomat and ruler. Indeed, the Princess could not have asked for a better suitor.

It was annoying.

'What say you, Captain Svenson?'

They'd been discussing their tactics for retaking Constantinople, and now the Emperor and Antonius were looking at Erik expectantly. Erik glanced at the man sitting opposite him...the man who was going to spend the rest of his life with the Princess. The latter thought was painful, but oddly he felt no bitterness towards the King. After all, how was he to know that Erik had fallen deeply in love with his betrothed?

He shook off the feelings. He needed to concentrate. The sooner he delivered the city from Demetrios's men, the quicker he could leave and try to get on with his life.

'I think that's a good idea,' he said. 'If we attack Constantinople from the east, we will take the rebels by surprise. They will fully be expecting us to sail up the Golden Horn, where we would be sitting ducks.'

'My thoughts exactly. But that would mean that we'd

have to leave the ships behind, and the infantry would be even more important. We'll need the Varangians to train the men in close hand-to-hand combat. Only you have the expertise to do that.'

Erik saw that Antonius was looking at him with something close to admiration. Damn it! The man was impossible to dislike.

'Certainly. But if we are to launch the attack next week, we will need to start training as soon as possible.'

'The men are ready. Shall we begin?'

'Yes. Show me the training field.'

Erik followed Antonius to a large arena-style space where almost a hundred men were training, some with swords and axes, and others with gladiator-style nets and lances.

'An impressive contingent,' Erik noted as he surveyed the yard. 'How many are novices?'

'About a quarter, I'd say. But they're hardy men, mostly farmers, and they are used to hard work.'

Erik nodded. 'Let's begin.'

'I thought we would start with a practical example. Perhaps you and I could provide a demonstration?' Antonius suggested, pulling off his shirt.

'As you wish.'

Erik inclined his head, discarded his own shirt, and gripped Skull-Splitter.

The two men squared up to each other, their legs planted firmly apart on the ground, warrior-style. Antonius had an impressive physique, Erik noticed with no little annoyance. They were evenly matched in stature, although Erik was broader and slightly taller. Antonius was lithe, but in spite of that Erik sensed he had strength.

Erik turned to the men. 'Keep your guard high at all times. Like this.'

He held his sword aloft by way of example, and Antonius took the cue and brought his sword crashing down on Erik's other side. He crouched as he brought his shield up to parry the blow, and had the satisfaction of seeing Antonius forced back several paces.

'Your opponent will seek to attack your weaker side, so you must be swift in defence,' he explained to the men.

The men cheered. 'More! More!'

He was just about to give another instruction when a flash of green on high caught his attention. He squinted up. Two women were watching the training session from the parapets. His heart gave a lurch. The Princess was leaning against the balustrade, looking as radiant as ever in a gown of emerald-green, her eyes resting on him. She was accompanied by a younger woman, whom Erik recognised as her cousin the Princess Adriana.

He tried to ignore the streak of competitiveness that flashed through him, and the fact that the man who stood opposite him was an ally, not an enemy.

Earlier, Adriana had burst into Thea's chamber.

'Oh! Thank goodness!'

Before Thea had been able to speak, she'd found herself being enveloped in a tight embrace.

'I was so worried about you! I told Papa that we should sail back for you, but he was adamant that the Varangians would rescue you. Oh, Thea!'

'Shh!' Thea had laughed as she'd returned her cousin's hug. 'I'm perfectly fine. And Uncle was right to do what he did. You needed to be protected.'

'Nonsense! Anyway, you're safe and well, which is the main thing. Tell me about the journey!'

Thea had hesitated. She would need to be very selective about what she told Adriana, and she would have to be doubly careful when she spoke about Erik, because it felt as if every time she thought about him her heart melted.

She had recounted the highlights of the story, only.

'You attacked a bandit?' Adrian's eyes had grown wide with shock. 'You could've been killed! Captain Svenson would've been able to protect himself!'

'The bandit came from behind. I had to protect him.' The words came out before she could stop herself.

Adriana looked at her sideways, her eyes narrowing. '*Protect* him? That's a strong word, cousin.'

'Nonsense! I was merely doing for him what he'd done for me. After all, he saved me from Demetrios—and that wolf.'

'Hmm...' Adriana did not look convinced. 'Are you sure you don't like this man? It's not something to be ashamed of! I've told you before—everyone talks about how handsome he is.' Adriana giggled.

'Oh, come, now!' Thea waved her hand in dismissal. 'I'm already spoken for.'

Adriana dropped her gaze, and a frown formed on her delicate features.

'Yes, Papa told me after we left Constantinople. How do you feel about that? I know you always hoped you'd be able to have some say in who you married.'

Thea sighed. Yes, she had thought her uncle would consult her, at least.

'I should be happy... I just wish I could have a bit more time to accept what it means for my future. I'll need to give up my work in the hospital, and I had so many hopes for it!'

Adriana put her hand on hers. 'I understand, cousin. But Antonius is a wonderful man. Indeed, I have spent the last few days getting to know him well. He is learned, polite and handsome. And he rules with integrity.'

'Thank you, cousin. As you say, Antonius is a good man—so I should be grateful, rather than sit here complaining about my lot. I will obey without question. I couldn't risk the political implications that would unfold if I were to refuse, and nor would I want to fall from Uncle's favour. You and he are the only family I have left, and I would not lose you.'

'There's nothing you could do that would ever anger me, Thea! Now, come—I have something that may cheer you up about your husband-to-be. Follow me!'

She'd had a mischievous glint in her eye.

'Where are we going?'

Thea had followed Adriana through a maze of corridors until they were outside, walking along the fort's walls. The clamour in the distance as they'd passed over the portcullis had set her on edge.

'Adriana...'

'Don't worry, cousin. It is just military exercises.' Adriana had come to a halt and pointed down. 'Every afternoon the soldiers train in the large courtyard down yonder.'

Now, as Thea peered down, she thought she recognised... *Erik!* And who was he talking to? Was that...? *Antonius*! Both of them were bare-chested and whirling their steel swords in the air as they faced each other. Seconds and then minutes passed as they fought on. The soldiers cheered and spurred them on, pumping their fists in the air as the two men crouched and leapt and feinted around the arena.

Thea could hardly watch, so afraid was she of either

man getting hurt, and yet she couldn't take her eyes off Erik. His moves were smooth and sinuous as a big cat, for all his hulk and muscle.

'Your captain fights well,' Adriana observed.

'He's not *my* captain,' Thea said, trying to hide the note of wistfulness in her voice. 'But I'll admit he is a seasoned warrior. I've seen him fight in real life, after all.'

'Up until now I have only observed Antonius training the men each day. Life here otherwise has been a bit boring!' Adriana sighed. 'It is fun to watch the two of them together…they are indeed evenly matched.'

The two women watched as the men continued to cross swords, and then suddenly it was as if Erik had felt her eyes on him, for he suddenly looked up and their gazes met.

For a fleeting second she saw a muscle twitch in his jaw, but otherwise he gave no indication that he had seen her. A sigh escaped her lips, closely followed by a gasp as she saw Antonius's sword come down on Erik's shield. But Erik had anticipated the move, and crouched instantly to parry the blow.

The sun was high in the sky, and its light bounced off his bare chest as he moved to and fro, continuing his swordplay. The sweat glistened on his golden skin as if he were Neptune, emerging from the sea. The image reminded her of the afternoon they'd spent together, and she ached to feel his touch again.

And now it was Adriana's turn to gasp, as Antonius was forced back several steps. The crowd of young soldiers watching seemed divided over which of the men they wanted to prevail. Then Antonius was advancing again, and he struck a blow that nicked Erik's arm, drawing blood.

'Oh! Must they continue like this?' Thea exclaimed, although at the same time Adriana gave a whoop of glee.

'This is madness! They should be training with wooden swords.'

Adriana touched her arm in comfort. 'Don't worry, cousin, this is usual when they practice. It doesn't get too serious. And, anyway, they won't be encountering wooden swords in a real battle, now, will they?'

Thea observed her cousin and noticed that she seemed much more grown up than when she had seen her last. Her time at the fort had obviously done her much good, for it had seemed to bring her out of her shell. Indeed, it was as if she was more open to adventure and the outside world.

She turned her attention back to the duel, and saw that Erik, filled with a vitality which reminded her of when he had fought off Demetrios's men, was now meeting Antonius blow for blow, driving him back until he was pinned up against the wall of the arena, Erik's sword at his throat.

The young men's shouts and cheers grew in intensity, and Thea could not bear to watch any longer. Finally, she heard the deep, booming voice of her lover.

'Do you yield?'

Antonius must have dropped his sword, for the crowd erupted in applause as both Erik and Antonius bowed and clasped arms, signalling the end of the fight.

Thea's heart sang. She was happy for Erik's triumph. But she kept her joy muted, for Adriana was looking at her rather suspiciously.

Chapter Thirteen

Thea sat quite still as Adriana fussed over her. Her dinner with Antonius was in less than an hour, and she didn't have a suitable outfit or any of the oils and cosmetics she would usually use when preparing herself for an occasion such as this. There were no amenities in the fort, but Adriana had managed to bring with her a few basic supplies before they were evacuated from Constantinople on the night of the coup, including some fine dresses, and she had lent her one for tonight. It was a deep royal blue and made of silk—a material much sought after in the region—and its needlework was exemplary, with golden strands stitched into the hems and the neckline.

'The colour looks wonderful on you, cousin,' said Adriana.

'Thank you. But don't you think it's a bit too much for just a dinner—?'

'It's not *just* a dinner!' Adriana looked scandalised. 'Antonius is going to speak to you about your upcoming marriage.'

'Yes, but it's hardly a secret. It's been written into the treaty. The rest is just a formality.'

'Be that as it may, you must look like a future queen.'

Thea again noted how recent events had changed Adriana. She was no longer a girl, but a mature and discerning young woman.

'Now, you look a bit fatigued—which is no surprise, given what you've been through. I dare say you could do with a touch of make-up,' Adriana remarked, as she rummaged through the contents of her cosmetics bag.

Thea caught sight of her reflection in the looking glass. Dark rings were visible under her eyes and her complexion was pale. She did feel tired, and according to Adriana it seemed she looked just as she felt. Having dinner with Antonius was the last thing she wanted to do, but she had no choice.

She sighed. Perhaps some light make-up would help mask her real feelings of desolation and sadness. 'Very well,' she conceded finally.

Adriana at once took charge, locating some kohl and carefully applying the black powder along and above the edges of Thea's eyelids, then using it to thicken and define the arches of Thea's eyebrows. Next she selected a bottle of paste containing red ochre and used it as a rouge, rubbing it into Thea's high cheekbones and onto her lips, too. Then she brushed her hair until it shone and fell in dark, glossy waves around her shoulders.

Adriana stepped back to survey her handiwork and seemed pleased. She beckoned Thea to observe her reflection in the looking glass again, and Thea was surprised at the transformation.

'What do you think?' Adriana asked apprehensively.

'A vast improvement—thank you, cousin,' Thea said, genuinely impressed.

'You're most welcome.' Adriana dabbed some fragrance on Thea's neck and wrists before giving her a tight hug. 'Rosewater and jasmine. It will help ease your nerves.'

Thea smiled appreciatively. 'Thank you.'

She gently disentangled herself from Adriana's embrace

and smoothed down her dress, knowing that if Adriana tried to comfort her any more she'd dissolve into a weeping mess. But she needn't have worried, for one of Antonius's attendants was soon knocking on the door, requesting that she follow him.

He led her through a maze of corridors, and it seemed like an eternity before they finally arrived at Antonius's quarters.

'You look exquisite, Thea.' Antonius rose from the fire-place where he had been sitting and greeted her warmly.

'Thank you, Anton.'

'Come.' He beckoned her to take the chair opposite him. 'Did you manage to rest?'

'A little.'

Antonius nodded. 'Do you have everything you need?'

'Indeed. Your staff have been extremely attentive. I could not have asked for more.'

'Good. You've had quite an ordeal, I hear. Captain Svenson relayed the events to us this afternoon. We owe the man a great debt.'

At the mention of Erik, Thea felt her chest tighten.

'Yes, we do.'

'It sounds like he is in your debt, too. He told me how you warned him of the burning beam that night of the coup, and how you dared to stop a bandit from attacking him.'

Erik had told them that! She felt her heart contract. They had been through so much together, and they hadn't known each other for much more than a sennight.

'It was nothing. I'm sure anyone in my position would have done the same.' Thea shrugged, not knowing what to do or say.

'I highly doubt that.' Antonius was looking at her warmly. 'You are truly an amazing woman.'

He paused for a moment and a veil of silence hung between them. Thea blushed and drew in a deep breath, knowing that the moment had finally come.

'Thea, until your uncle approached me recently marriage was not on my mind. It was not something I was actively seeking—at least not in the near future. But when Basil suggested joining our kingdoms through my marriage to you it struck me as the most obvious thing in the world. You are beautiful, intelligent and kind. A true prize. And we have been friends for a long time and have known each other for even longer. Quite apart from our marriage forging a strong alliance between our two nations, I see no reason why we cannot have a long and happy life together, and even come to love one another in time.'

He paused, looking at Thea expectantly. She met his gaze. She wanted to respond, but for the life of her could not find the words to do so.

'I... I—' She dropped her gaze. 'Sorry, I—'

Antonius clearly sensed her discomfort. 'Thea...?'

He frowned, reaching out to place a hand over hers. It was a reassuring gesture, but all it served to do was bring back memories of her time with Erik, and how it had felt when *he* had touched her like that.

'What's the matter, Thea? Do you not want this marriage?'

'Of course I do!' she blurted out.

She could not risk the downfall of her city just because of her selfish wants and needs. Just because she was in love with someone else. She was betrothed to one of the kindest, most selfless men in the region, and yet she didn't want him. Silently she berated herself, fighting to harness some logic. She ought to count her lucky stars that Antonius was the man she would be bound to. Other women fared much worse in political alliances.

She looked to the object of her thoughts and saw that he was observing her with a steady gaze, looking unconvinced.

'Come, Thea, you know you can tell me anything...just like when we were children.' He smiled softly. 'All my life I've been surrounded by sycophants, constantly subjected to flattery and dishonesty. People see me as "the King", and are only interested in what I can give them. But you... you have always had the courage to tell me what you *really* think.' His voice took on a melancholy tone. 'When I saw you in the hall earlier you seemed so cheerless...like a caged bird that can no longer sing. I fear that the prospect of this marriage is troubling to you, and that saddens me deeply.'

She opened her mouth to speak, but he gently squeezed her hand and continued.

'So I ask you now—not as a king, but as a friend—will you do me the honour of being my wife? If the answer is no, I will release you from the contract and there will be no hard feelings between us. You have my word.'

Thea dropped her gaze. He was such a good man. She didn't deserve him. She had played this moment over and over in her head for the last few days. And she had prepared herself for it.

Yesterday afternoon she and Erik had given each other a part of themselves, in an experience which she would carry with her for the rest of her days as an indelible memory. Her heart belonged to him. But she had resigned herself to her fate, and from now on she would do her best to be a good and faithful wife and reciprocate Antonius's goodwill to the fullest extent. She would do her duty to Constantinople, and to her uncle.

So she painted on the brightest smile she could muster, and responded as enthusiastically as she could.

'Thank you, Anton, but my release from the contract is not necessary. I would be honoured to become your wife. Forgive me if I have not shown it. I am only a little tired, I assure you.' She placed her hand on top of his.

His expression relaxed and he smiled. 'Of course. I should not have pressed you to dine with me when you should be resting and recovering from the journey. Would you prefer to retire to your chamber?'

'No, no, I'm fine. Besides, we must discuss arrangements for the ceremony...'

The rest of the evening passed in companionable discussion of the coming days. The wedding was to take place tomorrow afternoon and would be followed by a feast. After that the forces of both Macedonia and the Varangian Guard would begin their journey towards Constantinople.

And Thea was grateful that when she retired for the night Antonius did not attempt to make any advances towards her. Instead, he drew her gently to him and dropped a kiss on her forehead as he bade her goodnight.

As she made her way back to her chamber she thought she could hear her uncle's voice coming from behind one of the doors. She went over to knock, wanting to inform him that the day for the wedding ceremony had been agreed, but just as she was about to do so she heard the unmistakable low timbre of Erik's voice. She froze, remembering the promise she had made to herself. She must keep out of his way—for both their sakes.

She moved to walk away, but something about the tone

of the dialogue made her stay. Her uncle was speaking now, and he sounded sorrowful.

'We have indeed lost a great warrior in Harald.'

'Yes, Your Majesty, he will truly be missed.'

'Ah, well, you have kept your end of the bargain and brought the Princess home safely to me. A deal is a deal. I will have the gold brought to your quarters in the morning.'

'Thank you, Your Majesty. And Harald's?'

'Of course. I will include Harald's portion, too.'

'Thank you, Your Majesty.'

'It is the least I can do after the protection you have offered me and my family all these years. I suppose I can't persuade you to remain in the Guard after we take back the city?'

'I'm afraid not, Your Majesty. I have obtained what I need to. I am set on a new path.'

'Another great loss to the Guard! But it's fair enough. With the years you've put in, you must have quite a fortune now!'

'It is ample, Your Majesty.'

A cold dread crept over Thea. The conversation she had overheard left a bitter taste in her mouth. It sounded so… *transactional.*

'A deal is a deal.'

'I have obtained what I need to.'

Threads of the conversation whirled in her head.

Had everything she and Erik shared been a lie? Had his end goal always been to earn as much money as he could, even during those times when they had been intimate, through everything they had shared?

She felt her stomach contract, as if a fist were clenching it tightly. It must be so—especially as he was asking for Harald's share of the reward.

She felt her throat constrict, and hot tears spring to her eyes. How could she have been so stupid as to think that he could love her the way she loved him…? It was all just a job to him. Of course he didn't want her. He was still in love with Frida. She meant nothing to him. She had wondered why he seemed never to be able to express his feelings for her, and now she knew why. It was because he had none.

The doorknob turned, bringing her out of her reverie.

'I bid you goodnight, Your Majesty.'

She could hear a chair shuffling back. Terrified Erik would discover her in such a state, she fled, thankful for the cover of darkness. She was just about to breathe a sigh of relief at having made her escape unseen when she heard his voice.

'Princess?'

She swung round, her heart sinking.

'Erik.' She straightened her back.

'What are you doing, wandering the corridors at this hour?'

'I had dinner with King Antonius, remember? We are to be wed tomorrow.'

She saw his jaw tighten. There was a moment of silence so thick that one might have cut it with a knife.

'I see.' An iciness edged his voice. 'Please, allow me to escort you back to your quarters.'

'There is no need for that. After all, by delivering me to my uncle haven't you already fulfilled your duty? I am no longer your concern.'

He frowned. 'I don't know what you're talking about.'

'That is surprising. You said as much to my uncle just a moment ago. You have *obtained what you need to…*' she said, placing deliberate emphasis on the last part, imitating his words.

She saw his eyes widen in surprise—a sure affirmation of his guilt. It gave her the courage to continue to throw verbal darts at him.

'What we shared meant nothing to you.'

'That is not true.'

'Then why would you ask for Harald's share of the reward for my return? I knew of the Varangians' penchant for gold and jewels, but I did not believe it of you.'

Even in the dimly lit corridor, she saw his eyes grow dark with hurt.

'I have no need of that money. My intention has always been to give Harald's portion, and my own, to Leonora and her family.'

'A convenient excuse.'

'Believe what you want. As you say, I have done my duty in delivering you to your uncle and your betrothed. I wish you and King Antonius a happy life together.'

With that, he marched away, leaving her standing where she was. She heard his receding footsteps and felt sick with hurt. Trembling, she slowly made her way back to her quarters, where she sank down onto her bed and sobbed.

Dawn broke and Erik groaned in discomfort. An empty jug of mead stood at his bedside table, staring balefully at him. After his bitter exchange with Thea last night, he'd decided it was a good idea to quite literally drown his sorrows.

She had overheard his conversation with the Emperor, and had taken it completely out of context. How could she believe that all he'd been after was a monetary reward? That what they had shared meant nothing to him? Erik couldn't understand it. After everything they had been through, she had reduced their relationship to a cold, hard financial transaction, devoid of emotion or feeling. Her words had shaken him to his core, and the sting was like a dagger in his guts.

He wanted to punch the stone wall beside him. Thor's beard! She'd made his blood boil with her accusations. And not just her accusations... She had looked beautiful. Though in a different way, for he had never seen her wear make-up before. It had lent her an icy beauty, which had only served to emphasise her coldness towards him. Indeed, it had been as if a completely different person had stood in front of him...an ice queen.

'I had dinner with King Antonius...'

She'd been in Antonius's chambers—that was obvious. They must have discussed their upcoming nuptials—that also was a given. But had there been more? Was that part of the reason why she had acted so coldly towards him? Did she prefer his company? His touch?

His heart contracted in agony. It was as if unstoppable waves of anguish were crashing into him, one after the other, relentlessly. The thought of her with another man almost floored him. Even though he knew full well that he was her future husband, and that it was perfectly reasonable for him to want to be intimate with his betrothed.

He'd have to get used to the idea, though. The Emperor wasn't releasing him from the Guard until they'd successfully retaken Constantinople, so seeing Antonius and the Princess together would be a common thing from now on— or at least for the next couple of weeks. He'd need to steel himself—especially for today, since the Emperor had insisted that he attend the wedding ceremony. Not in his capacity as a Varangian, but as an honorary friend.

After a while his agitation cooled and he grew calmer. In all fairness, he was to blame for allowing himself to let her in...to let her beauty and charm and kindness make him break his cardinal rule—the personal oath that he had sworn to himself. He'd made himself vulnerable by falling for her.

To some extent his training in the Guard would help him cope. But could he learn to live the rest of his days in the knowledge that Thea thought him so base that he sought fiscal reward mindlessly, including stealing his dear friend's wages? That he would take advantage of physical intimacy with her in the process?

He could have told her everything. How he had no need for the money he'd earned as a Varangian Guard...how his father's legacy would be enough to sustain him and future generations twice over. But that would mean revealing more of his past—which he couldn't face doing yet. In any case, he shouldn't *have* to justify his actions. She should know him well enough to trust that he would never use her, or dishonour Harald in such a way.

But perhaps it was better that she thought of him like that. It might make it easier for her to conduct her life with Antonius, and for him to carry on with his, knowing that she was both physically emotionally out of his reach.

Frustrated, he disentangled himself from the bedclothes and got up to splash some water on his face. He regarded himself in the looking glass and saw that he looked as terrible as he felt. And to add salt to the wound he'd have to watch the woman he loved marry someone else in just a few hours.

He needed a distraction, so he made his way to the keep, where their hostage was being held in one of the prison cells. Yesterday he'd regained consciousness, but it had been brief, and before anyone had been able to interrogate him he'd fallen back into darkness. But it was a step in the right direction, and the prospect of his recovery was promising.

Erik decided to look in on him now. After all, he needed some way to vent his frustration.

The prisoner was asleep.

Erik tapped him on the cheek. 'Wake up!'

The man's eyes flickered open and he groaned.

Erik thrust a cup of water and a plate of bread and cheese in front of him. For a moment he did not move, his eyes still heavy with sleep. But when he recognised the items in front of him he eagerly gathered them to himself and downed the cup of water in one gulp.

'More…' he rasped, holding out the empty cup.

Erik took it and refilled it, and the man eagerly stretched out his bound hands to take it.

Erik held the cup just out of his reach. 'You'll get some more. But first you have to tell me why you attacked us.'

The man's eyes grew dark with contempt and he slouched back against the wall, pursing his lips.

'Very well. I'll try again tomorrow.'

Erik scooped up the platter of food and made to leave the room. But his tactic worked, and before he'd taken one step the prisoner buckled.

'Wait!' He licked his lips, his eyes darting from the food to the water. 'I'll tell you.'

'Go on.'

'We were approached by a man not long ago. He asked us to track the Varangian moving camp and to wait until we saw a woman who looked as if she was high born. He described her to us. She sounded like quite a beauty. After a few days, when a woman matching her description arrived with you, we knew we had found our bounty.' He smiled smugly, skating his tongue over his teeth. 'And what a bounty she was... I wouldn't have minded if she'd warmed *my* bed—'

Whatever he had been about to say next was stifled when he saw Erik take a threatening step towards him.

'Do not speak of the Princess in such a way.'

'Princess?'

'That is the Emperor Basil's niece. You will do well to know your place. Now, who was this man you spoke to?'

The prisoner whispered something, but it was inaudible.

Erik bent down, the better to make out his words. 'Repeat the name.'

He cocked his ear to one side and the prisoner spoke again.

A cold sheen of sweat formed on Erik's forehead. He turned on his heel and rushed out, ignoring the plaintive cries of the prisoner as the food clattered to the floor.

'Your Highness, may I come in?'

Thea awoke to a light rapping on her bedroom door. She rose, bleary-eyed, and opened the door, to see a handmaiden just outside.

'Yes?'

'Your Highness, this has just arrived for you.'

She handed Thea a small missive.

'Thank you.'

The maid bobbed a curtsy and left, while Thea broke the wax seal.

Princess—one of the men has been injured in a training exercise. Please hurry and bring your medicine bag. We are near the ruined Temple of Athene, two furlongs north of the fort. Erik

Thea got dressed at once, grabbed her medical supplies and rushed to the stables, where Belle was tethered.

Her heart gave a flutter at the thought of seeing Erik again. She was a little nervous about facing him after their encounter last night, and her mind was still jumbled. In the cold light of day she'd admitted to herself that accusing Erik of using her for monetary gain was a low blow, even though she was still hurt that he had so eagerly accepted the reward. But he had sworn that both portions were to be handed over to Leonora, to help support her and her family, and when she had challenged him his gaze had met hers, unflinching.

Was he telling the truth?

She had definitely read anger and pain, in his eyes, and a hurt far deeper than she would ever have guessed. That look had been more than she could bear. But the old demons of her past had taken her over last night. She had let her wariness of men overcome her—and, worse, she had let the traditional view of the Varangian Guard, who were known to have a thirst for gold, cloud her judgement.

Deep down, she somehow knew this wasn't true of Erik. She ought to have believed him rather than jumped to conclusions. And now, when she thought back to everything Erik had done for her, she felt stupid for her childish outburst, and the churlish words she had hurled at him. She'd use this opportunity to apologise to him.

Before long, the ancient ruins that Erik had mentioned in his letter came into view. Tethering Belle to a nearby column, she went in search of Erik and the injured soldier.

Soon enough, she heard the sound of footsteps. She turned, expecting to see them. But it wasn't Erik. Instead, a hooded figure appeared on the other side of the stone altar which stood in the middle of the circular space.

Very deliberately, he pulled his hood back. At first she could not recognise the man standing opposite her, so dis-

figured was he. The man had clearly been badly burned...
Then, with a start, Thea realised who he was, and her expression registered shock and disbelief.

'What's the matter, *Princess*? Haven't you seen burns before?'

'Demetrios...?' The word left her mouth in a tiny whisper. It couldn't be. She'd watched him recede into the flames at the wards. 'I thought—'

'You thought to find your Varangian?' He laughed softly. 'I'm glad my little note found its way to you.'

'Wha—?'

'Yes. I have been watching. Waiting patiently for the right moment to present itself. And finally it did.'

'You wrote that note?'

Thea looked around in panic. They were alone. *It was a trap.* For a second time she found herself at the mercy of Demetrios.

She took a step back, her eyes darting around the crumbling ruin, looking for an escape route. Behind her, Belle sensed her agitation and stamped her hooves. But she would not be able to get to the horse and mount Belle in time, and she certainly wouldn't be able to outrun Demetrios. Apart from his facial scarring he seemed mobile, and the glint of steel at his waist told her that he was armed. She, on the other hand, had only the pair of small pruning shears that she used to cut herbs.

Her skin prickled as cold apprehension crept over her. 'I don't understand how—'

'How I found you? How I survived?' Demetrios smirked. 'I'm sure you're disappointed that I didn't meet my demise that night, aren't you?'

'No, I'm a healer. I wouldn't wish ill on any person, even if that person was you.'

'Always so noble, Thea. When will you learn that the world doesn't work like that?'

He slowly took a step along the edge of the oval altar. She backed away in the opposite direction.

'No, Demetrios, it is only your world that works in such a way. Now, be gone. You will be spared if you surrender. King Antonius and the Emperor are only a league or so away, and the Varangians are with them.'

He laughed softly. 'I know exactly where they are, my dear. I've been tracking you and those filthy Norsemen all the way from Constantinople. I have spies everywhere. I was just waiting for the perfect moment to get you on your own.'

'You have no hope of overcoming them.'

'Oh, don't I?'

There was a dangerous edge to his voice, and his smug expression set her on edge.

'My dear Princess, my army waits just beyond that hill.' He nodded in a direction behind her. 'They'll attack the stronghold at noon today, when I hear preparations are to be made for your wedding. The fort will be taken completely unawares. You didn't think I was going to let you go so easily, did you?'

A surprise attack… Apprehension turned to alarm, and Thea's heart was in her mouth. Erik would be trapped, too! She'd never have a chance to make everything right between them!

Her stomach churned in anguish. She had to buy some time and try and talk some sense into Demetrios.

'You're not serious…'

'I've never been more serious in my life.'

And she saw that he was.

'Demetrios, stop this madness. There has been enough bloodshed already.'

'Yes—but only because your foolish uncle won't acknowledge that he is not fit to rule. He could have prevented this.'

'Please leave—and tell your army to surrender.'

'Never!'

'If my uncle finds out that you are here he will surely kill you. And the Varangians will show you no mercy— you know that.'

Her words seemed to antagonise Demetrios further, and his scarred face grew even more contorted.

'They are vile, worthless pagans.'

'Their worth outstrips yours a thousandfold!' Thea threw back.

'Ha! After today they'll all be gone. And I will take back what is owed to me. You were always meant to be mine, Thea, and you know it.'

Frightened, and trapped, Thea tried not to lose hope. Although it seemed that Demetrios had laid a cunning plan which he'd already put into motion. Sick at heart, she could not rid her mind of the memory of the hurt in Erik's eyes last night, and nor could she bear the thought that the last words she had said to him were ones of bitterness.

Chapter Fourteen

Erik worried at his lip, trying to work out what Demetrios's likely plan would be now that his capture of the Princess had been thwarted. They were in a reasonably strong position. Since joining forces, the Guard and the Macedonians would be mighty adversaries. But if Demetrios had already been able to make contact with assassins so far from Constantinople it must mean that he had been following them and was nearby.

The Emperor and King Antonius would be targets, of course, and he'd need to get a warning to them as soon as possible. But Erik knew for certain that there was only one person upon whom Demetrios would choose to exact his revenge first.

He cursed, wishing he had stayed and finished him off that night at the wards. If anything happened to the Princess he would never forgive himself. He hadn't been able to save Frida, and now another woman he loved was in danger. And once again it was his fault.

The only thing he could do was try and mitigate the fallout.

With his heart in his mouth, Erik rushed to the section of the fort where the royals were residing.

A handmaiden met him at the entrance, and his worst

fears were confirmed when she told him that the Princess had received a letter early in the morning and had left her quarters.

He took the stairs three at a time, until he was at the Princess's bedchamber. He flung open the door, ignoring the sound as it squealed angrily on its hinges, and rushed in. He was in search of one of the Princess's garments.

On a chair at her bedside was the gown she had been wearing last night when they had argued. The memory cut like a knife. But he forced his emotions aside and took it, for if she'd left the fort the hounds would need a scent to track her.

Then he went to the keep, where he donned his armour and quickly scribbled a note, asking one of the stable boys to take it, post haste, to the Emperor and King Antonius.

Finally, he ordered the kennel man to call out the hounds. They gathered around Thea's gown and soon enough began hurtling towards the gate and scratching eagerly at it.

Erik's jaw tightened. So she *had* left the fort.

She could be anywhere…

He bit back a cry of despair as he saddled Mercury.

'Erik, what are you doing?' Leif approached him, an expression of surprise on his face as he looked around at the commotion.

'Rally the Guard. We have company.'

'Who?'

'Demetrios lives, and he will have brought reinforcements. Split up the Guard and search the surrounding areas for signs of military presence, but retain a core group to protect the Emperor—and wake the Macedonian guards, too.'

Leif needed no further explanation and sprinted off.

Erik's fingers clenched around the fabric of Thea's gown,

his face deathly pale as he rode out. Surely she couldn't be far away. The thought raised his spirits, and he urged Mercury to an even faster gallop.

He cast his mind back to their encounter last night.

Perhaps he should have worked harder to overcome his self-loathing and revealed to the Princess the responsibility he felt for Frida's death, which he linked inextricably to his noble birth. Maybe then she would have believed him when he'd said that he did not thirst after money or reward. And they would not have parted ways so unfavourably.

Perhaps he should also have told her how much he loved her...that he could not live without her...

He suppressed a strangled groan of anguish at the possibility that he might never be able to say that to her...that their last words to one another had been so hurtful.

His thoughts were interrupted as a clearing came into view. It was still some distance away, but the hounds were indicating that someone was ahead.

Erik dismounted from Mercury and tethered him to a nearby tree, making his approach stealthily on foot.

'Let me clear your muddled wits, Demetrios. I'll never be yours.'

Thea continued to regard the man who stood in front of her with resentment, trying to play for time by engaging him in dialogue.

'Oh, you will. And you'll learn to obey me.'

'You'd have an unwilling woman?' The words erupted from her mouth as she felt every fibre in her being recoiling at his smug smile.

'I'd prefer you willing. But if not I'll have you anyway.' His gaze bored into her. 'You'd do well to forget your Varangian.'

Thea frowned. What did he mean?

'Yes, Princess, I know what you've been up to with that barbarian. My men saw you together.' He paused as his lips drew upwards in a cruel, twisted smile. 'Ah, well, bedding a virgin has never been any fun for me, so I can look forward to enjoying you even more now.'

She was shocked and disgusted at Demetrios's words. But if these moments were to be her last, then she would not renounce Erik now. Besides, what she had shared with Erik was special, and to hear Demetrios reduce it to mere carnal pleasure angered her.

'You know nothing of what passed between us,' Thea said, appalled. 'And I'd rather die than be anywhere near you—let alone in your bed!'

She drew in a long, deep breath, tamping down on the surges of panic that were rising up within her in wave after wave. She must stand her ground. She must delay him long enough for her absence at the fort to be discovered.

Demetrios ignored her protest and took a step closer as they continued their game of cat and mouse around the altar.

'Tell me…what's so good about that Varangian anyway?' he asked.

'You wouldn't understand, since you possess none of the qualities that he does.'

'That is true. I am not a filthy foreigner. And my bloodline is pure.'

'Your bloodline is traitorous, and you're a coward. Erik is kind, honourable and brave. He is the only man I will ever love. I would love him in this world and the next.'

'*Love?* You speak of love? You are truly a creature to be pitied, Princess. That loathsome Varangian wanted nothing more from you than your body.'

'That's not true. He is not like you,' Thea spat back.

'It doesn't matter what you think. I've ordered my men to bring him to me alive, so he can watch as I have my way with you. Before I slit his throat in front of you.'

It was clear that Demetrios was beyond listening to reason or logic. Thea's throat felt so dry she could scarcely speak, but she gritted her teeth and mustered the only thing Demetrios could not take from her: her courage.

'He'll kill you before you lay a finger on me.'

'We'll see.'

'It's not over yet.'

It can't be over.

Erik's pulse quickened as he approached the ruins in the clearing.

Please let her be safe.

He would get her back. He focused on that aim. It was the only option. For if he entertained the possibility of an alternative, even for a moment, he was sure he'd lose his mind.

But then he saw Belle tethered to a column, and he breathed a sigh of relief. He slowed his pace and silently unsheathed his sword. He flattened himself against one of the stone walls and peered around it to gauge the situation. He could clearly make out Thea, her expression a mixture of anger and fear. Opposite her was a man he didn't recognise, so misshapen was his face.

But then he heard the cold, familiar undertones of malice, and knew that he'd found his quarry.

He quickly scanned the area and saw that the only thing separating Thea from Demetrios was a stone altar. He gritted his teeth, a wave of protectiveness washing over him, while at the same time he suppressed a cry of savage satisfaction at the thought of ridding the world of Demetrios once and for all. He'd never be able to threaten Thea ever again, nor Alexios, and Erik would finally be able to avenge Harald's death.

The thirst for retribution was pressing, but he forced himself to resist the impetus to charge in and slay the man. He'd have to be patient, and give Demetrios as little warning as possible. If Erik tried to advance too quickly, Demetrios might lash out at Thea, who was well within reach of his sword's blade. He'd need to wait until Thea had manoeuvred herself further around the altar, then he could snatch her away and position her behind him.

Come on, Thea. Move just a little more…

Erik cocked his head to one side to try and make out the words that passed between her and Demetrios. He heard the word 'Varangian', spoken in the scornful tones of Demetrios's voice. The Princess was standing her ground, arguing back. And now Demetrios was speaking again.

'So he can watch as I have my way with you.'

Erik's grip tightened around the hilt of his sword. The thought of Demetrios taking Thea by force was enough to send him into a murderous rage. But he fought for restraint. Thea was almost where he wanted her, and everything depended on the next few moments.

One more step…

Finally she was within his arm's reach.

He grabbed hold of her, pulling her protectively behind him.

'Stay behind me!' he commanded.

He registered a moment of surprise in Demetrios's expression, which quickly turned to rage and then contempt.

'Well, well, well… Speaking of filthy Varangians.'

'Yes, Demetrios, I am here. And now, instead of preying

on defenceless women like a coward, why don't you finish this with me, man to man?'

'Gladly.'

A cruel smile twisted Demetrios's features, rendering them even more grotesque. And Erik stepped away from the altar and watched as Demetrios came to meet him.

Thea had staggered behind the stone column that Erik had propelled her towards, not quite believing that he had come for her, let alone actually found her. And now she watched as the two men faced each other.

The cold glare in Erik's eyes was unmistakable, and it was as if the surrounding area also felt it…for the atmosphere in the ruined temple seemed to ice over.

Thea had come to know that look well. She knew it meant death.

'I hear you've had your way with that harlot,' Demetrios sneered as he jerked his head towards Thea. 'She's a fiery one, isn't she? I look forward to experiencing her skills.'

'Speak of her like that again and I will make sure I give you a slow and painful death rather than a quick one,' Erik warned.

'Your blood shall stain my blade just as Harald's did!' Demetrios spat. 'Sinking my sword into his back made everything else I suffered that night worth it… To think that the Emperor thought to replace *me* as General with that scum is beyond belief.'

'You are the scum, Demetrios. You may have slain one of our greatest warriors, but you acted only as a coward would.'

Outraged, Demetrios lunged forward with savage zeal. But Erik was ready for him, parrying the blow easily as he sidestepped him, while simultaneously delivering a slice to

Demetrios's arm with Skull-Splitter. Yet Demetrios fought on recklessly, his expression a mask of hatred and outrage.

Another slash from Erik opened a rent across his chest, and now the madness in his gaze gave way to desperation. Gone was the defiance, the confidence. Grimacing, he clapped his hand to the wound as he fell to his knees, leaning on his sword for support. There was a long moment of silence, until finally he dropped his weapon and raised one hand in surrender.

'Mercy! Mercy! You win, Varangian.'

Erik paused and lowered his sword.

'Get up and put your hands on the altar,' he commanded.

'As you wish…'

Demetrios licked his lips, and only then did Thea notice the cunning in his eyes. But she was too late to warn Erik, for in a split second Demetrios had scooped up some of the sand by his feet and flung it into Erik's eyes. Erik stumbled back, temporarily blinded, and Demetrios pulled a scimitar from his boot and leapt up, swiping at Erik's side, drawing blood. Erik grunted, but recovered his balance in an instant. He lunged past Demetrios's guard, driving the point of his blade into his shoulder while knocking the scimitar out of the other man's hand.

Demetrios cried out in pain as he was forced back onto his knees—and then the edge of Erik's blade was at his throat.

'What are you waiting for, Varangian? Do it.'

Erik's gaze hardened, and Thea saw something strange flit across his features.

'First you will apologise to the Princess for your insults.'

She watched as Erik slowly forced Demetrios's head in her direction, and then Demetrios's cold stare was upon her. His mouth gaped open in a cruel smile.

'I'd rather die than apologise to that whore—'

His last word ended in a choking rasp as Erik drew back his sword arm and thrust.

'Then you shall,' Erik muttered as he let the body fall, surveying it with anger and disgust.

Thea watched her lover sheath his sword and saw the last remnants of ferocity in those ice-blue eyes diminish as he turned towards her.

He closed the distance between them in two strides, and before she could speak gathered her to him tightly, desperately.

For the space of several heartbeats neither of them spoke.

Then, 'Oh, Erik, you came for me!' she cried, burying her head in her chest.

'Of course. As soon as I realised you were in danger.' He glanced at the slain body of Demetrios. 'Did he harm you?'

She shook her head. 'No, you found us before he laid a finger on me. I can hardly believe he's dead…'

'Yes, it's over now. And I will not pretend I'm sorry I killed him.'

'I didn't wish for things to happen this way…for a life to be lost on account of me. But he gave you no choice.'

Erik observed this woman who was like no other. He tenderly cupped her cheek. 'Your goodness really knows no bounds. How can you pity someone like Demetrios after what he made you endure…?' He pulled back, a look of softness in his eyes. 'You really are an angel. But for my part I am content that Harald's death is now avenged in full. And Demetrios will no longer be able to harm anyone else.'

'That is true.' She looked up at him. 'Erik, I am sorry for how I acted last night. I should have given you a chance to explain yourself rather than jump to conclusions. When

I found myself trapped by Demetrios, and I thought it was the end, the only thing I wanted to do was to make things right between us.'

'So did I. When I heard from the hostage that Demetrios might be nearby, and then did not find you in your quarters, I was beside myself. If I'd pursued him that night in the wards this would never have happened!'

He crushed her even deeper against him, but she gently pulled her head back so that she was looking at him.

'Stop, Erik. None of this was your fault.' She paused, searching his face, locking her gaze with his. 'And you must not blame yourself for things that were outside your control. You must believe that nothing of what happened to Frida was your fault.'

At those words of hers he felt an overwhelming sense of relief, as if a burden was being lifted from his shoulders. This was the moment when he could finally free himself, give the Princess the last piece of the puzzle about his past, his status, his shame.

'Thea, about last night—'

But just as he was about to speak the sound of hoof-beats could be heard. He quickly disengaged himself from the Princess as flashes of crimson evidenced a Varangian presence, and soon Sigurd and Leif appeared in the clearing, accompanied by a host of others from the Guard, their steeds foaming at the mouth.

'Leif, Sigurd… What news?'

'The Emperor is safe, but he was worried about the Princess and sent us out to find you. Though I see he had no cause to be,' Sigurd managed, as he drew rein in front of Erik and fought to catch his breath. 'Our scouts have found the rebels. Indeed, they are led by Demetrios. Where is he?'

'Demetrios died by my sword.'

Erik stepped aside, and as Demetrios's body came into view the Varangians cheered, glad that Harald's death had been avenged.

Eventually Erik held up his hand to silence them.

'The Emperor does not want any further bloodshed,' he told them. 'The rebels will be dealt with diplomatically. Hopefully, once they see that their leader is dead, they will be deterred from their cause. Leif, you'll come with me. We'll take the majority of our men and ride out to meet them. Sigurd, you and a handful of the cavalry can escort the Princess back to the fort.'

Sigurd nodded. 'Yes, Captain.'

Erik turned to face her, fighting to keep his expression stoic. There was so much left unsaid between them. But he couldn't risk divulging his feelings for her in front of the others, even though he felt as if his whole world was collapsing with uncertainty.

'Come, Princess.'

He helped her mount Belle, and he got back on Mercury. She was looking at him expectantly, as if waiting for him to say something. Or perhaps she was wanting to say something herself.

After a few moments, she spoke.

'Captain?'

Erik swung Mercury around. The sun glinted off his chainmail and his golden hair, which whipped at his face with the sudden movement, and he was magnificent. He seemed as he had been that first time she'd seen him, in armour at the wards, like a Northman from the Norse sagas.

For a split second she glimpsed something in his eyes— a look which told of a deep, unspoken emotion that melted her heart. But just as quickly the Varangian mask replaced the man she loved with the soldier who was wont to distance himself from her.

Thea's heart leapt to her mouth. She wanted to rush over to him, to tell him so many things. And she'd felt as if he, too, had been just about to open up to her about something important. She wished she'd had longer with him before the others found them. What had he wanted to tell her? And when would she see him again?

I love you. I love you, my Varangian.

The words burned on her tongue. She wanted him to know. But they were not alone, and she wasn't sure what effect her revelation might have on him.

'Be safe, Varangian,' she told him. And that was all.

Sigurd and the others escorted her away, and before long the fort's entrance came into view. Adriana, her uncle and Antonius were waiting for her inside the keep. Adriana, her eyes red with tears, immediately enveloped her in a tight embrace. Her uncle, too, came forward and placed a hand on her shoulder.

'Thank goodness, Theadora, we were all worried sick. Are you harmed?'

'No, I am well. Captain Svenson found me in time.' She managed a weak smile.

'We owe Captain Svenson a life debt. And what of Demetrios?' her uncle queried.

'Captain Svenson found us just as he was about to kidnap me. They became engaged in a duel. Captain Svenson offered mercy, but Demetrios spurned it.' She looked at the floor. 'He died by Captain Svenson's sword.'

'It is never good to hear a life has been lost, even when it belongs to someone such as Demetrios, but Captain Svenson did the right thing.' Her uncle was solemn.

'There is more, Uncle. The rebels are camped nearby.

They are due to launch a full-scale assault on the fort shortly, but Captain Svenson and some of the Varangians have ridden out to meet them.'

'Very well. I will ride out, too, with Sigurd and the others.'

'But Papa, is that safe?' Adriana said with concern. 'What if there is a conflict?'

'All will be well, daughter. I am Emperor, and it's imperative that I am visible, and that the rebels swear allegiance afresh to me.' He gave her a reassuring smile. 'Come, Sigurd.'

'I will see you out, Papa.' Adriana said, leaving Thea alone in the room with Antonius.

'My dear, can I get you some wine to ease your nerves? Perhaps some cheese and figs?' Antonius steered her to the chaise longue nearby.

'Some wine would be good,' she said gratefully, and he immediately left to attend to her request.

Alone for the first time that day, Thea stared ahead of her, focusing on a tiny speck on the wall. Today was meant to be her wedding day, and the thought made her feel sick. After this morning's events, when she'd thought she might have lost Erik for good, she was more certain than ever that there was only one man to whom her heart would ever belong, even though she could never hope to have a future with him.

And then there was Antonius. He was a good, kind person, and they'd known each other from childhood. She was about to take the sacred oaths of marriage with him, but she was in love with someone else. It didn't feel right to keep that information from him. She owed him the truth, at the very least.

She was jolted out of her thoughts as Antonius walked back in, bearing wine.

'How are you, my dear?' He handed her a cup and she drank deeply, trying to find liquid courage.

'I... I—' She fought to find words to express herself. Where could she start?

'Thea, come... You know you can tell me anything. Since you arrived I've sensed your disquiet. I asked you before, and you said it was only tiredness from the journey.' He paused, and thumbed away the tear that was silently rolling down her cheek. 'I know you have been through more than anyone can imagine with Demetrios. But something else is bothering you.'

There was nothing for it. She needed to unburden herself, no matter the consequences. It wasn't right to mislead Antonius.

'It's our marriage,' she admitted.

There was silence, but when she looked up at him she saw that he was smiling at her gently.

'My dear, I thought as much. It was foisted upon you, and you had no choice in the matter.'

'It's not that, Anton. I know I have a duty to the city, to my uncle. I have prepared myself for a marriage of convenience and all that comes with it all my life. I know I'll need to give up my nursing. I am prepared for that too.' She looked up at him, uncertain how to continue. But he was making it easy, his expression encouraging and kind. 'Marriage to you would be an honour—truly. But... I must be transparent.'

She took a deep breath, wondering how to find the words to explain that she was in love with another man.

'Come...tell me, Thea. There were never any secrets between us as children. You can speak freely, knowing you will not be judged.'

'I… I cannot give my heart to you.'

'There is someone else?'

There was no accusation in his eyes, no resentment in his voice. Just a note of enquiry.

'Yes.' She breathed a sigh of relief. There. It was out. She had admitted it out loud, to herself and to her betrothed. 'But I have not played you for a fool,' she went on. 'My feelings for this man took root well before I knew of our marriage. I give you my word. In any case, a future with him is impossible.' She clasped her hands tightly together in her lap. 'I just thought that you should know.'

'Thank you for telling me, Thea. It takes courage to be so honest. But you need not fear my displeasure, for I know that you would not conduct yourself with malicious intent.'

He put an arm around her shoulder and his understanding and generosity were too much. She finally gave way to the emotions that were whipping up within her and sobbed.

'Hush, Thea. Come, let's discuss the matter further and see if we can find a solution.'

He refilled her cup of wine and poured himself one, too, then he sat back on the divan, deep in thought. After some moments, he spoke.

'The alliance between Constantinople and Macedonia was made at your uncle's request and predicated on the need to counter the threat of Demetrios and his army. But now Demetrios is dead and the rebels are sure to surrender. The threat of Demetrios no longer exists.'

He looked at her pointedly, but she didn't understand.

'Theoretically,' he continued, 'Demetrios's death means that there is no longer any need for your uncle to rely on

Macedonian support to take back Constantinople, nor for a marriage that unites the two states. Not if all parties to the alliance agree.'

Thea wasn't sure she'd heard correctly. Was he presenting her with a way out of their marriage?

'You have a choice, Thea. I would be honoured to have you as my wife, but if your heart is set elsewhere it wouldn't be fair to force you into a union that you do not want. Besides, as I have said before, were it not for the alliance I would have happily waited a few more years for marriage myself.'

He winked at her.

She couldn't believe what she was hearing. She searched his face and saw there was only genuine kindness there. He was truly a good man, and in her view deserved much more than she could offer him.

For a split second Thea allowed herself to imagine a future with Erik, allowed herself the thought of being married to him, bearing his children and growing old with him... She would give anything to have all that...to be bound to him for ever.

But her uncle would have to agree to dissolve the alliance first. And even if her uncle allowed her to withdraw from her marriage to Antonius as a result of Demetrios's downfall, he would never sanction her marriage to Erik. The rules were clear. She'd be expected to marry someone who would enhance the power and standing of Constantinople. Someone who hailed from their own region, not the Northern lands. If she willingly chose to ignore all that she would jeopardise her relationship with her uncle, who had treated her like a daughter and was the only family she had left. She'd likely be banished from court, and she'd lose Adriana, too. And all that was on the assumption that Erik even wanted to wed her!

Doubts and misgivings clouded her mind once again. 'Oh, Anton! I don't know what to do.'

'You don't have to do anything now. When the rebels surrender—and surrender they shall—your uncle will no doubt want to return to Constantinople to show his presence in the city. I am sure all decisions will be postponed until he is back. So you will have time to think on it.'

He placed an arm on her shoulder.

'Be that as it may,' she said, 'I cannot have a future with this man. At least not without severely disappointing my uncle.' She frowned.

'Thea, your uncle is so fond of you. Speak to him. I am sure he can be persuaded. Is this man really so unworthy?'

'He is an honourable man, but not of our blood or lineage. And even if by some miracle my uncle did allow it, I am not even sure this man shares my feelings.'

Antonius let out a booming laugh. 'I would be astounded if he did not, Thea. But why not speak with him on the topic? This man might be feeling exactly the same way. Women can be just as hard to read as men, you know.'

She managed a weak smile. 'Thank you. I am truly grateful for your understanding and your kindness.'

'I care for you, Thea, and I want you to be happy— even if your happiness is not with me. Now, you must be exhausted. I will leave you to rest while I go and see how your uncle and the Varangians have fared with the rebels.'

She nodded, her heart full of emotion. She felt a little lighter, as if a burden had been lifted from her. She'd finally told someone of her love for Erik, albeit without divulging his identity. And, moreover, there might be a way out of her marriage to Antonius if her uncle was amenable to it.

But could she dare to hope for a future with Erik? Could she risk her uncle's displeasure and, with it, the possibility of losing the only family she had? And if she made this sacrifice for Erik would it be worth it? Could he finally put his past and whatever troubled him about it behind him and love her?

Chapter Fifteen

As predicted, the rebel army was quick to surrender and disband once the soldiers discovered that Demetrios was dead. Most had sworn allegiance afresh to the Emperor, and there had been no further bloodshed. It had been decided that the royals and the Varangians would return post-haste to Constantinople, so that the Emperor could be reinstated.

Erik hadn't seen the Princess since their encounter with Demetrios, but he'd heard from Sigurd that she was travelling in a carriage with her cousin. There'd been no opportunity for him to ascertain how she was feeling about her return to Constantinople. Or, indeed, how she felt about him.

But every step of the journey, as they retraced their steps towards Constantinople, stirred a memory or triggered an emotion.

They rode past the glade where he'd saved Thea from the jaws of the wolf, the night he'd first realised he'd loved her, and the memory cut like a blade. They passed through the abandoned settlement where he'd first seen her naked, in all her beauty, and the hut where she'd let him give her pleasure. He was still proud that he had been the first man to show her the heights of such enjoyment, and that she'd subsequently trusted him enough to give herself to him completely.

The days were torture. He felt drained by the intensity of the emotions that had ensued since he'd last seen Thea. He'd almost wept with joy when he'd found out that her wedding was to be postponed, since the priority was to return the Emperor to Constantinople. But that feeling of joy had been only temporary, and had soon been eclipsed by sheer desolation at the prospect of losing her... The wedding couldn't be put off for ever.

And then there were the words she had uttered at their last meeting. She'd looked him straight in the eye and told him not to blame himself for Frida's death. He hadn't realised how much he'd needed her to say that with such certainty, to absolve him of the guilt he'd carried for years. Of the shame he'd felt because of who he was.

In a moment of piercing clarity, he'd realised that he loved her more than life itself. After Frida's death, he had vowed never to put someone else in danger again by virtue of being connected to him, nor ever allow himself to love someone so much that he'd put himself in a position of weakness. But now, since the Princess had shown him that both of those things were surmountable, there was no longer any excuse for him to deny what he felt for her. He'd realised after all these years that even though love might expose one to vulnerability, it could be deeply empowering, too.

He was now at a crossroads. He'd lost Frida, and there was nothing he could do to bring her back. But he had finally managed to allow himself to open his heart to love again—a love that was about to be cruelly snatched away from him. Could he allow himself to let that happen? Could he live with knowing that he hadn't at least tried to save that love?

He'd spent the last few days thinking long and hard about his options. And, after much deliberation, he'd made his decision. The consequences would be serious, the outcome uncertain, but of one thing he was absolutely sure—whatever the result, it would be worth it.

Just then, the imposing Theodosian walls of Constantinople came into view. Scouts had ridden ahead to inform the citizens of the Emperor's victory and his return, and even as they entered the Golden Gate there was a carnival atmosphere, with townsfolk rejoicing in the streets, waving and cheering.

Erik steered his way through the crowds, with Leif and Sigurd at his side and the rest of the Varangians behind them. There would be no rest or celebrating for them yet. They needed to secure the palace and the surrounding areas, ensuring that the rebels were well and truly suppressed, so they got to work.

The September evening was a chilly one and Thea shivered, wrapping her shawl around her more tightly as she looked at what remained of the wards. She surveyed the damage with sadness, her feet crunching on shattered medicine bottles. She saw that although much of the interior had suffered major damage, the structure of the building was still intact. Perhaps it could be rebuilt in time. Indeed, beneath the general smell of burnt wood she could detect the underlying aroma of her herbs. And despite everything the atmosphere retained its stillness, its calmness.

There had been much merrymaking that afternoon, as the palace had celebrated the Emperor's safe return, but although Thea was pleased for her uncle, she herself felt heartsore. She'd seen Erik at the banquet. It was the first time they had crossed paths since he'd saved her from Demetrios. He'd divested himself of his Varangian clothing and donned a dark blue tunic, which had only served to bring out the warmth in his ice-blue eyes. He'd looked so handsome, and the image of him had taken her breath away.

They had not spoken, but when she'd happened to catch his eye he had acknowledged her with a slight nod of the head and a huge knot had formed in the pit of her belly. Because one look from him was enough to undo her...enough to allow all the memories they had built together to come flooding back. Their first kiss. The warmth of being encircled in his arms. How he'd made love to her so tenderly in the woodcutter's hut, and then again more passionately.

Subconsciously, she put her hand to her mouth, as if that would bring back the feel of his lips on hers. The emotions, the love, the doubts, the happiness, the misery...all threatened to overwhelm her.

Although there'd been no opportunity for her to speak to Erik since they'd left Antonius's fort, she had spent the last few days mulling over every possible scenario and outcome. She needed to see him in private—one last time. There was still so much left unsaid between them, ...she needed confirmation that her instincts were right.

So she'd slipped away and come to the one place which had always been her sanctuary. The place where she could think when it all became too much. She came to the space that had been her study. Her desk was still there, albeit blackened with char. Fingering it tenderly, letting her fingertips draw a trail through the ash on its surface, she remembered how she'd tended to Erik's wound when they'd first met and her heart gave a little tug.

'We can make you a new one.'

She swung round.

'Erik!'

For a moment, neither of them spoke. But then he was striding towards her, filling the room with his presence until it felt as if it had shrunk to the size of a closet, just like that first time she'd encountered him. And soon he was crushing her to him. Nothing loath, she reached up on tiptoe, hungrily searching for his mouth, eagerly reciprocating when she felt his tongue plunder hers.

Finally, she felt him gently disengage himself from her. 'I had to see you again, Thea. I must speak with you.'

'Oh, Erik, and I with you!' She buried her head in his chest, savouring the familiar feeling of security she always felt when she was in his arms.

He gently raised her chin, so that he could look at her. 'The ghosts of my past no longer haunt me. You banished them for me, Princess,' he said softly, his eyes dark with emotion.

Even in the twilit haze she could see that he was struggling with how to express whatever was to come next. So she waited patiently, stroking his arm, wanting to reassure him in whatever way she could that he could trust her.

'I have told you about Frida and Bjorn. But I have not told you everything about my past...' He paused. 'My father is a jarl.'

'A jarl?' Thea tried to remember what that term meant from her history lessons.

'It means a chief, of sorts. He rules over a large kingdom in Norway, which is mine by birthright. I was betrothed to Frida when we were both babes. My father and hers wanted to join kingdoms. When she came of age, she travelled across the country to wed me. You know what happened next...' He paused again, his voice tight with emotion. 'I have never forgiven myself for what happened to her. It was my birthright that caused her death and our child's. If I hadn't been the son of a jarl she would not have been betrothed to me... She would never have left her home and travelled to mine, contracted the fever there. It was an even greater blow when I learned that her home was in a part of our country that had escaped the worst of it. I have been ashamed of who I am ever since.'

'Oh, Erik!' Tears sprang to her eyes at the thought that he had been carrying such a burden around with him. 'None of that was your fault!'

'I know that now,' he said. 'But I couldn't tell you when you confronted me about coveting Harald's reward that I have no need of riches.'

'No, it is I who should apologise for jumping to conclusions,' said Thea. 'For allowing *my* ghosts to cloud my judgement.'

'You have nothing to apologise for. The fault is mine for not being open about my past. For keeping my heart locked up. When I lost Frida and Bjorn I promised myself that I would never allow myself to love again, to become vulnerable in that way. Until... I fell in love with you.'

Her heart sang. *In love with her?* Had she heard correctly?

For a moment Thea was quite still, and his heart leapt to his mouth. Did she feel the same way? His gaze searched hers, seeking the answer to his unspoken query.

'Oh, Erik! I love you too.'

Her eyes grew soft and warm with emotion. She reached

up on tiptoe as she drew his head down to kiss him. It was a long, lingering, tender kiss, which sent his senses spiralling.

A wave of relief crashed over him and his heart swelled as she spoke of things he had never thought to hear. He couldn't believe that he had earned her affection, let alone her love. He gathered her to him tightly, revelling in the warmth and feel of her body, even knowing in his heart of hearts that these were likely the last moments he would ever have with her. But being able to freely express his feelings was exhilarating, and it was as if the shackles around his heart had come undone, letting the floodgates open.

The prospect of losing her to Demetrios had almost destroyed him, and while he knew he might now lose her in marriage to Antonius, he realised in a moment of piercing clarity that to have such love for a woman and for it to be reciprocated was worth the pain and heartache of that loss a thousand times over.

'I have dreamt so many times of a life with you...' she was saying.

'Indeed—and what, pray, would that life entail?'

'We would be surrounded by a brood of children. Sons who have eyes as blue as the midwinter sky, like their father, and girls—'

'Who have their mother's beauty and spirit,' Erik finished for her, his heart full.

It tore him apart to know that he might never have that with her. That it might be someone else's children she'd rear. It didn't bear thinking about.

Unaware of the direction of his thoughts, she continued her musings. 'We would rebuild the hospital together and add a new wing for orphans.'

His heart swelled with love for this kind, selfless woman.

He might be about to lose her, but he felt lucky to have had her in his life, even if it had been short-lived. He squeezed her more tightly at the thought, and loved it when she nestled further into the warmth of his chest as a result.

'What are you thinking, my love?' He stroked her hair.

'I didn't know how much I needed to hear you say you love me,' she said huskily, as she gently drew her head away from his chest and faced him. 'All this time I've been trying not to hope for the impossible...for your love, for a life together...'

'My darling, I have loved you from the day I set eyes on you here in the wards. You were radiant. So intelligent, beautiful, brave. I'd never met a woman like you.'

He looked down at her, still not believing that this woman loved him.

'I never thought I'd be able to give myself and my heart to a man. But now it feels as if it was never meant for anyone else but you.' She paused. 'Erik, the treaty...'

His heart plummeted. Would she choose duty over love? He would respect her wishes, but every fibre in his body wanted to beg her to choose him. He had worked out a plan—a plan that might give them a shot at a life together. All she needed to do was to choose him.

He forced himself to remain calm, and told himself again—just as he had kept telling himself for the past few days—that whatever happened he was lucky to have known her, and to have been loved by her. He'd rather have known her and lost her than never have known love like this at all.

He waited with bated breath.

'I have spoken to Antonius and told him that my heart lies elsewhere.'

'You have done what?'

'I said that I couldn't go through with our marriage without telling him that I was in love with someone else. He will not stand in our way.'

'Oh, my brave Princess!'

He crushed her to him again. He knew this didn't solve everything, but the fact that she had risked incurring Antonius's displeasure on account of him melted his heart. And at least that eliminated one significant obstacle...

'But Erik...' She grew quiet, a slight frown settling on her delicate features.

'What is it, my love?'

She sighed. 'It is only...since my parents died, my uncle has been like a father to me. He has treated me as one of his own and allowed me liberties I could only dream of—like working as a healer. But he is still the Emperor. Just because Antonius is willing to release me from the contract, it does not mean that my uncle will. And even if he does, he will likely not sanction our union. To disregard his wishes would mean that I would risk losing him and Adriana. They are the only family I have. It would break my heart all over again. And yet...' She looked up at him. 'To lose you would do the same.'

'I understand, my love. I know what it is like to lose a family. But if you choose me, I promise I will love you for the rest of my days. We can start a family of our own. I will never forsake you, Thea.'

'I believe you, Erik. But... I do hope my uncle will understand and give us his blessing.'

'I have spent the last few days trying to work out a solution,' he told her. 'It is helpful that Antonius will not stand in our way, and I have a plan that may help with your uncle. But if it is to work we will have to hurry...we don't have much time.'

* * *

They rushed through several darkened streets and a maze of passages that led to the eastern part of the palace. Thea looked to Erik, to try and ascertain what he might be feeling, but his expression gave nothing away.

Soon they arrived at a dome-shaped building with a line of tall, fair-haired men-at-arms at its entrance.

'Captain Svenson.'

'At ease, Varangian. I need access to the Treasury for a short while.'

The Varangian nodded and stepped aside, and Thea saw Erik pull out a large brass key from the pouch at his waist. He slotted it into the keyhole, and two of the other Varangians helped him drag it open, for it was heavily reinforced with iron.

He offered her his hand as he ducked his head to avoid the low-hanging beams. 'Come, Princess.'

Thea saw that beyond the entrance a narrow stone staircase curled down into darkness, and as they began their descent underground the air became dank and close. She felt as if she couldn't breathe. The stairs were steep and narrow, and dimly lit, so Thea hung on tightly to Erik's hand on her left, and to the hand rope on her right.

Each step felt like torture. She wasn't sure whether that was to do with the fact that she was in a tunnel, or whether it was fear of what they were about to do.

Erik must have sensed her hesitancy, for he asked, 'Thea? Are you all right?'

'I am uncomfortable in dark, enclosed spaces...but I'm all right.' She tried to sound stoic.

'I know, my love. It is only for a short while, I promise.'

The endearment filled her with warmth, and it was enough to stave off the darkness and cold. They continued to follow the trail of torches that flared at intervals on the walls. Deeper and deeper they went, until it felt as if they were descending into the very bowels of the earth.

'Almost there, my love.' He turned to her and dropped a kiss on her forehead. 'This is a safe place, Thea. The safest place in all of Constantinople,' he said softly.

Soon they came to another squat door, with more Varangians guarding it. Torchlight silvered the curves of their battle axes and bounced off their helmets in a yellow halo.

'Captain.' One of them nodded, before opening the door leading to another staircase.

As he led her upwards the air became less dense, and Thea glimpsed shafts of light coming from above. They walked along a small tunnel that forked off the main one, and soon they were almost back at ground level. She felt a little calmer.

'We're here,' Erik said at last, and Thea's knees almost buckled with relief. She wanted to get this over with. 'Are you well, my love?' he asked.

'Yes…a bit better now.'

'Good.' He held her tight, cloaking her in his warmth. 'Now I will need to retrace my steps and enter through the main entrance.' He lifted her chin. 'I'm sorry I had to take you through the secret passages, but I had to get you inside without being noticed.'

'I know, Erik. I will wait.'

'I won't be long. I promise.' He hooked his hand around her neck and brought his mouth down to hers. 'It will all be all right.'

But Thea could sense the tension in his voice. It was the first time she had ever seen him afraid of something.

'Erik, I love you. Whatever happens…know that.'

'And I love you, my darling. See you on the other side.'

In the dimness, she could just make out his crooked smile, and with that he was gone, his footsteps soon lost in the abyss.

Erik made his way back through the maze of corridors that led out to the open air and hurried to the main entrance of the Royal Treasury. He was only a few steps away from his fate.

All manner of outcomes entered his head, and he tried to ignore the worst one—being accused of high treason. Because ultimately that was what he would be found guilty of when he professed his love for the Princess. And a barbarian daring to pursue a relationship with one of the Emperor's female relatives was a crime punishable by death.

Whatever happened to him, he would need to ensure that the Princess's reputation remained unstained. But other than that, and armed with the new knowledge that the Princess loved him, he was prepared for battle.

The ceremony to swear the Emperor back in was almost at hand—a ceremony that would need to take place to re-establish his sovereignty. There was only a short time before this event took place—a time during which the Varangians were allowed to enter the Royal Treasury and take whatever they could carry out of it as a reward for their past services.

He approached the large wooden door where the Treasurer was already waiting, and the man led Erik to an antechamber.

The Emperor was already there. 'Ah, Captain, I knew you'd be the first here. Always prompt.' He chuckled good-naturedly. 'Come, tell me—what news of the city's condition?'

Erik bowed. 'All is well. There is some damage, but

nothing that cannot be reversed. I have left instructions for the next General.'

He offered the Emperor a scroll, upon which he'd carefully written down everything he could think of in terms of the administrative running of the Guard—duties, responsibilities and proposed restoration works.

'Have you given any thought to whom that might be?'

'Well, I was hoping it would be you…but I suppose you are still set on leaving the Guard?'

'Yes, Your Majesty. It has been an honour to serve you as a Varangian. But I believe I am now at the end of that journey.'

'Very well. I shall always be in your debt. You saved my life once, and now you've saved not only my beloved niece, but also the fate of Constantinople.' He spread his hands, gesturing to the door that led down into the underground chambers of the Treasury that held the city's wealth. 'Well, you know the custom. Take whatever you can carry, Varangian. I thank you for your service and release you from the Guard.'

Erik saluted him, bowed, and then entered the underground chamber beneath the foyer, his heart thudding wildly in his chest. The Emperor was fond of him, but what he was about to ask for was worthy of the gallows.

The Princess was waiting for him where he had left her. There was no need for further words. It was time.

He scooped her into his arms and walked back into the antechamber where he had left the Emperor, who was now standing with his back to them, looking out over the courtyard. Erik's heart pounded, but Thea's closeness gave him courage.

'Your Majesty, I ask for only one thing. One thing more precious than all the gold and jewels in the world, and something I do not deserve, but I can carry it out of the Treasury. I ask for the Princess Theadora's hand in marriage, if she will have me.'

The Emperor swung round, at first clearly not registering what he had heard. 'What on earth…?'

Erik set Thea down on her feet, and for a moment nobody spoke. A thick cloak of silence fell over the room as Erik saw a myriad of emotions flit across the Emperor's features, from surprise, to curiosity, to sternness.

He looked from one of them to the other. 'Thea, what is this? What is going on?'

'Uncle, this is the man I love…the man I want to marry.'

'But this is most irregular!' the Emperor spluttered, sitting down on the chair at the writing desk that stood beside him.

Rarely had Erik ever seen the Emperor at a loss for words. He felt bad for him that he'd had to find out about their love in such a way. But a Varangian's right to a reward from the Treasury was as absolute as his loyalty to the Emperor. Would Basil respect that right? Or execute him? There was only one option that he allowed himself to entertain, and he would fight for the Princess until his last breath.

'I am Erik Svenson, son of Sven Haraldson, Jarl of Bergen. I am not of these lands, and nor do I offer the opportunity to ally your kingdom with a powerful neighbouring state. But my lineage is worthy, and my love for your niece knows no bounds. A union such as this would not be irregular, since you once betrothed your own sister in marriage to King Vladimir of the Rus.'

The Emperor's gaze bored into him. There was a long period of silence. Neither man spoke.

'I am disappointed with you, Erik Svenson,' the Emperor

said at last, steepling his hands in front of him. 'The Princess is betrothed to King Antonius—you know that. To ask for her hand in light of this is high treason. I'm surprised you would even ask, knowing the punishment.'

'I am aware, Your Majesty. But it is a risk I am willing to take. I love your niece more than anything. I would not be true to myself if I did not declare it. Even if it meant my death.'

Now Thea stepped forward. 'Uncle, since Demetrios has fallen, there is no longer an urgent need for Macedonian support. Antonius is willing to release me from the marriage contract, and I hope that you will find it in your heart to do so, too.'

Again, silence. The Emperor's brows were knitted together in a deep frown. Several times he opened his mouth to utter something, but closed it again.

Finally, he spoke. 'Captain, leave us. I would speak to my niece alone.'

Thea's heart thudded in her chest. She'd chosen Erik. Now she had to be prepared to acknowledge that with that choice she might lose her family. Her uncle had never been stern with her before—but then, she'd never disobeyed him.

'My dear, what is the meaning of all of this?'

She saw he was not angry. In fact, his expression looked almost sorrowful.

'Are we not close enough, you and I, that you could tell me of this?'

'I wanted to tell you, Uncle, but it all happened so quickly and was extremely confusing...' She sighed. 'My feelings for Erik took root even before the coup, and the journey to the Varangian travelling camp only made them stronger. That was before I knew about my betrothal to Antonius. But I wanted to do right by you and fulfil my duty to the city. Then…when I faced Demetrios and realised that it might be my last day on this earth… I knew I would only ever want to spend it with Erik. I love him, Uncle. But I fought against that realisation for so long for fear of disappointing you. I do not want to lose you, or Adriana. You are the only family I have left…all that reminds me of my mother—'

Her uncle was now by her side, taking her hand in his. 'My dear, you could never disappoint me, and I will always acknowledge you as my family. I am only sad that you have had to carry this burden with you for all this time. Oh, don't cry!' He wiped a tear from her eye. 'I was foolish. I thought that you would welcome marriage to Antonius. He is a good man, and you have been well acquainted with him from childhood… Will you forgive me?'

Forgive him? Her uncle was seeking *her* forgiveness? She could not quite believe her ears.

'Oh, Uncle, there is nothing to forgive. I never want to lose you. And you are right, Antonius would have made a fine husband. If it weren't for Erik…'

'Ah, yes, Erik… He is an honourable man. His loyalty to me is without question. But do you know the man beyond the Varangian mask?'

Thea smiled softly. 'Yes, Uncle, I believe I do. It took some time, but I understand him and I love him. I cannot imagine life without him.'

'You are quite sure that you seek marriage with him?'

'I have never been more sure of anything in my life, Uncle.'

'And you are happy?'

'The happiest I have ever been since before Mama and Papa died,' Thea said truthfully.

Her uncle was silent, and Thea saw that his eyes were glassy with emotion.

'Thea, my dear, you have served Constantinople well. You have carried out your duty to the city and to me flawlessly. To acknowledge your devout service I am willing to allow you to follow your heart. I give you my blessing to wed Capt—' He corrected himself. 'Erik.' He smiled.

'Oh, Uncle!' She threw her arms about his neck and dropped a kiss on his cheek. 'Thank you! I was so worried I might lose you!' she exclaimed, thinking she could never be happier than she was in this very moment.

'My dear, you are my niece—we are blood. You will never lose me. Now, come… Why don't you summon your betrothed and put him out of his misery?'

Erik lay on his bed as he mulled over the events of the day, starting when he'd heard a knock on the door.

It was the Princess.

'My love, what are you doing here?'

Erik pulled her in, peering around the door and checking the corridor from side to side. Once she'd entered, he shut the door behind them.

She stood there, wearing a hood over her features, a glint of mischief in her eyes.

'Why, I am spending my last night as a single woman with the love of my life.'

She laughed, and his heart exploded as he gathered her to him.

'We'll get into trouble. We are meant to be spending the night before our wedding apart,' he said, planting kisses down the gentle slope of her neck.

'Mmm…' She made a soft mewling sound. 'You mean

that we should be chaste and good before our wedding night?' She playfully nipped the corner of his mouth.

'Yes...' He followed her lead, indulging in her roleplay.

'Just like we were in the woodcutter's hut?' She nuzzled his neck.

'Yes, just like that.'

His arms were around her waist in a vice-like grip, and he could feel her soft, delicate curves.

'Erik, I want you to take me. Here. Now.'

He gazed into her eyes and saw the need and the desire there. It was too much. He growled, and pulled her even closer, plundering her mouth with his, stealing into it with his tongue. When she wrapped her arms around his shoulders to steady herself he picked her up and felt her legs curl around his waist. It drove him wild crazy.

He stumbled towards the bed and set her upon it on her knees. She fumbled with his breeches until they were puddled by his feet. Then she brought both her hands up to cup him in her palms before taking the length of him in her mouth. He groaned, both shocked and delighted at how wanton his wife-to-be was. He'd never felt pleasure like this before.

The thought brought him back to his senses, and he gently disengaged himself from her.

'What is it, Erik? Do I not please you?'

He laughed throatily. 'On the contrary, you please me too much. I want to prolong my pleasure and start yours.'

Even as he spoke he unfastened her gown and brought it over her head, so she was completely naked in front of him, still on her knees, looking up at him with those big, beautiful brown eyes. He got onto the bed so that he was on his knees too, and they were facing each other. Hungrily, he trailed his hands all over her body, cupping her breasts, grazing his fingers over the hardened peaks of her dark nipples, in awe of how easily his large hands encircled the smallness of her waist. When he reached her secret place, one touch evidenced her slickness and how ready she was for him.

'How do you want me, Erik?' she asked, her eyes pleading with him to take her, to make her his. This time permanently.

A low, guttural sound emanated from his mouth, and the thought of finally taking her completely, spilling himself inside her, was almost too much to bear. In answer to her question, he sat back and brought his hands behind her, to grasp her firm bottom, moulding her to him. With a decisive but gentle movement he lifted her and set her upon his hard length, easing her down and waiting for her to settle and accommodate him.

She moaned, throwing her head back in carnal pleasure, and he kissed the curve of her neck as he rocked her back and forth on his lap. He was patient, but demanding, and this time she rose to meet his demands, her palms roaming over his shoulder blades, down the planes of his back and then along his pectoral muscles.

'Oh, Erik, I'm so close...'

He was about to lose control himself, so he lowered her down, so that her back was supported by the bed, and pinned her wrists above her head as he drove into her. She was crying out now, pleading, begging him to give her what she wanted. Her legs were still hooked around his waist and she used her position to pull him even deeper into her, showing him how much she wanted him.

Finally, he felt her climax, and she let out the sweetest, most feminine moan and clenched around him—evidence of her satisfaction. Safe in the knowledge that she had derived her pleasure, and that this time there was no need to withdraw, he let himself go, a cry of savage joy escaping his lips as he emptied himself inside her in a series of powerful throbs.

'Thea, you're fully mine now,' he said softly as he lowered himself beside her and gathered her into him, so they were spooning side by side.

'And you're mine,' she answered happily, nestling into his body.

'I love you, Theadora. I can't wait to have you beside me until my last breath. I swear to love you, and to try every day to make you the happiest woman alive.'

The look of love that she gave him in return told him everything he needed to know.

His kiss was gentle, loving, and at the same time so utterly consuming that she lost herself in it as they melded as one. She felt love emanating from him. It was there in the steady, reliable beating of his heart against her bosom, in his soft words of endearment and in the passionate lovemaking they had shared. And now, as he lowered his head to hers, it was there in his gaze. A love that was as immeasurable as the expanse of the sky and as unfathomable as the depths of the sea.

Epilogue

Spring, 980 AD, Constantinople

Erik led Thea to the rebuilt hospital as the first pink rays of dawn cast light upon its façade. It had taken a few months to restore the city to its former state after the rebellion, and the wards had suffered damage on a large scale, but yesterday they had finally completed the refurbishments, and Erik had wanted Thea to be the first to see it.

'Thank you for helping the men with the building.'

Thea turned to Erik, her eyes full of love.

'It was an honour. After all, the place is special to me. It's where I first met you.'

He gave her one of his winning smiles, which made her heart soar. She didn't think she would ever get tired of seeing them.

'Come, let's go in.'

Erik let her enter first, and he smiled widely as he saw her expression of delight.

'Erik, this is wonderful! There's not a trace of the destruction it suffered.'

She moved around the main ward excitedly.

'I'm glad you like it, my love. But come… I want to show you something else. Close your eyes.'

She did as she was told, and let him lead her down a corridor.

'All right, you can open them now.'

In front of her was a brand-new wing, and at the top of the doorway an inscription read *The Georgios and Helena Wing for Orphans*.

She looked at it in wonder, speechless.

'I knew of your dream to build a new wing for orphaned children, so I commissioned it and named it in your parents' memory,' Erik explained.

Tears sprang to her eyes. She'd always wanted to expand the hospital and prioritise a section for orphans. She was glad that they'd adopted Alexios, but she wanted to do so much more. And the fact that Erik had thought to name it after her parents made her heart turn over. They'd be with her every day now, as she carried out her duties.

'You are truly the love of my life.' It was all she could say in return.

'And you're mine.'

'I can't believe you did this for me.'

'Well, you will be spending a lot of your time here, after all.'

She looked at her husband, grateful that she had married someone who appreciated her independence.

'Thank you for allowing me to continue my vocation, Erik. I truly appreciate it.'

Erik still couldn't believe that Thea was now his wife, and that she loved him as much as he loved her. When he had first set foot in Constantinople he had just lost a family. Now, years later, he had gained one.

He had decided to pursue his trading enterprise from Constantinople, rather than move to Cyprus. And with his experience in the Varangian Guard he had made connections with the Rus in Kiev, the Angles and Saxons in Britannia, and of course he had his local contacts in Norway. With such a network he had already established a passage from Scandinavia through the river system in Russia down to Constantinople, and the company was thriving.

There really wasn't much else he could want or wish for.

'As long as you still have time for your husband and our son,' he said now.

'Always.' She kissed him on the cheek. 'And maybe for one more…'

She gently brought his hand down to her stomach. His eyes widened, and she answered the query she saw there.

'Yes, Alexios is to have a brother or a sister soon.'

Erik felt his heart swell with joy and love. Once, the Norns had snatched away everything he had held dear, but now they had restored his loss in full measure.

* * * * *

The Viking's Royal Temptation
*is Roxy Harper's debut for
Harlequin Historical*

*Be sure to look out for her next book,
coming soon!*